PRAISE FOR NJ BARKER'S THRILLERS

THE HONESTY INDEX:

"A well-written thriller with a superb hook."
Wayne Brookes, Pan Macmillan

"I ended up reading it in two sittings! I thought this was a perfectly paced thriller, brilliantly commercial and with such a clever and high concept premise."
Sam Eades, Orion

"The writing and plotting were really pacy and engaging, and it reminded me of TM Logan."
Joel Richardson, Michael Joseph

KENNEDY LOGAN THRILLERS:

"The Catastrophe Test is a fast-moving, clever, well-written novella that will only leave you wanting more of Nigel's writing."
Jennie Godfrey, *Sunday Times* bestselling author of The List of Suspicious Things.

GENIUS CLUB

NJ BARKER

For Claire and James x

AUTHOR'S NOTE

Genius Club is fiction, but the technological developments in the book are based on actual scientific breakthroughs and theories that happened around the time of the narrative.

All external scientific papers, reports, studies, tests and programmes referenced are real.

“Genius is 1 percent inspiration and 99 percent manipulation.”

- *Anon.*

1

NOW

TUESDAY, 11 JUNE 2019

Raynes Park, London

PROFESSOR MATTHEW STANFORD CURSED UNDER HIS BREATH. SHOULD he get off and run? It was only another mile until his home stop opposite the train station, but the bus was edging through the rush hour early-evening London traffic, barely outpacing the pedestrians. He hit redial and waited, counting the rings until it flipped to his son's voicemail.

'Hey, this is Alfie. Here's the beep. Knock yourself out.'

Still no answer. Matthew stared at the last text messages from his son.

I had a missed call from Mum. I can't get hold of her.

He tried his son again.

'Hi, Dad,' Alfie's voice sounded hesitant.

'Hey, Alfie, are you okay? I'm only a few minutes away now.' He heard Alfie swallowing.

'Mum always messages or calls me back...' Alfie trailed off.

Matthew's shoulders tensed, and fear began to scratch inside his stomach. He glanced out the window and silently swore at the car stranded across the roundabout, blocking the bus.

'I had a missed call, too,' Matthew said, trying to sound calm. He decided against mentioning the voicemail he'd received from their friend and fellow scholar, Sammy, telling him Lucy hadn't turned up for their coffee catch-up earlier that day. Lucy hadn't responded to Sammy's messages. He cleared his throat. 'Are you at home?'

'Nearly.' He sounded younger than his twelve years. 'I'm just walking up our road.' There was a hesitation before Alfie spoke again. 'Do you think something's wrong?' Matthew's heart thumped. The car had finally driven off, and the bus was moving again. Rain began to sweep down against the window. 'Dad?' His son's voice was strained.

Matthew swallowed and dropped his voice. 'I'm sure Mum's fine.'

He walked down the aisle of the bus as it slowed towards the stop, hating himself for using such a platitude with his son. Lucy hadn't left him a message, which was unusual in itself, but she hadn't rung off before the call connected. He'd listened to the recording several times, and while she hadn't said anything, he could tell she was upset. That wasn't like Lucy at all.

He was less than five minutes away from home. He stepped off the bus and started to jog along the road, twisting to see the traffic so he could dart across to the other side. 'I'm nearly home.' He heard his voice; the cold air, asthma and physical activity had triggered a wheeze already.

'I'm going in,' Alfie said. 'I'll see you in a minute.'

'No, wait for me,' Matthew said. He was sprinting now. He flew by the parade of shops and the group of teenagers hanging around on their bikes, spun up the road, his feet splashing through the shallow puddles until he reached the flat. He fumbled for the keys, knowing his son was on the other side of the front door.

His phone's ringtone burst to life, and he scrambled to pull it from his pocket, but it wasn't Lucy; it was Alastair. He'd forgotten that he had been due to meet his friend for a drink at the local pub. He buried his phone back into his pocket.

He opened the front door and stepped inside. The entrance hall was bare and unloved. There were two doors – theirs and the ground-floor neighbour's. Alfie was leaning against their front door—his son —all the hope in his heart, all the fear in his stomach.

'I'm sure Mum's just lost her phone. Something like that,' Matthew said, his swallow catching in his throat. 'I'm going in, okay. You stay here. I'll be back down once I've spoken with Mum.'

There was a barely imperceptible nod from Alfie. Matthew unlocked the front door, walked through, and pushed it to behind him. Then he sprinted up the stairs.

'Lucy.' His shout died against the walls of their hallway. His wife's red duffle coat was hanging on the peg, but her black trainers, which always rested on the shoe rack next to Matthew's slippers, weren't there.

He called out again as he moved forward. No answer. He spun around in the empty kitchen and moved into the bathroom. Nothing. The bedroom door creaked as he pushed it open. He swallowed. No Lucy. He turned into the living room, sweat now dripping down his back. She wasn't there.

There was only one room left to look in—Lucy's study. Breathing heavily, he reached out towards the chipped brass handle. He gripped it expecting resistance, but it turned smoothly. His chest squeezed in, and he could hear the blood rushing in his ears. The door swung open.

THE FLOOR TILTED, and Matthew reached out towards the wall to steady himself. Lucy was lying on the floor, stretched out on her back. She was dressed in the jeans and the yellow tunic top he had watched her pull on that morning. He could tell immediately that she was dead. Yet seeing her there, devoid of life, made no sense. No sense at all.

It was as if he was watching himself momentarily, looking at her and waiting to see how he would react. He was dimly aware of his knees smashing into the laminate floor as he reached for her, knowing though that it wasn't her any longer, knowing that she was gone.

His fingers fumbled towards her neck, but her skin was cold, and the only pulse he could feel was his thumping against his temples. He rested his head on her chest, but her arms didn't comfort him; her fingers didn't tangle in his hair. Already, those memories belonged to a different lifetime.

One of Lucy's arms was folded so that her hand supported her head on the floor whilst the other was flung backwards as if she were mid-stretch. Matthew pushed himself back into a sitting position and pulled out his phone to call an ambulance. The conversation was a blur. He heard himself say the words *Sierra Whiskey Twenty*. He tried to focus.

'No, she's not breathing,' he said.

He moved her arm, placed the palm and heel of his hand on her chest and started compressions. One, two, three, four. He tilted her head, pinched her nose and covered her mouth with his. Breath. Breath. Then, back to compressions.

Lucy's eyes were closed, and her expression calm—was it still her expression when there was no emotion to show? But there was no shudder of life rebooting, no flinch as her heart restarted. There was nothing.

It was then that Matthew spotted it. A clear plastic tube with the plunger jammed down to the bottom. His body tensed. His instinct was to reach towards it, but he forced himself to continue to beat out the compressions whilst staring at the syringe. He knew he shouldn't touch it, that there were rules about evidence, but what force did rules have in a situation like this? He wanted to smash it, to destroy what had taken his wife.

He was numb as he continued with the cycle of compressions and breaths until the ambulance siren cut through the air. Seconds later, he heard voices downstairs.

God, Alfie.

Matthew stood and moved towards the doorway as the paramedics crowded around Lucy's body. He could tell from their reaction that Lucy was gone. He closed the door behind him and walked down the corridor. Alfie was standing, motionless, halfway up the stairs. Nothing could have prepared Matthew for that moment.

It took Alfie less than a second to read Matthew's expression. 'No.'

'I'm so sorry, Alfie.' Matthew took a step towards him.

Alfie didn't move. 'No,' he said. 'She can't be dead.' He was blinking away tears. 'She can't be dead,' he repeated, his words spinning around the hallway.

Matthew stepped down and reached for his son. 'I'm sorry.' He didn't know what else to say.

He pulled Alfie into an embrace and buried his face in his son's hair. He had seen the questions in Alfie's eyes, but he was mainly witness to his son's deep anger. It would change him; Matthew knew that. He had never felt so utterly powerless.

'I want to see her.' Alfie pulled himself free from his father's hug and slipped past him.

'Alfie, wait.'

Matthew wasn't quick enough, and Alfie was at the entrance to the study before Matthew caught up with him. Alfie froze in the doorway, watching the paramedics working diligently on his mother. The paramedics looked so sure of their actions, well-versed in dealing with death. The older-looking paramedic walked over and led Alfie down the hallway, talking softly.

The paramedic speaking to Matthew looked younger than Matthew, perhaps in his mid-to-late thirties. Matthew barely registered the words as he struggled to focus on what the man was telling him.

Lucy was dead. The paramedics would notify the coroner, and a post-mortem would be needed. An inquest would follow to determine the cause of death.

None of it sounded real.

The paramedic seemed to think that Lucy had taken her own life. That was the apparent explanation. Except, if something was obvious, it was easily understood. Matthew's mind searched for the building blocks needed to develop the very idea—depression, a secret that tormented her, or perhaps some other illness. Yet, nothing seemed plausible.

Matthew stepped inside the room. Lucy's writing desk was pushed against the window that overlooked the garden. A black notebook and a Bic biro lay on the table. The paramedic was still talking, but Matthew tuned him out. The diary felt cold as he picked it up. Was he right to want to look inside it? He had never wanted to fall in Lucy's estimation, but that was now forever frozen—or wiped away entirely. His body shook as he looked again at Lucy, prone on the floor.

After a moment, he tossed the unopened diary back onto the desk.

2

THEN

MARCH 2001

Cambridge

BENJAMIN CAESAR PERCHED ON THE EDGE OF THE SEAT, HIS FACE illuminated by the green glow of the computer screen. The blackout blinds were lowered, and music pulsed through the speakers resting on the bookshelves lined on either side of the room. As the music wrapped around him, he sat, staring at the list. He tapped on the keyboard and scrolled down until he saw the names of three children who hadn't made it.

Two of them had fizzled out. They would never know what they had let slip through their fingers. The other case had been more ... delicate. The mother had asked too many questions, and questions were not encouraged by the programme. Her child had to be removed. Regrettable but necessary. He highlighted the three names and, with a click, deleted them from his spreadsheet.

That left those he was minded to invite to interview for a scholarship. He pushed back the chair and stood, taking a moment to stretch. The music was louder now, the insistent one-chord refrain echoing around the room.

The final selection was a question of balance. He had hoped to know his mind by now, yet he was only sure about five students.

He barely heard the chime alerting him to a new email. Scout Three had sent him a voice memo about one of the children he was still undecided on—an interesting case, Matthew Stanford. He clicked on the attachment, and a woman's voice filled the room. Scout Three spoke with a slight lisp and a Gaelic lilt.

'Update file on Matthew Stanford from Scout number three. Recorded on 18th March 2001. I can report that Matthew is an exceptional child. His mathematical ability is undeniable. He took part in the British Mathematical Olympiad and scored full marks. He was invited to join the British training squad for the International Mathematical Olympiad, which takes place in South Korea in July. However, his father has refused to allow his son to participate. End of report.'

There was a subtle click, and Ben closed the file. That information was enough for him to make his decision. Matthew was gifted—there was no limit to what he could achieve with the proper support and development.

Six students had been selected now; tomorrow, he would send them their invitation for a scholarship interview. Six was his original target, but he was leaning towards selecting a seventh. It wasn't his natural preference to trade symmetry for contingency, but he sensed it was the right choice.

The final candidate was the most brilliant of them all, but she also troubled him the most: Dylan Steele.

He knew all the test results from memory, and Dylan was top in all but one category. Yet, in that one category, she was way below the others. That alone should have been enough to eliminate her. He sighed as he clicked on the tab showing the reports from the scouts.

Dylan Steele: Codes faster, more beautifully and in more languages than most postgraduate computer scientists. Two years ago, she developed a software programme to timetable A-level courses for the school. The school offered to buy her software for £50. She let them have it for free so they could license it to other schools for a profit.

His finger hovered above the delete button. The music was relentless. One chord pounding into his brain, the same harmonic set of notes, again and again, each building on the last and offering something new. He balled his fist and shook his head. Maybe he would regret it, but one had to make exceptions for the exceptional.

He highlighted Dylan's name and moved her to the 'interview' column. A warmth weaved itself across his chest as his breathing shallowed.

The music stopped, and the room was silent apart from the hum of the computer. As he turned away from the screen, there was a knock on the door. He glanced at his watch. His guest was twenty minutes early.

He saved the file and switched off the computer screen. His deadline for the final selection was tomorrow, but he couldn't risk not taking this meeting now. It was as important as the selection itself—yin and yang. He pulled up the blind on the window, and the shock of the daylight made him squint and turn towards the door. He walked over, released the security chain, and pulled down on the cold, metal handle.

Ben took in the man opposite him. He hadn't laid eyes on him for nearly ten years, and he'd forgotten just how tall his friend was. His head barely reached the other man's shoulder as they embraced. After a moment, they released each other.

'Hello, Henry,' he said.

The tall man smiled and made a slight adjustment to reposition his glasses. 'Now then, Ben, tell me what was so important that it couldn't wait.'

3

NOW

TUESDAY, 11 JUNE 2019

Raynes Park, London

Matthew was sitting at the kitchen table, trying to make sense of what was happening. He looked up as the door swung open, and Alastair walked in.

'Okay, Alfie's in his room. I've spoken with his headmaster and to your work,' Alastair said. 'I've also told the gang. Sammy wanted to come over, but I suggested she hold off. They're all devastated and want to help however they can.'

Alastair was his best friend and a world-leading psychologist. If anyone knew what to do, it would be Alastair, but some things were impossible.

'No one can help,' Matthew said. His elbows were on the table, with his head in his hands.

'I know.' Alastair sighed. 'I couldn't get hold of Caesar, so I left him a message. I hope that's okay?' Matthew nodded. 'Do you want me to stay?' Matthew didn't know what he wanted other than to turn back time or to witness a resurrection, but nothing from the realm of the possible. 'How about I get you something to eat?'

Matthew closed his eyes but couldn't shut out the image of Lucy lying on the floor. He pulled a tissue from his pocket and blew his nose, wiping his eyes with his sleeve.

'I'm not hungry,' he said. He sniffed. 'It just doesn't make sense.' Nothing did. Lucy's death. The prospect of life without her. The world would keep turning, and everyone would go about their regular business. How could her death be so *incidental?* His shoulders began to shake.

He felt Alastair's hand on his arm. 'Do you think Lucy could have been depressed? Is it possible that she hid it from you?' His voice was quiet.

Of course, it was *possible,* Matthew thought. Just highly improbable.

'Didn't her mother...'

Matthew finished Alastair's sentence in his head. *Take her own life after suffering for years with depression.*

'Lucy is nothing like her mother.' He squeezed his eyes shut and fought the urge to correct himself. He knew Alastair wouldn't push the family medical history or Matthew's use of the present tense.

'What about any recent appointments with doctors or therapists? Anything like that?' Alastair asked.

Matthew sniffed again. 'She mentioned a doctor's appointment a couple of weeks ago but didn't say anything more about it.' He let the possibility settle. Could it have been something significant that he'd missed? He didn't think so but didn't know for sure because he had never asked. 'I don't believe she took her own life.' He heard the defiance in his voice. He was silent for a few seconds. 'Alfie and I both had missed calls from her,' he said.

'Yeah. Alfie told me.'

Matthew cleared his throat. 'She didn't turn up for her coffee meeting with Sammy.' He tapped on his phone screen and held his phone out to his friend. 'The missed call went to answerphone,' he said.

Alastair raised his palms. 'I don't know if I-'

Matthew selected the speakerphone button and hit play. There was a click, and Lucy's shallow breathing filled the room. After a few seconds, there was a sharp intake of breath, and then the call ended.

'Do you think it's her?' Alastair asked.

'Yes,' Matthew replied. 'It's hard to explain why, but everything about it is familiar.' He rubbed his forehead. 'I could tell she was upset. Something was wrong. She wanted to tell me something but didn't want to leave a message. I can't recall her ever doing that before. I left for home immediately.'

'If she was that upset-'

'Lucy didn't kill herself,' Matthew said.

Alastair nodded and waited for a few seconds before speaking again. 'Did you play the message to the police?'

'Yes,' Matthew said. He watched his friend pace around the room. 'None of this makes sense.' The words caught in his throat.

Time stretched as if Matthew was watching a slow-motion video recording of the world. He was aware of sitting in the kitchen, discussing his wife's death. Part of him was involved in the conversation. Another part of him was observing it, trying to rationalise not what had happened but his reaction to events.

His face was wet from his tears—no doubt he was devastated, yet the rational part of his brain was still trying to do what it always did: analyse, sift through data, and search for patterns. His talent, however, lay in numbers and abstract thinking rather than trying to divine why humans did what they did. As was so often the case when he tried to understand human behaviour, he came up with nothing.

'Matt.' Alastair's tone was enough to signpost that he was about to say something his friend wouldn't like. 'I know you think Lucy didn't take her own life, but it has to be worth looking into her recent appointments.' The silence hung in the air. 'I think you should try and find out what you can.'

'Her doctor won't tell me anything,' Matthew said. 'Patient confidentiality.'

'If she was having treatment for depression, you'll find something.

Prescription drugs, medical records, a journal.' Alastair leant back on the chair. 'You should try and find out, Matt, even if it's to demonstrate to the police that it's not what they think.'

'Okay,' Matthew said. 'I will.' He didn't like it, but he knew Alastair was right; he nearly always was.

4

THEN

MAY 2001

St Albans, London

MATTHEW SCOOPED UP THE POST FROM THE DOORMAT AND CARRIED IT through to the kitchen, sorting through the envelopes. His pulse quickened when he saw that one of the letters was addressed to him. He had no idea what it was about, but he couldn't remember ever receiving his own letter before.

His father rarely made it up before Matthew left for school. Matthew preferred it that way; he enjoyed the peace, and it gave him time to think. He didn't want to risk his dad coming down early. There was something intriguing about the unsolicited letter, and, whatever the contents, he wanted to savour the moment, free from interruption.

He shoved a piece of toast in his mouth, snatched up his school bag, and auto-piloted down the driveway and towards the bus stop. He peeled off down the back road when he approached the high street. The smell of fresh bread from the bakery made his stomach rumble, so he walked further along the pavement before stopping next to a shopfront boarded over. His hands trembled as he opened his school bag and pulled out the letter. His letter.

Dear Matthew

My name is Benjamin Caesar, and I am the founder and patron of a new scholarship. I am writing to invite you to an interview for the scholarship, which will be available to students entering higher education in September 2001. The scholarships are highly selective and offered only to students who have exceptional promise in their chosen area and have also faced additional challenges in childhood.

Matthew's brain cycled around, firing off question after question. Who was Benjamin Caesar? How had he even heard of Matthew? What challenges?

The scholarship entitles the scholar to full funding of academic and living expenses throughout their undergraduate studies. Additional support and funding will be available to scholars once they graduate.

A tingling sensation began in his hands, spreading up his arms—a golden ticket to university.

The key requirement for a scholar is an exceptional intellect with unusual levels of proficiency in one or more specialist areas. Consideration for the scholarship is by invitation only.

Matthew couldn't believe what he was reading and braced himself for the punchline or the punch in the gut.

Individuals selected for a scholarship will be noteworthy for their academic achievement, but in particular, their character, ability to respond to adversity, and drive to make a positive impact in the world.

Drive to make a positive impact in the world? Matthew barely created a ripple in his bathtub. Would it be enough that he could answer virtually every question any teacher asked him?

He folded the letter back into the envelope and slipped it into his bag. The bus would be coming in a few minutes. He'd go to school and wouldn't say anything to anyone. When he was alone he would work out how to get to Cambridge for the interview because he had been given an opportunity and he wasn't going to let it slip through his fingers. Not when it could change his life forever.

London King's Cross Station

LUCY GLANCED AT HER WATCH. She had eight minutes before her train to Cambridge was due to depart and three hours before her scholarship interview with Benjamin Caesar.

The middle-aged man sitting beside her in the station waiting area had been speaking loudly on the phone about debt funding before starting on the *Times Crossword*, only to put it down, incomplete, twenty minutes later. His coat was draped over the back of his seat. He stood up, stretched and looked around. He dropped the newspaper on his chair and caught Lucy's eye.

'There must be a mistake in that one. I always complete them in under fifteen minutes. I'm a crossword expert.' He nodded as if to confirm his self-assessment and then headed towards the toilets.

Lucy smiled and said nothing. Once he was out of sight, she picked up the paper and scanned his answers and the clues. After approximately ten seconds, she spotted his mistake and corrected it. She worked her way through the remaining clues until the crossword was complete. She checked her time—two minutes and thirty seconds. Not bad, she thought, placing the newspaper back onto the man's chair.

She spotted *Crossword Expert* walking back over to collect his coat. He picked up the newspaper and scowled.

Lucy stood up and slipped the shoulder strap of her bag over her shoulder. 'Have a lovely day,' she said. Then she headed off to catch her train.

5

NOW

TUESDAY, 11 JUNE 2019

Raynes Park, London

There weren't many places in the flat where Lucy could have hidden anything from Matthew; the last remaining place was the wardrobe in their bedroom. He pushed away his guilt as he flipped through her dresses hanging on the rail before squatting down and searching through the boxes at the bottom of the wardrobe. Tucked away at the back, on Lucy's side, underneath some old trainers, Matthew found a small white plastic container. He pulled out a pair of navy trainers to give himself room to slide the box out.

He frowned as he ran his hands over its top. Then, he pressed the catches on the side, lifted the lid, and peered inside. It contained a set of white headphones. There was a pinch between his shoulders. He removed the headphones from the box, and only then did he realise that the two circular pads weren't in the correct place. The device had a curved T-bar with a small cross pad at the base, which appeared designed to rest at the base of the skull. The strap ran up over the top of the head and down over the forehead whilst the broader bar fitted horizontally with the two discs resting just beyond the eyes, near the temples.

He reached back into the box and removed a device resembling a smartphone. He pressed the power-on button and waited for it to boot up. A moment later, he was looking at the home screen, a green background with a white sine wave curving around the word *electro-flow*. Whatever the device was, he was holding the controller. Matthew let out a breath. He pressed on the icon, and a menu appeared.

Your Progress

Set New Goals

Profile

He hesitated before clicking on *Your Progress* and scrolling through Lucy's report. She had been using the device for periods of more than thirty minutes for years. Matthew shook his head. The first entry was recorded on 2 September 2007, seven months after Alfie was born, and the last entry was that morning.

His arms were trembling. Alastair had said he would find something. Matthew stared at the device. He'd accepted his friend might be correct, but he'd never considered that when he unearthed some evidence, he would have no idea what it meant.

MATTHEW STARED at the computer screen. His answer was written clearly in white text on a black background. The electro-flow website claimed that using an electric current to stimulate the temporal lobes could counter depression. It cited various clinical trials which supported the view that the electro-flow device was a more effective treatment for depression than antidepressants. Matthew clicked on one of the reports referenced and started to read.

"Transcranial direct current stimulation (tDCS) of 20- or 30 minutes are efficient for treating mild and moderate depression; the effect of 30min stimulation exceeds that obtained from 20min."

Matthew chewed his lip. There were two facts. Lucy had used an electro-flow device, and that device was advertised as a treatment for depression. The two statements pointed to an obvious conclusion but weren't compelling. That conclusion wasn't inescapable. He thought back to his conversation with Alastair. If Lucy had hidden a struggle with depression, she would likely have sought medical support.

It was already late at night, but Matthew stood up and opened the loft hatch. Lucy had filed away their old medical records a few years ago. It only took him a few minutes to locate the box file and carry it down from the loft. He placed it on the kitchen table next to his laptop and opened it. The box was full of documents, and Matthew picked up the document from the top of the pile. It was a slim, bound volume labelled as a medical report from Heartfield Health Clinic.

He had forgotten that Lucy had been for a check-up every year after graduation, and she'd been sent a report after each appointment. He read the report and studied Lucy's vital statistics and the BMI, cholesterol, and cardiac risk graphs. There were also pages with audio graphs, analysis of lung function tests, and eyesight results. Finally, there was a pathology report.

Matthew flicked back to the cover letter. The conclusion was that Lucy was in good health, and there was no mention of depression or any mental health challenges. The report was dated August 2007, the month before her first recorded device use.

He read through all the reports in the box, which covered every year from 2007 until the final report, dated August 2011. None of the reports mentioned any physical or mental health issues other than low-level concerns over Lucy's weight and lack of exercise.

The signatory of the reports was Dr Henry Bannister. Matthew recalled the name immediately. Caesar introduced them to Bannister, his private doctor, when they joined the scholarship programme. Lucy had liked him. She had first seen him at university in Cambridge and continued to see him at his Cambridge practice, even when she'd moved to London. She'd also encouraged Matthew to see him, but he hadn't heard her mention the doctor's name for several years.

Matthew sat back down in his chair and opened Google on his laptop. He typed in the doctor's name and hit search. The third hit was an obituary.

Doctor Henry Bannister, a doctor and an academic, died aged 53.

He scanned through the text, not knowing what he was searching for. His head jerked back to the penultimate paragraph of the obituary.

Professor Hunter, who tutored Dr Bannister at Cambridge University, recalled: 'He was an exceptional, brilliant and radical man. He liked to push medical boundaries and challenge conventional thinking. He died too young. He was destined for great things.'

A knot twisted in Matthew's stomach. Lucy started using the device in September 2007, when she was still seeing Bannister for her annual medicals. tDCS treatment wasn't universally accepted by the medical profession, at least not over a decade ago. Had Bannister prescribed the treatment to Lucy, an example of him pushing medical boundaries, and kept it from her official medical records? And if so, why?

MATTHEW DECIDED to rake through everything he could find on the uses of tDCS machines. He started reading online articles. Several studies appeared to show that the treatment reduced depression symptoms in patients, yet Matthew was sure he would have known if Lucy was struggling. He also clearly remembered her telling him she wouldn't take her mother's chosen path—ever.

He was aware people who were depressed could hide it well, even from those they were closest to, but there had been no changes in Lucy's appetite or sleep pattern and no loss of interest in activities.

He shook his head and tried to focus on the facts. There wasn't a single suggestion, or even a hint, that his wife had been suffering from depression, but she had been using a tDCS machine for over a decade. The only explanation was that she was using the device for another reason—but what? He began to scroll through the research papers and paused at a headline from October 2018.

Would you zap your brain to improve your memory? Scientists study attitudes toward brain stimulation.

An article dated August 2014 made a similar claim.

Northwestern Medicine researchers have discovered that using high-frequency repetitive transcranial magnetic stimulation to indirectly stimulate the hippocampus portion of the brain (which is involved in forming memories) improves long-term memory.

Then he found a third, from March 2019.

Online repetitive transcranial magnetic stimulation during working memory in younger and older adults: A randomized within-subject comparison.

Matthew changed his search terms, and immediately, he was presented with page after page of articles on transcranial magnetic and direct current stimulation being studied as possible methods for boosting intelligence. He sat back and let out a deep breath.

Could Bannister have suggested using the machine not to treat depression but to attempt to boost Lucy's intelligence even further?

That would explain why there was no medical record of depression. It would be consistent with no mental health issues whatsoever. He rubbed his forehead. Bannister *had* treated Lucy, a doctor described as radical and a man who liked to challenge conventional thinking.

Matthew raked his fingers through his hair. What had this guy done? What had Lucy signed up to?

With Lucy and Bannister both dead, only one person might have the answers to all his questions. He needed to speak to Ben Caesar.

6

NOW

WEDNESDAY, 12TH JUNE

Belgravia, London

IT HAD BEEN A COUPLE OF YEARS SINCE MATTHEW HAD LAST VISITED Caesar's London home. Alastair referred to it as *Caesar's Palace* because it was located on one of the most exclusive roads in London, which meant it was also up there in the world ranking. The building was faced with white stucco, and thick pillars framed a vast black front door. There was a balcony at the front of the first floor with Corinthian columns supporting the floors above.

Caesar still hadn't contacted Matthew. It was unlike him not to respond. Given Lucy's death, it was close to unforgivable. His upset at Caesar was only partly mollified by a growing concern about what had happened to their patron.

Matthew pressed the doorbell and heard the chime reverberating deep inside the building. A minute crawled by with no answer. He tried again before stepping off the porch to look through the windows. No lights were on. Knowing that Caesar preferred to camp out in the basement, which was kitted out as a full-on library and office, Matthew waited another few minutes to give Caesar time to climb up the spiral staircase. It was a fruitless wait.

Sighing, Matthew pulled out his mobile phone and called Caesar's number. He held his breath, thinking through what he was going to say. The call connected but went to voicemail. Where was he?

'It's Matthew. I'm sure you've heard about Lucy.' He paused to suck in some air. 'I would really like to talk to you. I'm outside your house right now. If you're here, please let me in. If you're somewhere else, please call me back. Thanks.'

He moved his shoulders to try and release the tension in the muscles at the base of his neck. He turned away, and his phone beeped to signal a missed call. The number was withheld, so he hit the button to play the message.

'Hi, Matt. It's Sammy.' There was a pause. 'Look, I can't imagine how hard things must be for you right now, and I wondered whether it would help to get away for a couple of days—you and Alfie—I don't know. You can use our holiday place if you want. Okay, well, it's just an idea. I'm at work if you want to talk. Take care, Matt.'

Matthew stuffed his phone back into his pocket. Perhaps a couple of days away would be good for Alfie. A change of scene might also benefit Matthew; it would give him the space to think.

He dialled Sammy's work number.

'Hello. Matt, I'm so sorry.' There was a slight hesitation before she continued. 'You know Daniel and I are here for you.'

'Thank you.'

'Where are you?' she asked.

'No. I called round to Caesar's house, but he's not in. Have you spoken to him recently?'

'No. It's very odd that he hasn't been in touch with you. He's been out of the country but was planning to be back for our meeting in a couple of weeks.'

The meeting had slipped Matthew's mind. Every year, Caesar hosted a formal get-together, and they'd all received their invitations for this year's event a month ago. Would there even be a meeting now when Lucy wouldn't be there? He could still see her so clearly—freckles and blue eyes—laughing as easily as she did everything else.

He pushed out a breath. 'If you hear from him, will you tell him I need to speak to him?' he said.

'Of course,' Sammy replied. 'Is there anything I can do?' Matthew hesitated, thinking about Lucy's self-treatment, but before he could decide whether to say anything, Sammy continued. 'Have a think about taking a few days away. You can use our place whenever you want. Open invite.'

'We might drive there tomorrow,' Matthew said. 'Perhaps stay a couple of days.'

'Great,' Sammy said. 'Yeah, that's great. I'll call our neighbour and let her know. She's got a key.'

'Thank you.' Matthew stopped, realising that he didn't know what to say next.

'Call me or Daniel anytime. For anything. You understand?'

'Yes. I understand. Thank you.'

Matthew slipped the phone back into his pocket and looked at Caesar's house again. He balled his hands.

There was still no sign of anyone inside. Where was he? And why had he disappeared at the same time as Lucy's death?

7

THEN

MAY 2001

Cambridge

BEN WATCHED SAMMY ANGEL WALK OUT OF THE ROOM. SHE HAD PASSED the interview and passed easily, but she was less confident than some of the others, so she wouldn't know it. As the door closed behind her, he reached into his pocket, pulled out a pair of headphones and slipped them into the socket of his desktop computer. Sound burst into his ears. Two voices with some background distortion. He tapped on the keyboard to lower the volume. He could just about make out the conversation.

'...I don't know, I found him hard to read,' Sammy said.

Ben smiled because he could read her; that was all that mattered.

'But you want the scholarship, right?' That Scottish lilt must be Alastair Niven, next in line for the hot seat.

'God, yes. This would change my life. Just the financial support alone, and that's before you even consider what his patronage might-'

'Slow down. I get it. You want it.' There was a pause. 'That's nice.' Alastair sounded just a touch too offhand. Interesting, Caesar thought.

'So, what about you?'

There was no answer, but Ben imagined that Alastair had shrugged. That would be him all over—too cool for rules. Sammy was his polar opposite. She stayed at home, devouring texts on investing, accounting, and finance. She was an early adopter of the AOL chat rooms, posting to investment blogs under the name Gabriel. She was smart, driven, and loved a challenge.

'You're Scottish?' Sammy asked.

'Aye, lassie.'

Ben pictured the easy smile he had seen in the photographs with the scouts' reports. Everyone wanted to be in Alastair's gang—perhaps apart from Alastair himself. Regarded as the 'cool kid,' he hit top grades without paying attention, working, or sometimes even turning up.

But no matter how casual, how disengaged Alastair might seem, Ben knew the truth. The scholarship was the chance to change the course of his life. He lived with his parents in Govan, Glasgow. He'd applied to Oxford University to study Psychology, Philosophy and Physiology, but he was unsure whether he would secure the loans and bursaries he would need to be able to afford it. His parents didn't have the means to support him. That's why the scholarship changed everything. It offered him full funding and ongoing support for his undergraduate degree and beyond—a post-graduate promise of no student debt. Money couldn't buy you love but could buy almost everything else.

'Right, well, good luck, I guess.' Sammy sounded irritated.

Ben scratched his beard as he slipped off the headphones and placed them in the desk drawer, taking out a piece of paper and placing it in the middle of the table. Then, he waited.

Ben didn't stand as Alastair entered the room. Alastair was the only one of the boys to opt out of wearing a suit - casual shirt and no tie - no doubt because he liked to think he was different. He had long and untamed dark brown hair. Sunglasses. Half bored, half smiling. A modern-day Mona Lisa.

Alastair strode over to the empty chair and slid into the seat without waiting for an invitation. He scanned the room, taking in Ben, and then his gaze settled on the solitary sheet of paper on the table.

Ben leant forward, placed his hand on the paper, and slid it towards Alastair as an introduction. 'Can you solve that?'

Alastair took a second to digest the equation neatly laid out on the paper in his hand before dropping it back on the table.

'Yes.'

'Go on then.'

There was a pause, and Alastair looked Ben straight in the eyes. 'No.'

Ben suppressed a smile. Edge. Oh yes, plenty of edge. 'No?' He raised his eyebrows but kept his voice even.

'Look, why waste both our time? I know I can solve that equation. You know I can solve that equation. Why don't you ask me a real question?'

There was a long pause before Ben spoke. Let's see just how much edge you have, Mr Niven.

'What is courage?' he asked. It was an invitation; the only question was whether Alastair would accept it.

Alastair didn't react for a moment. Then he glanced towards the window. His mouth twitched before settling back to a neutral expression. He didn't speak but pushed back his chair, stood up, and walked out of the room.

Touché, Mr Niven, Ben thought. Touché.

Aylesbury

LUCY HEARD the footsteps on the stairs and instinctively slipped her book under the pillow on her bed. She picked up the crimson jumper next to her and started folding it. The bedroom door creaked open.

'Lucy, this letter came for you.'

Her aunt had never wanted a child, and Lucy had lived with that sentiment every day. It was as if her aunt blamed Lucy's mother, her own sister, for dying.

Aunt Kathleen's hair was tied back in a bun. Her glasses frames were strawberry-coloured, which might lead one to believe she was a joyous soul. The truth was that Aunt Kathleen didn't care much for any shade of red, and Lucy knew that those particular frames had been on offer at the opticians. She reached out to take the envelope and threw it onto her pillow.

'Aren't you going to read it?' her aunt asked.

'You've already read it.' Lucy's natural warmth was chilled by her aunt's presence.

'It's a scholarship offer.'

Lucy fought to control the excitement which bubbled up inside her. If that was true, then...

'Read it.' Aunt Kathleen's tone didn't anticipate resistance.

Lucy's interview had been smooth, but she hadn't dared to believe she might have passed. Benjamin Caesar had been so hard to read. She had tried everything she could to connect with him, but she'd come away unsure. She could click with most people, but there was a veneer with him that she hadn't been able to break through.

Aunt Kathleen would be relishing the release of the burden her sister had placed on her; she would hope to see the back of her adopted daughter. For Lucy, it was the dream of further education—to push herself and seek out knowledge. She had long wanted to escape the gravitational pull of home, and a university scholarship would provide the rocket fuel to propel her to reading English at Oxford University.

'Why do you have to open my post?' Lucy knew she would lose the argument, but she was determined to hide her exhilaration from her aunt. That would have to be victory enough.

'Because it was posted through my letterbox. Just read it.'

Lucy sighed and reached over. Isn't it *our* letterbox, she thought? She slid the letter out of its envelope, unfolded it and began to read.

Her conviction to hide her joy evaporated. She had been successful. She could go to Oxford knowing that a full scholarship would cover all her costs. She almost reached out to hug her aunt, only catching herself at the last moment.

Aunt Kathleen was smiling—if you could call it that- but Lucy knew it wasn't a smile of joy; it was a smile of relief.

8

NOW

THURSDAY, 13 JUNE 2019

Southwold, Suffolk

MATTHEW SAT HUNCHED OVER THE DESK, STARING THROUGH THE window out to the sea. As soon as Sammy made the suggestion, he realised he needed to get away with Alfie, but he also wanted to feel close to Lucy, which was why Sammy and Daniel's Suffolk coastal holiday home was perfect.

Matthew, Lucy, and Alfie had stayed there several times before, although not for a few years. It was a quiet day; the wind had stayed home, and the sun was glancing around, lazily playing hide and seek with the clouds. The pebbled beach was deserted, and the lifeguard's flag awaited a wind to bring it alive. Matthew twisted away as the sun blazed suddenly into his eyes, and catching sight of the necklace he'd brought with him and left on the desk, he instinctively picked it up. The delicate silver links tumbled through his fingers. Lucy had worn that necklace practically every day since he'd bought it for their first anniversary, whether she was walking on the beach or dressing up for an evening out with him or friends in town. He wrapped his fingers around the coral pendant. Its spikes pushed into his hand.

Just over ten years ago, he had sat there watching her through the window. She'd been wearing a red summer dress and walking barefoot with Alfie, turned towards the sea and away from Matthew. Alfie, two years old, was sitting on the beach, just at the water's edge, where the waves tickled his toes. His laughter was her laughter.

Matthew squeezed the necklace as tightly as he could and closed his eyes. His chest tightened, and his face went taut—two whole days. Goodness only knew how many minutes—too many to bear, too many for her to be gone. Giving the necklace one last squeeze, Matthew opened his eyes.

He saw a family had made their way down onto the beach: mum, dad, and two children. There was a splash of water, and Matthew spotted the family dog thundering through the waves. The couple were walking hand in hand, their children trailing tiny footprints in the wet sand, and the dog stopping to deliver a body-shaking, powered water shower. Cries of delight, smiles, laughter.

Matthew felt the bitterness hovering over him and tried to push it away. Why shouldn't they be happy? He didn't even know them. They had no link to what had happened.

Matthew was no closer to understanding what Lucy had been doing with the tDCS device, but he was sure she hadn't been depressed; she hadn't taken her own life. There were only two other possibilities: it had been an accident, or she had been murdered.

Matthew couldn't believe it had been an accident, which left murder. The famous Sherlock Holmes quote ran through his mind: *When you have eliminated the impossible, whatever remains, however improbable, must be the truth.* There was no suggestion of a break-in or sexual assault. He shook his head. Who would want to kill Lucy? Everyone loved her; everyone in the Genius Club adored her. A thought pushed its way into his mind.

He put down the necklace and reached for his laptop. A few minutes later, he typed the name Kathryn Farthing into the search bar. Kathryn had been a member of the Genius Club, although she had only joined after Dylan's departure.

The first hit was the three-year-old news report he knew by heart.

Detectives are investigating the murder of a 35-year-old woman who was stabbed to death in her own home in Kingston. Kathryn Farthing died from a knife wound to the chest on Tuesday, 27th June. Her young daughter, who was at home and witnessed the attack, was unharmed.

Inspector Darlington said: "We are now appealing for witnesses to come forward if they saw anyone in the area at this time, or if they have any further information that may help with the investigation. Extensive enquiries are still ongoing."

The other articles all told the same story. There were quotes from Kathryn's colleagues at Birkbeck, where she had taught History of Art, but there was no news of an arrest.

Matthew tried to order his thoughts. Kathryn's murder was three years ago. Neither Matthew, Lucy, nor any of the others had been close to Kathryn. She wasn't one of the original scholars and had never bonded with the group. Kathryn had been a scholar for less than a year when she opted out. There was no dramatic exit or fall-out. She had told them she felt she couldn't operate at their level and wanted to take a different path.

Matthew pulled his phone from his pocket and video-called Alastair.

He started speaking when his friend's face appeared on his phone screen. 'Kathryn Farthing was murdered.'

Alastair looked puzzled, and there was a pause before he responded. 'Yes, she was,' he said.

'I think Lucy was murdered, too,' Matthew said. Alastair's lips thinned. 'Did you hear what I said?' Matthew asked.

Alastair nodded. 'I heard you.'

'You think I'm delusional?'

'No, of course not.' He paused, frowning. 'The police seem to think Lucy took her own life.'

'No one knew her like I did.'

'I know, Matt,' Alastair said quietly. He rubbed his chin. 'So, with Kathryn and Lucy, you're wondering what the odds are of two scholars dying unexpectedly?'

'The odds don't matter,' Matthew said.

'How do you mean?'

'I mean, asking what the odds are is the wrong question.'

Alastair's expression softened. 'Okay, yes. The right question is whether there's a connection between the two.'

Matthew briefly wondered whether that was what Alastair had meant in the first place. He was often told he was too literal. 'I should tell the police about Kathryn's murder,' he said. 'Explain that she and Lucy were both scholars.' Matthew ran his hands over his face. 'There could be a link.'

'Between Lucy and Kathryn?' Alastair asked.

'Between their deaths and the scholarship,' Matthew said.

'I can't think of any reason someone would want to target us. Hardly anyone even knows about the Genius Club.'

'Just the scholars,' Matthew said, 'and Caesar.'

'Precisely,' Alastair said, nodding. 'And I can't believe it's any of us.'

'There were others besides our group of friends.'

Alastair stared at him. 'You mean Jason Tanner?'

'Yes, for one, but there might have been more.' Matthew shuffled forward on his seat. 'Jason and Kathryn weren't introduced until Dylan left at the end of the first year, but we know they were interviewed at the same time we were.'

'You think there were other candidates, perhaps ones who failed the interview.'

'Right.' Matthew tapped the fingers of his free hand against the table. 'What if there was a screening process? There could be others who knew about the scholarship but weren't selected for interview.'

'It's possible,' Alastair said, but his eyes were distant, 'although none of us knew anything about the scholarship before we received our invitation to interview.' He paused. 'I don't know. It's a long time for someone to hold a grudge. And to kill people?' He shook his head. 'I can't see it.'

'Jason was pretty upset when he was kicked out,' Matthew said.

'Exactly. *When* he was kicked out, that was nearly two decades ago.'

Matthew swallowed. 'You remember *why* he was expelled, though, right?'

Alastair shrugged. 'Yeah. Of course, I remember.'

Matthew let the idea settle in his mind, and then he sighed. 'You're right. It's unlikely. Still, I'll ask Caesar when I finally see him.' He heard the door creak. 'I have to go.'

Matthew ended the call as the door swung open, and Alfie poked his head into the room. He looked at his father and spoke so quietly that Matthew struggled to hear him.

'Hey, Alfie,' he said softly. 'What did you say?'

'I fell asleep.' Alfie's face was pale, and Matthew could see distress in his eyes.

He stretched out his arms in an awkward invitation. He saw a flicker of confusion ride across Alfie's face before he nodded and moved into the room. He buried his face in Matthew's jumper whilst Matthew put his arms around his son and held him as tightly as he dared. He clumsily patted his son's hair.

After a moment, he felt Alfie's hands on his jumper and realised his son was trying to free himself. Feeling guilty at his slight sense of relief, Matthew let go. Alfie leant back and looked into Matthew's eyes.

'I can't believe that I'll never...' his voice was scratchy, '...never be with her again. Ever.'

Matthew cleared his throat. He went to speak but couldn't find the words. He pulled his son back towards his chest and hoped Alfie wouldn't notice that his dad was crying.

THEY WATCHED a couple of films together in the room Alfie was sleeping in, with Alfie succumbing to sleep just before the end of the second one. Matthew had watched it to the end and then turned off the TV. He kissed Alfie on the head and slipped out of his bedroom, closing the door behind him. He found himself back at the desk, looking out over the beach. This time, a glass of whisky was his companion. He'd never liked whisky, but Lucy had been a quiet connoisseur. He swirled the drink around his mouth as he imagined appropriate and swallowed hard, trying to ignore the bitter aftertaste.

Alfie had surprised him earlier by telling him he wanted to return to school on Monday. Matthew argued at first, but Alfie was intractable, and Matthew couldn't point to any hard evidence that having time away from school was the best answer. Ultimately, the conversation twisted off in another direction without them agreeing explicitly.

Just then, his phone buzzed. He looked at the screen to see an email from Caesar. He blinked, tapped on the screen, and started to read.

Matthew,

I'm sorry I haven't returned your calls. I have been very unwell and too weak even to call.

I've heard the awful news about Lucy. I don't know what to say; I'm not sure there are any words.

I am so deeply sorry.

I still intend to meet with you all – health permitting. Lucy's tragic death has made me reconsider everything we have done and everything we are doing. I want to share my thinking.

In the meantime, you and Alfie are in my thoughts.

Ben Caesar.

Matthew blew out a breath. Caesar's health had been patchy for the last couple of years and had clearly worsened recently. At least he had finally made contact, and Matthew would hopefully see him at the scholarship meeting, if not before.

He put his phone down on the desk, took another mouthful of whisky, and reached for the black notebook he'd left on the table. He'd brought it with him, and until that moment, he hadn't been sure that he would look inside it, but he needed to find some answers—for Alfie and for himself. He opened the notebook, and a single sheet slipped free and floated to the ground.

Matthew crouched to pick it up. He turned it over, and then he was looking at a photograph of a woman he hadn't seen in person for nearly two decades. There was a tremor in his hand as the image pushed into his mind. He stared at the photograph: short, bleached white hair, angular features and grey-blue eyes—impassive as if she didn't care, which was her all over.

Dylan Steele.

9

THEN

SEPTEMBER 2001

Cambridge

MATTHEW HAD ARRIVED EARLY FOR THE FIRST RESIDENTIAL WEEKEND scholars' meeting, which was good for him. It forced people to speak to him when they arrived, and he needed all the help he could get to break the ice. He'd arrived so early on the interview day that the previous candidate, Lucy Summerton, was still waiting to be invited in. Something about her had snuck into his brain and lodged itself there. Scratch that—everything about her.

He was used to girls ignoring him and, most of the time, he didn't mind, but Lucy had greeted him as if they'd been friends for years. He had smiled back, knowing that he'd probably looked goofy, but he never could pull off appearing cool. They had chatted for a couple of minutes and, for once, Matthew hadn't had to try. His emphasis on making conversation had always been on the 'making' element. He used building blocks to try and open up discussions, but people's answers often confused him, and he found he didn't know how to layer on top of what had just been said. Sometimes, he wouldn't respond at all. Speaking with Lucy was different. Action and reaction. Call and response. Over and over.

Matthew peered into the room. Books covered the walls, and ornate, padded chairs were spread around as if set up for a reading group meeting. He paused, took a deep breath, and stepped into the room.

'Hello, again,' Lucy said in a voice that was all sunshine and moonlight at the same time. She took his outstretched hand between hers.

'Hi,' he said, warmth spreading across his chest. He waved at Daniel, who nodded while listening to the woman beside him.

'This is Vanessa,' Lucy said, pointing to the woman chatting to Daniel. She had long, red hair swept over her face, partially covering her eyes, and she brushed it away before introducing herself.

'Hi. Vanessa Wordsworth. Most people call me V.'

Her warmth was different from Lucy's. Lucy pulled you in emotionally. Matthew imagined it was how it would feel to be hugged. Meanwhile, with Vanessa, it was more like standing next to a generator. He saw her eyes during the whirlwind introduction, and they looked bloodshot. He felt sure that she'd been crying. Lucy was watching her, too, and Matthew saw a small crinkle form on Lucy's forehead.

The group had fallen silent as the door creaked open. Matthew would have hated to walk into the room in such circumstances, with everyone staring and silent. He saw the woman's cheeks turn pink as she waved to them.

'Hello, everyone. I'm Sammy.' She pushed at her glasses and smiled from beneath her frizzy fringe.

Lucy had started to move before Sammy spoke, and they shook hands seconds later. Matthew felt a dull stab in his stomach that Lucy had greeted everyone as she had greeted him, but when he spun the thought around, he began to feel better. He held back as Sammy introduced herself to the others.

'Shall we grab a drink and sit down?' Lucy suggested. Without waiting for a response, Lucy picked up the tray of glasses and held it out towards Vanessa.

Matthew passed on the offer of champagne and lowered himself into the nearest chair. He held his breath while Lucy finished her waitressing and sat in the chair beside him. He let the air out as slowly as he could.

A few minutes later, the final two scholars arrived. They made a striking couple. The man was tall, slim, and wearing a leather jacket and black jeans. His dark hair was styled with classic rock-and-roll nonchalance. He wasn't smoking, but somehow it seemed as though he should be.

He nodded in greeting and then took a swig from his beer bottle. He paused and extended his arm towards the group, waiting for the woman to walk ahead of him in some display worthy of a rock star for the modern generation.

The woman was wearing a T-shirt that looked a couple of sizes too large. It was a violent yellow, and the message 'Error 404, not found' was emblazoned across the chest in black letters. Her hair was short and dyed blue, her skin pale, and her eyes looked straight ahead, focused only on the future. She didn't respond in any way to the man's gesture, but after a moment, she reached into the back pocket of her green camo trousers and pulled out what looked like an oversized calculator, which puzzled Matthew because she appeared to be reading it.

The man shrugged, took another swig of his beer, and strode over to introduce himself. For whatever reason, he chose to hold his hand out to Matthew first.

'Al Niven. Good to meet you.' He grinned, and Matthew saw him wink at Vanessa, who fired him back a wink of her own.

'Matthew Stanford.'

'Nice one, Matt.'

Matthew shuffled on the spot, unsure how to respond to being glossed with the closest thing he'd ever had to a nickname. He'd never considered himself a Matt, and he was pretty sure the rest of the world hadn't either.

The other new arrival was still standing inside the door, staring at the machine in her hand, making no effort to connect with the others in the room, but Lucy was nearly across to her.

'Hi. Good to meet you. I love your hair. I'm Lucy.' She held out her hand for what seemed like an eternity. A couple of revolutions of the earth later, the woman shook her hand.

'Dylan Steele.'

'Come on, Dylan. Meet the others.' Lucy gently pulled on Dylan's arm, and to Matthew's surprise, Dylan followed her.

At that moment, he heard the door click shut, and Matthew looked around to see Benjamin Caesar for the first time since accepting the scholarship.

CAESAR WORE A BROWN SUIT, a rust-coloured shirt, and a hazel tie with flecks of gold. His beard and moustache were neatly clipped, his hairline receding with flecks of grey peppering his dark hair. He was smiling, and Matthew thought he had the air of a journalist who knew he was about to break a major news story. Caesar shook everyone's hands before inviting them all to sit down while he remained standing.

Matthew tapped his fingers against his palms as Caesar started speaking.

'Welcome to the inaugural meeting of the scholarship group. The scholarship has been designed to provide you with every opportunity to help you fulfil your potential. You've been selected because you show immense promise, and whilst you excel in different areas, I hope you will learn from each other and focus on what differentiates you.'

Matthew glanced around the group, but everyone was glued to Caesar's every word. Their patron pointed to the shelf closest to him, which spanned the entire room and was packed with books.

'These are the biographies of some of the greatest minds in history. Scientists, philosophers, poets, revolutionaries, artists, and dreamers. Some of them were world-famous, others relatively unknown. Some had been touched by the hand of God, others haunted by madness, yet every last one of them was extraordinary. I want you to aspire to join them.

'I want to be clear that this is the start of my long-term commitment. My life experience taught me how difficult it can be for those who have to strive for every penny. The scholarship is designed to support you through university and beyond. In exchange for the ongoing support of the scholarship, I ask that you agree to two commitments. Firstly, you will not have sexual relationships with any other scholar.'

'Really?' Alastair asked. Matthew wasn't sure Alastair had meant to speak aloud, but he looked like he wanted a reply.

'Yes, really,' Caesar said. 'This group has been carefully selected, and the investment that will be made in you all will be considerable. The balance and harmony of the group are of critical importance. You will naturally develop friendships, but intimate physical contact will likely fracture the group dynamic. I appreciate that we cannot easily enforce this, but I want to be clear. Anyone who has broken the rules will be expelled from the scholarship.'

Matthew stared at Caesar, partly because he couldn't quite believe what he was hearing and partly to prevent him from looking at the others.

'The second commitment is to support the scholarship in its broader work to democratise intelligence.'

'What does that mean?' Vanessa asked.

'My vision is to help as many people develop to their potential as possible. There are many interesting research projects in the areas of intelligence, education, and personal development. I would like you each to assist with research into some of these areas.'

'Will we be able to choose which ones?' Vanessa was sitting bolt upright.

'There are a number of areas of study,' Caesar replied, 'but within those areas, yes, there will be scope to define your projects.'

'Can you give us some examples?' Daniel asked.

Caesar turned to face him. 'One example would be research into game theory in the context of human behaviour and psychology.

Another is to understand why China performs so well in the International Mathematical Olympiad.'

'What's that?' Lucy asked.

Matthew swallowed as Caesar looked straight at him. 'Perhaps you could explain, Matthew.'

Matthew felt his face redden. 'It's an international maths competition.'

'Matthew was selected for the British team,' Caesar said, 'and was invited to represent the UK in the international event.'

Lucy turned to face him. 'That's amazing.'

'China has achieved the highest team score six times this decade alone,' Caesar continued. 'I'm interested in understanding how they perform so consistently well.'

'So, we each get to choose our research area?' Sammy asked.

Caesar nodded. 'We will have a discussion, and you'll be given a choice from a few options. All I ask is that you commit to spending some time on whichever research area we agree upon.'

He paused and looked around the group, but there were no more questions. 'Every month, I will arrange for us all to get together for a weekend here in Cambridge. I will cover your travel costs, and there's enough room for everyone to stay here. During those weekends, I will have a one-to-one conversation with each of you to see what, if any, support you need.' There was a general murmur from the group and a nodding of heads. 'Okay, then. Well, if that's all clear, it's time for some friendly competition.'

THE DOORS SWUNG open and the doorman walked in, carrying a stack of boxes. Matthew could see that they were chess sets.

'Who's playing?' Sammy asked.

'You all are,' Caesar replied.

'Yes, but who's playing whom?' Sammy had edged forward on her seat. The doorman was setting up nine boards.

'I've split you into a group of three and a group of four. Within each group, you are going to play each other simultaneously.' A silence fell over the room until Caesar continued. 'Once you concede or lose one game, you forfeit your remaining game. Then, the two winners play each other. Matthew, Lucy, and Sammy are in group one. Alastair, Dylan, Daniel, and Vanessa are group two.'

Alastair kicked his feet forward and rested them on the table that separated them all. He'd finished his beer and was working his way through a glass of champagne. 'Christ, chess? What sort of party is this?' he whispered. 'They had clubs at school for this sort of stuff that I avoided like the plague.'

'Nervous, Al?' Vanessa raised her eyebrows.

'Aye, maybe. But not about playing chess.' The edges of his mouth twitched.

Matthew could sense a change in the atmosphere but couldn't quite identify it. Sammy and Daniel had warmed to the task, Alastair seemed unimpressed, and Dylan hadn't even been listening.

Five minutes later, Matthew was the first to lose. He underestimated Lucy, and she immediately punished him for a sloppy move. Sammy was concentrating hard, while Alastair was laughing and looking like he wasn't trying. Dylan had plugged in some headphones and was nodding along to whatever music rocked her world, seemingly not paying her games any attention. Her focus was on reading her email pager. Several times, one of the others had had to prompt her to take her turn.

Within a few minutes, Lucy conceded, putting Sammy into the final. Daniel and Vanessa were already out from the other group. Matthew turned to watch Dylan and Alastair battle it out. Alastair was playing aggressively, taking risks that would probably be his undoing but might just see him win. Dylan's play was unpredictable. There was no pattern or structure. It was like watching someone playing for the first time with each move credited not with genius, but with increasing beginner's luck. Matthew guessed it was an approach based on first principles, a response to raw data, rather than a learned tactic. Dylan slipped off her headphones and looked directly at Alastair, who shrugged. Dylan moved her bishop, and their game was over. Alastair was out.

They all crowded around the final game. After a few moves, Sammy flinched very subtly. Dylan couldn't have seen it because she was, at the time, staring intently at her pager, but she raised her head to look at the board, then her opponent.

Sammy shook her head. 'I concede. I don't think we need to keep everyone waiting while we play out the next twelve moves.'

'Four, but okay.' Dylan slipped her headphones back on and turned her attention back to the pager.

10

NOW

FRIDAY, 14 JUNE 2019

Southwold, Suffolk

MATTHEW KNEW THAT LUCY HAD STAYED IN TOUCH WITH DYLAN, BUT she hadn't mentioned her for a long time. The photograph looked recent; he guessed it was perhaps only a couple of years old.

Something inside him shifted: a hollowing out of his stomach and a stretching of his chest. Looking for an explanation for why Lucy had the picture meant finding the woman who had left the scholarship after the first year.

He placed the photograph on the desk and focused on the diary. His fingertips left marks on the black cover, and as he turned the pages, he could feel Lucy watching over him. He nearly closed it again, but he knew he had to look. The first flick-through confirmed that it was an appointment diary rather than a personal journal. The wave of relief that flooded through his body surprised him. Had he, on some level, prepared himself to read Lucy's thoughts and discover that he didn't really know her? He had already lost her, and he couldn't face the thought that he'd never truly had her at all.

Matthew turned back to the first page. Monday through Wednesday covered the left-hand page, and Thursday through

Sunday were on the right-hand side. Various appointments were recorded, but his attention was drawn to a handwritten entry on Monday consisting of one word: Dylan. He turned the page, and his eyes sought out Monday again. There it was—Dylan. He flicked forward. She was there every week.

The diary fell closed over his fingers whilst he processed the information. Dylan had walked out of the scholarship after the first year. Lucy and Dylan had forged a friendship over that year, and whilst Matthew and Dylan would never be great friends, Lucy had stayed in contact. She rarely mentioned Dylan, and Matthew assumed that was because they weren't in regular contact, yet Lucy's diary showed that she had been meeting Dylan every week.

It was dark outside, and he could only distinguish the sea from the sky by the faint shimmer of the ocean. His eyes searched for the horizon, and a thought spun in his mind, taking a moment to form.

Monday was the day Lucy went to choir practice. Almost without fail, she'd head off to church on Monday afternoons. He'd been to most of her choir's concerts, and there'd been no sense that she didn't fit in or that the others looked at her as if she shouldn't be there. He was sure she was a regular. He couldn't imagine she'd skipped practice every week to meet Dylan rather than rehearse, but he knew who to ask to confirm. Matthew glanced at the time and then made the call.

Sammy answered immediately. 'Hi, Matt. Is everything okay?'

'Hi, Sammy. Yes, we're all ... we're both fine.' He swallowed hard and pushed on. 'I wanted to thank you and Daniel again for letting us stay here. It's just what we need.'

'I'm so glad you agreed to go. You can stay as long as you like. We won't get to the coast for a few weeks.'

'Thank you.' He paused. 'Alfie wants to go back to school on Monday. I'm not sure what to do.'

'Perhaps it's best to let him deal with things his way. Going back to school might be the best thing for him.' Matthew didn't know what to say, so he stayed silent. 'Well, I hope you've made it down to the beach. It's lovely at this time of year.'

The beach—where families played with the angels looking on. Where his own family once played. But no longer.

'Not yet,' he said, his voice cracking. 'I wanted to ask you a question about choir.' He didn't know how to build up to it, and now he'd just blurted it out. He chewed on his lip.

'Choir?' He heard confusion in her voice.

'I was thinking back to some of the concerts. Lucy used to love her practice.' He wasn't lying. She would come back home every Monday evening, having picked up Alfie from his after-school computer club, and her eyes would shine whenever their son chose to join her in a duet.

'Yes, she did. I'm afraid I haven't been going much the last year, but she was one of the group's mainstays.' There was a silence, and Matthew wondered whether Sammy was holding something back. 'We all miss her, Matt. The choir won't be the same without her. We need to treasure those memories.'

'I don't think she ever missed a rehearsal other than when we were on a family holiday,' he said.

'No.'

He caught what he thought was a melancholy gloss over her confirmation. Or was it hesitation or even a suggestion that Lucy hadn't attended practice? He shook his head. No. Sammy was just handling him gently.

'I wanted to ... um, this may sound a bit strange, but do you have contact details for Dylan?'

'Dylan Steele?' Sammy said the name as if it was a conspiracy theory. 'No. Why do you ask?'

Matthew coughed. 'I guess I thought ... after Lucy's, after what happened, I thought she might like to know.' His words tailed off. His explanation didn't carry the same conviction as Lucy's diary entry, but he wasn't ready to share that.

'I don't think any of us will have her contact details. Lucy was close to her, wasn't she, but if they didn't keep in touch, I can't imagine that ... maybe, Alastair?' She sounded like she was trying to help without believing she could. 'I'd be very surprised though.'

There was another pause. 'Maybe it's best to leave Dylan in the past.'

It was almost certainly best, but now impossible, thought Matthew. Could Dylan have been hiding in plain sight in the choir? No, Sammy would have recognised her, and Matthew himself would have spotted her at the concerts. It had to be something else. A weekly call, maybe.

He realised he hadn't replied to Sammy. 'I'm sure you're right,' he said in a rush. 'It was just a thought. Well, thanks again, Sammy. I'll call you again soon. Give my best to Daniel.'

He ended the call and fired off a text to Alastair.

A wave of tiredness hit him, and he lowered the blind over the window before heading towards the master bedroom. On the way, he leant around the other bedroom door to check on Alfie and watched for a moment. The duvet rose and then fell – if only the daytime were so peaceful. He turned, and at that moment, Alastair's response arrived.

Dylan? Yeah. We go clubbing every Saturday night.

Matthew stared at the text, and his phone vibrated to signal a new arrival.

Or, no, I haven't seen her for years.

A third buzz.

It's definitely one or the other. Take a guess. Night, mate.

Matthew powered off his phone. None of them were in contact with Dylan, other than Lucy, who appeared to have an appointment with her every Monday. It didn't make any sense, but Matthew knew there must be an explanation. He just needed to find it.

11

THEN

JANUARY 2002

Cambridge train station

It still made Lucy smile that Dylan could have gone to any university in the UK, but she'd chosen Abertay University because they were the first to offer an undergraduate degree in ethical hacking—whatever that was.

Lucy stood on the platform and watched the train pull in. It was funny to think of her friend doing something as ordinary as catching a train. Dylan didn't value the same things as most others did. Tradition, convention, and worrying about how she made people feel had all been given a Viking funeral early on in Dylan's formative years.

Lucy saw the silver headphones glistening amongst the disembarking passengers, and she started waving as Dylan made her way through the crowd and over the bridge. Lucy weaved along the concourse and threw her arms around her friend. She was used to being shrugged off, but she didn't mind. That was as enthusiastic a response as she would ever get from Dylan.

'Love the hair,' Lucy said. It was the first thing she'd ever said to Dylan and was something of an in-joke. For someone who didn't care about what people thought of her, Dylan changed her hair more often than most people. But Lucy thought that the red suited her.

'Thank you for coming at short notice. Matthew was meant to be here, but he had to go home to visit his dad this weekend.' She paused as the secret bubbled up. No. Not now. She should stick with her plan.

'Always happy to be second choice,' Dylan deadpanned.

'Second? Um, well,' Lucy's expression dropped, and she pursed her lips. 'Sammy was busy, and I couldn't get hold of V.'

'Lucy Summerton, you couldn't lie even if your life depended on it.'

The comment made Lucy pause. She linked arms with Dylan's, knowing she hated physical contact with anyone other than Lucy, and leant in towards her. She dropped her voice to a whisper as they turned out of Cambridge train station and headed towards the city centre.

'It's funny you say that. Something happened in my last meeting with Caesar. It was a bit weird.' Dylan said nothing, and so Lucy pushed on. 'I hadn't told him about me and Matthew, for obvious reasons, but he asked me whether we were sleeping together.'

Dylan stopped and turned to face Lucy. 'Are you serious?'

'Yes. He asked it in a very matter-of-fact manner, without any build-up. He caught me unprepared, so I just told him the truth.'

'Which is?'

'No, of course not,' Lucy said. Dylan stopped walking and fixed Lucy with a stare. 'We aren't.' Lucy glanced around, conscious that she was talking loudly.

'Okay.' Dylan continued to look at her friend.

Lucy felt heat in her cheeks. 'We've talked about it.'

'Talked about it, as in, tell me what you want to do to me, talked about it?' Dylan's eyes were dancing now.

'Dylan!' Lucy's hand flew to her mouth, and she scanned the nearby pedestrians for signs of shock.

'Oh...' Dylan's eyes widened. 'You mean you actually discussed when would be the right time.'

'What's wrong with that?' Lucy asked. 'Why are you staring at me?'

'Just promise me you will always continue being Lucy Summerton.'

'I don't even know what you mean.'

'Exactly like that. Never change.'

'You're mocking me.' Lucy was sure of it, even though Dylan wasn't smiling.

'Only because I love you.'

Lucy punched Dylan on the arm, and they started walking again, but she knew that Dylan had spoken the truth.

'It's weird though, right? That he should ask me that?'

'Yes. He has no right to ask you anything like that, whatever pathetic rules he might have for his precious scholarship. If he asks you something similar again, tell him where to go.'

'Be more Dylan and less Lucy?' She smiled at her friend, who looked back at her, tilting her head.

At the time, Lucy had felt surprised more than uncomfortable. She hadn't mentioned it to Matthew because she knew he would be upset that she had answered.

'Are you still thinking about what it might be like to be more Dylan?' her friend asked.

'No.' Her conversation with Caesar wasn't important compared to her real news. Lucy pulled her friend over to the side of the pavement, away from the flow of human traffic. She was sure that her expression had already made the announcement, but she wanted the thrill of saying the words. And so, lingering over each syllable, she revealed the secret she wanted to shout to the world. 'Last weekend, Matthew proposed to me.'

Dylan blinked. 'Wow. I'm guessing you said yes.'

Lucy grinned. 'Of course I did.' Then she scrunched her nose. 'But I'm worried about Caesar.'

'What's it got to do with him?'

'I don't want us to be kicked out of the scholarship. It's been good for us.'

'There's an easy answer.' Dylan paused. 'Don't marry Matthew.'

Lucy rolled her eyes. 'I'm going to have to tell him. I was thinking back to what he said on our first day—that he was worried about rocking the group dynamic, but I can argue that this won't do that. It's not like it's a one-night stand.'

'That's true,' Dylan said. 'You haven't reached that milestone yet.'

'You're not helping.' Lucy grabbed Dylan's arm and pulled her towards the tower of the University Church of St Mary the Virgin. 'This is where he proposed to me.' She saw Dylan raise an eyebrow. 'Don't you dare say it,' she said. 'Come on. We're going to the top.' She started climbing the steps.

Lucy had said yes to Matthew before he had finished asking the question. They belonged together. She knew he wasn't a people person, but it wasn't because he didn't care about others – once she had learned about the challenge of his mother leaving him early in life and his father struggling to demonstrate affection, she could see how it would happen. Matthew had told Lucy she was the first person he could ever remember hugging him. Eighteen years of memories, and not a single one registered a hug—it was simply unfathomable. Even thinking about it made her arms ache to hold him.

Lucy and Dylan reached the top of the stairs and walked over to take in the view. Dylan stared out towards the Radcliffe Camera.

'Amazing, isn't it?' Lucy said. 'I could look at this view forever.'

Dylan nodded, seemingly fixated on the building. Lucy was glad she'd told Dylan, even if her friend hadn't swept her up in an excited hug or squealed with joy. This was Dylan Steele, after all.

'I told Matthew I want at least five children.' Lucy spoke to the back of Dylan's head, but her words made her friend turn around.

'You do realise you will have to sleep with him to do that, right? Probably several times.'

Lucy stuck her tongue out. 'Funny girl.'

Dylan tilted her head as she regarded Lucy. 'I can so see you as a mum.'

The wind carried away Lucy's laughter, but she hoped her friend was right. She saw a shadow fall over Dylan's face. 'What's wrong, Dylan?'

Dylan shook her head slightly. 'It's nothing.'

'Come on. You can tell me.'

But Dylan didn't reply. Lucy knew there was no point in trying to change Dylan's mind, but she tucked away the thought for another day. Something was troubling Dylan. She'd come back to it. But right then, she would continue to soak up the view and dream of the future.

12

THEN

FEBRUARY 2002

Heartfield Health Cambridge Hospital

Matthew shuffled in his seat. There wasn't much in the room. Weighing scales, a blood pressure machine, and a tall, thin trolley stacked with narrow drawers. Everything felt clinical.

Lucy had talked him into coming; she'd already seen Doctor Henry Bannister herself after Caesar had recommended him to all the scholars. Matthew's asthma hadn't improved, and Lucy suggested he make an appointment. The doctor was scribbling on a pad and talking as he did so. He tore the piece of paper free and handed it to Matthew.

'Let's try this prescription for a few months. I want you to take it with your current prescription, particularly if you have something stressful coming up.'

Matthew took the folded paper and slipped it into his pocket. 'Thank you.'

'Is there anything else?' The doctor spoke in a tone that suggested his thoughts were already turning to his next patient.

Matthew shook his head and mumbled another thank you before leaving the surgery.

He was due to head back to his college at Oxford that evening, and he'd already said goodbye to Lucy. He fastened his coat buttons, swung his bag over his shoulder and stuffed his hands into his pockets.

He pushed on towards the station, trying to ignore the cold seeping into his bones. He'd been making the trip almost every other weekend for the best part of a year, and he still couldn't quite believe his luck in finding Lucy. Not only that he'd found her, but that she'd agreed to marry him. He shook his head and laughed. Sure, they were young to commit, but he'd never been more certain of anything.

Matthew glanced up as he approached the station. He smiled to himself. He was even magicking her up now. The woman standing at the entrance looked exactly like her. She started to run towards him.

'Lucy?' It was her. 'What are you doing here?' She clutched his arm as she stopped in front of him. Her face was flush, and she was shouting, 'Slow down. I missed that. Is everything alright?'

Lucy paused for a breath, seemingly trying to do as he asked. 'Dylan's leaving.'

'Dylan's leaving?' he echoed. 'What do you mean?'

Lucy was talking quickly. 'She's quit. She's told Caesar she's not coming back.'

'How do you know?' Matthew took a moment to guide Lucy to a quieter part of the pavement away from the main entrance.

'She called me. She didn't say much; you know what she's like.'

'Wow.' But even as he spoke, Matthew realised that he wasn't surprised. Dylan never seemed to need a good reason for her actions; she just did what she wanted whenever she felt like it. He wouldn't mourn her departure but knew Lucy would be upset. He also knew better than to push Lucy for information. If she had little to say, it was because not much had been shared.

'Do you want me to stay in Cambridge? I could catch the train back early tomorrow.'

Lucy shook her head. 'No.' She stretched up to kiss his cheek. 'I still need to finish my essay. But thank you.' She rested her head on

Matthew's chest as he wrapped his arms around her. 'I just wanted to see you.'

Lucy's words were muffled, and he felt her pull her head back as if she were about to say something else. Then she relaxed back into him and squeezed him tight. After a few moments, Matthew rubbed her back before releasing her.

'I'd better head to the platform,' he said.

He saw her smile. She knew he liked to be early, sometimes so much so that he caught the previous train to the one he was aiming for.

'Hey, how was Doctor Bannister?' she asked.

'Fine,' he said, leaning back in towards her.

They kissed goodbye, and then Matthew turned and walked into the station.

13

NOW

MONDAY, 17 JUNE 2019

Fulham Broadway, London

IT WAS ALFIE'S FIRST DAY BACK AT SCHOOL SINCE LUCY'S DEATH, AND he'd been adamant that he wanted to go to the computer club. Matthew had found it hard enough to drop his son off at school, but the wait to pick him up again had been even worse.

Matthew didn't much like driving, so he'd left before rush hour to avoid the worst of the traffic. There would be at least a fifty-minute wait for Alfie to come out. He'd parked the car a couple of hundred yards down the road from the school gate and was trying to pass the time by reading an academic paper. He shook his head as his mind drifted once again. How on earth would Alfie have coped with school with his mother's death such a raw memory?

After a few minutes, he looked up to see some school kids drifting home. Alfie was walking down the road. Matthew pulled the keys from the ignition and climbed out of the car.

He called out to Alfie, who hadn't seen him and was striding down the hill. A couple of other students turned to look at Matthew, but Alfie didn't so much as flinch. Matthew pushed his glasses on his nose. He could see Alfie had headphones on. He started to jog after him, but almost immediately, his chest tightened, and he had to stop to catch his breath. He gave himself a few seconds, hands resting on his knees, before setting off again. As he walked, watching his son pull away in front of him, his mind began to explore an idea. An idea that made his chest crush even tighter.

Matthew shuffled along the road, no longer fighting to close the gap to Alfie. He wondered what Lucy would think of him sneaking after their son. He fought the urge to argue his case. There was so much that he could say—her diary, her self-treatment—but it wasn't helpful. He had to bite back on his emotions and wait.

They were walking towards the river. Wherever Alfie was going, it seemed likely to be somewhere in Putney. His son crossed over the street and turned down a side road. Matthew slowed his pace slightly, pulling back. Alfie walked up a driveway, and Matthew ducked behind a tree, close enough to see.

He heard Alfie speak. It sounded like 'hello.'

Matthew felt sick. Monday, every week—the appointments weren't for Lucy but for Alfie.

Matthew peered around the tree trunk. It hit him the second before he saw her. Swamped in a baggy T-shirt over black leggings, she stood with her arms around his son as if she had every right to hug him.

Dylan Steele.

MATTHEW LOST count of the times he stepped towards Dylan's front door, but on each occasion, he held back. Lucy would never have done anything to put Alfie in danger. Alfie himself was as intransigent as a twelve-year-old could be. He simply wouldn't have met with Dylan under duress.

After a while, Matthew decided to walk back to the car. Every step took him further away from his son, but it was the emotional distance that hurt him. Lucy and Alfie had their secrets, yet Matthew couldn't think of a single thing he'd kept from Lucy. Could Lucy have told him about taking Alfie to see Dylan, and he'd forgotten? He didn't think so.

The irony was that he used to have the perfect answer in situations like this: Lucy. Even though she was no longer there, he could hear her telling him not to charge into a discussion with Alfie. He climbed back into the car and tried to bury himself in one of his students' latest theorems. After ten minutes, he saw Alfie turn the corner and start the walk back up the hill. Matthew kept his head down, and Alfie walked past the car and back into school.

Computer club wasn't due to finish for another ten minutes, and Matthew was confident that Alfie would reappear then. There had been something different in Alfie's countenance as he walked past. Matthew hadn't turned to get a close look, but he could have sworn that Alfie had been crying.

Matthew sunk his head into his hands. He needed help. He didn't like confrontation and didn't want to put Alfie in a position where he might lie to him. He needed to speak to someone other than Alfie, who might have had contact with Dylan. He knew none of his fellow scholars had stayed in touch with her. There was only one other person to ask: someone who had always had his back and his family's.

He hit the dial button and waited. Voicemail again. Matthew tossed his phone into his lap, feeling slightly sick. Just when he needed him the most, Ben Caesar had disappeared from the face of the earth.

14

NOW

TUESDAY, 18 JUNE 2019

Raynes Park, London

MATTHEW DRIED HIMSELF AFTER HIS SHOWER, PULLED HIS CLOTHES back on, and headed to the kitchen. He looked at his watch. It would take him approximately an hour and a half to walk to Dylan's, giving him plenty of time to decide precisely what he would say.

He made himself a cup of coffee in a mug that Lucy had given him. It bore the caption 'All you need is LOVE' with four graphs of mathematical functions spelling out the letters in LOVE. As he sat down at the kitchen table his mobile phone started to ring.

'Hello, Professor Stanford. It's Mary Burton from the coroner's office.'

Matthew's mouth went dry. He was grateful he was already sitting down because he didn't feel he would've had the strength to continue standing. He listened, almost mute, to the procession of technical words that sounded like a recitation of a pharmaceutical brochure.

Midazolam. Vecuronium bromide. Potassium chloride.

His brain processed the information as if it were footnotes to the conversation. One. A sedative. Two. A drug to paralyse her muscles.

And three, to complete the death row trifecta, a chemical designed to stop her heart.

The last three words dulled everything around him. They pulled the sunlight from the sky and buried it in the ground. *Stop her heart.* He thought he could never know anything as strong as his wife's heart, but apparently, all it took to stop it was an injection of potassium chloride. He heard the conclusion, delivered in layman's terms.

'All the evidence points to your wife having taken her own life.'

Matthew slumped in the chair, clutching the phone to his ear, waiting for something to make sense, but it didn't happen. The coroner's office confirmed what the police had previously told him.

'There'll be an inquest into the death, which will likely be in a few months. We typically need that time to conduct our investigation.' Matthew began to zone out. 'Professor Stanford? Are you still there?'

'Yes, sorry.' Matthew swallowed. 'This is very difficult.'

'I'm very sorry, Professor. I was just saying that you'll likely be required to give evidence at the inquest.'

'Okay.' He heard himself speak but already knew what the coroner expected to conclude.

The police had told him that there'd be no criminal investigation: a dead body, a syringe, and a toxicology report. There were no signs of a break-in or a struggle. There was no evidence of another person having been in the building. Except that, to Matthew, it was anything but clear. It was a series of loosely connected statements which had led to a conclusion that defied who Lucy was. It simply wasn't enough. There were too many jumps. If it had been the work of an undergraduate, Matthew would have graded it a fail and given them a lecture on the nature of proof.

The police had listened when Matthew explained that Kathryn Farthing, a victim of a brutal murder, had also been a member of the same group of scholars. Still, he could tell from their tone that, while they said they would follow up with their colleagues, they didn't believe there was a connection.

The call with the coroner had ended, but Matthew hadn't been fully conscious of the fact. Ms Burton had been professional and polite, and yet the only facts that Matthew could take away from the verbal report were that Lucy was dead and that it had been a dangerously high cocktail of drugs injected into her bloodstream that had killed her. That was it. Everything else, each opinion, every inference, and the conclusion itself, was not demonstrably true.

He had scanned his every interaction with Lucy over the preceding months but had found nothing—no distress or despair. There wasn't anything to make Matthew even suspect she might have taken her own life.

Then there were the things that didn't fit with their conclusion. Firstly, Lucy was wearing her trainers when he found her. She never wore her shoes indoors. He knew it sounded inconsequential, but it was entirely out of character.

Secondly, the police's protestation that it was easy to order the deadly cocktail on the internet hadn't been swayed by Matthew stating that Lucy had rarely used the internet. There was no history in the internet browser on her phone, but Matthew was confident Lucy hadn't visited an Internet café or snuck onto another computer. No. She didn't order the drugs, and she didn't inject herself.

Lucy had been murdered, and whoever had done it wanted it to look as though she'd taken her own life. They'd done it well enough to satisfy the coroner and the police, but not Matthew.

He stood up and shuffled over to the sink to empty the remains of his coffee. He turned on the tap for a few seconds to wash it away, lost for a moment in the sound of the water hitting the metal. He sighed and twisted the tap closed.

The only good news from the coroner was the confirmation Lucy's body was no longer required for the investigation, which meant that the funeral could move ahead once Matthew had formally identified the body.

So, he would bury Lucy, he would wrap his arms around his son, and then he was going to hunt down whoever had murdered his wife.

15

NOW

TUESDAY, 18 JUNE 2019

Putney, London

MATTHEW PRESSED ON THE DOORBELL AND WAITED. AFTER A FEW seconds, the door opened, and he stood face-to-face with Dylan Steele.

She looked like the photograph in the diary with the addition of a pair of silver headphones. Slowly, very slowly, Dylan slid the headphones off.

'Hello, Matthew,' she said.

'I need to talk to you,' he said. Pleasantries didn't feel appropriate. Dylan didn't answer, so Matthew decided to get right to the point. 'You know about Lucy.' He said it as a statement, and Dylan nodded in acknowledgement. 'I need your help.' He swallowed. 'I don't expect you to do anything for me, but this is for Alfie.' He paused. 'And for Lucy.'

He studied Dylan's face, partly to gauge her reaction and partly to dull the pain of thinking about his wife. After what felt like a couple of orbits around the sun, she moved back inside and fully opened the door. Matthew stepped into the hallway and followed her into the kitchen. The room was sparse. There were no pictures, no rugs, and little furniture.

'How do you think I can help?' Dylan asked. She offered no drink, seat, or warmth.

'I don't know. Maybe you can't.' He shuffled on the spot. 'Would you mind telling me why you meet with Alfie?'

He heard himself. So apologetic. Shouldn't he be shouting, *what the hell are you doing with my son?* But somewhere, he could hear Lucy telling him to trust Dylan. Lucy did, and so Matthew had to try.

'Lucy asked me to teach him coding.' A flicker of confusion on Dylan's face was a rare display of emotion.

'Computing club.' Matthew said it as if reading the punchline to a joke he finally understood but still didn't find funny.

'It was Lucy's idea. He'd come here after school, and Lucy would pick him up after choir practice.'

Matthew felt something release inside him. That made sense. Some sort of sense, at least. Dylan was a genius with computers, and Alfie would learn more with her in an afternoon than a whole term attending an after-school club. But there was still a knot in his stomach.

'She wanted to tell you, but I asked her not to.' She stared at him, her eyes unblinking.

'Why?' His tone was sharp.

'Because I thought that you'd stop Alfie from coming.'

She was right. At least he would have started at that point. 'Lucy would have won that argument,' he said.

'I know, but I didn't want her to argue with you. Especially about me.'

Matthew nodded. Lucy knew he had struggled with Dylan since she asked Lucy to quit the scholarship with her. He could still recall how much Lucy had wrestled with the decision, and while she had chosen to stay, Dylan's encouragement to leave the scholarship, even if Matthew stayed, had cut deeply.

'There's no way she took her own life,' Dylan said.

Matthew stared at her. Somehow, Lucy had always been, and

continued to be, the one thing they always agreed on. 'Have you said that to Alfie?' he asked.

'No.' She stared at him.

Matthew thought of his son walking back to the school in tears and blew out a deep breath. 'I don't think she took her own life, either.'

'She called me,' Dylan said. 'The day she died. I was out; I missed the call.'

Matthew's head jerked up. 'Did she leave a message?'

Dylan shook her head. 'No. Nothing.' Matthew swallowed. Lucy had called him, Alfie, and Dylan, but she hadn't left a message with any of them. 'You realise, if she was killed, statistically, you're the most likely suspect,' Dylan said.

As his brain raked over what he knew to be true versus accepted facts, he heard himself say, 'Well, it wasn't me. You're next on the list.'

She blinked again. He didn't need her to deny it. He didn't suspect Dylan, but it did shine an uneasy light on the list of suspects.

'She was the purest person I ever met,' Dylan said.

Her response made tears prick Matthew's eyelids. 'I can't think of a single reason why anyone would want to kill her,' he said, looking at the floor.

Dylan was silent for a moment. 'How did Caesar react to Lucy's death?'

Matthew frowned. 'I haven't been able to speak to him. He sent me an email, but he's too unwell to speak,' he said, meeting Dylan's impassive gaze.

Time stretched until, eventually, she walked out of the room. Matthew knew that people sometimes found him socially awkward, but Dylan took it to another level. She reappeared a few minutes later and held out a small mobile phone.

His eyes narrowed as he reached to take it. 'What's this?'

'If we're going to help each other, I want to use a secure channel for our communication. Don't use my name when we speak or in texts. Don't use this phone for anything else but communicating with me.'

Part of him wanted to protest, but on some level, he knew that this was a massive compromise for Dylan. She turned and stared out of the kitchen window. She didn't seem to be registering anything that Matthew was saying. It was as if she had slipped her headphones back on. He hesitated. He'd found out much more than he had expected to, and all in all, Dylan had been civil. Perhaps their personal Cold War was over.

'Why did you ask about Caesar?' he asked.

'Do you know why I left?' Dylan didn't turn around, but Matthew could see her looking at him in the reflection in the glass.

'Yes, Lucy told me.'

'What did she say?' Her voice was so quiet that Matthew had to strain to hear it. He coughed. It wasn't exactly a topic he was comfortable discussing with anyone. Certainly not Dylan. 'Actually, it's okay. You don't need to say. It doesn't matter anyway.' She turned to face him. Matthew wasn't sure, but it looked like her eyes were wet. 'I never told Lucy the full truth. It would have upset her.' The hairs on the back of Matthew's neck stood up. 'Towards the end of that first year at university, I was suffering from chronic stomach cramps. Some days I couldn't get out of bed.' Her voice was monotone now, as if she were dialling down the memory and damping down the pain. 'A scan revealed severe endometriosis. I was advised to have an operation.' A shadow passed over her face. 'I had both ovaries removed.'

Matthew flinched. 'I'm sorry.' It didn't feel anywhere close to adequate. A cold shiver crept down his spine.

'When Caesar found out, he kicked me off the programme,' she said.

Matthew didn't move. He'd always thought Dylan had quit, and he was sure that was what Lucy had told him at the time.

'He wasn't explicit, but I think it was because I wouldn't ever be able to have children.' Dylan turned around to stare out of the window once more, as if face-to-face contact was as dangerous as staring at the sun.

Matthew stood there awkwardly. Lucy would have known what to do, but all Matthew could do was ask. 'I'm sorry, Dylan. What should I say?'

'I'm not telling you for sympathy. I'm telling you because I don't trust Caesar.' She wrapped her arms around her chest. 'Benjamin Caesar isn't the man you think he is,' she said.

'What do you mean?' Matthew said. 'He's supported all of us, ever since we were selected.'

'That may be true, but there's another truth, too. I think he wanted to pair people up; that was his plan from the beginning.'

'What?' Matthew shook his head. That didn't make any sense. 'His core rule was that relationships between us were forbidden. You were there when he told us.'

'No casual sex; that's what he was against. Caesar cultivated relationships.' Matthew opened his mouth to speak but didn't know what to say. 'Think about it. You and Lucy. Sammy and Daniel.'

'What about Alastair and Vanessa? Caesar was never happy about them.'

Dylan shrugged. 'Maybe that fell short of the relationship Caesar wanted to endorse.'

'What do you mean? Endorse, how?'

'You'd have to ask him,' Dylan said, 'but look at Alfie, the child of two scholars. Caesar is oddly focused on his schooling, to the point where he even helps fund it.'

Matthew's head was spinning, and he let the fact that Lucy had told Dylan about their financial arrangement pass without comment. He frowned. 'Why mention this now? Surely you don't think he could be involved somehow with Lucy's death?'

Dylan shrugged, which was way short of a denial. Matthew's mind slipped into overdrive. Caesar had introduced Bannister. Could Caesar have known about Lucy's use of the electro-flow device? Matthew's heart thumped against his chest as a thought wormed into his head.

'Do you remember the name of the doctor who treated you?' he asked.

'Of course I do.'

It was as if she was insulted that he'd suggested she might have forgotten a fact from two decades ago. A cold shiver crept down Matthew's spine as he braced to hear Dr Bannister's name.

'Sharon Callaway,' Dylan said.

Matthew blinked. It wasn't Henry Bannister, but the broader implication of Dylan's exit from the club twisted in his guts. He started at the doorbell ringing.

'I should go,' he said, putting the mobile phone in his pocket. 'Thank you. I'll be in touch.'

'Matthew,' Dylan said as he turned to leave.

'Yes?'

'I'd prefer it if you didn't talk to the others about me.'

'Okay,' he replied. He couldn't see how that would cause any problems.

Matthew opened the door to find a man standing on the doorstep with his hand raised. He had weathered skin and silver hair.

'Sorry,' the man said, smiling. 'I was about to knock. Almost tapped you on the nose.'

Matthew turned towards Dylan, who hadn't moved.

'Come in, Adam. Matthew's just leaving.'

16

THEN

SEPTEMBER 2002

Cambridge

It was the first time Matthew had seen all the other scholars together since the end of the first year, and they were back at Caesar's house in Cambridge. But it wasn't seeing his friends for the first time in a couple of months that had Matthew on edge; it was the two new scholars standing next to Caesar. They were in the library, the room of the inaugural meeting, but there were no chessboards, and there was no Dylan Steele. Matthew exchanged a glance with Lucy as Caesar signalled for quiet and began to speak.

'I have decided to introduce two new scholars to the group.' He nodded towards the two students. 'Kathryn Farthing and Jason Tanner. I'll leave you together to get to know each other. As you know, I place enormous value on the harmony of this group, and I know I can trust you to make them feel welcome.' Then he turned and walked out of the room.

Lucy was the first to react, walking over to the two newcomers and holding out her hand. Matthew tailed Alastair, who was introducing himself to Jason, and the party quickly fractured into three sub-groups. Alastair and Jason looked not dissimilar with a mop of dark hair, but whereas Alastair was wearing black jeans and an untucked T-shirt with *Hard To Explain* printed on the front, Jason was wearing a very slim black suit, a white shirt and a long black tie.

'Welcome to the Genius Club,' Alastair said, grinning.

Jason shrugged. 'Yeah. Not sure what to make of it all.'

'It's great,' Matthew said. 'Everyone's very supportive.'

'Okay.' Jason dragged the word out, and Matthew wondered whether he'd said something wrong.

'Where are you studying?' Matthew asked.

Jason looked at him momentarily and then pointed towards the other group. 'What's her name? The blonde girl.'

Alastair flicked a look at Matthew. 'Lucy. The guy over there's name is Daniel. The one-'

'Lucy,' Jason said, nodding so slowly that Matthew felt a knot form in his stomach.

'I assume Caesar ran over his rules with you?' Alastair asked, keeping his tone neutral.

Jason laughed. 'Yeah. But what he doesn't know can't harm him, right?'

'Lucy and I are engaged,' Matthew said.

Jason turned back to face Matthew. 'Sorry? What did you say?'

'We're engaged.' Matthew tried to hold his gaze, but after a few seconds, he looked at the ground.

'You've done well there, mate,' Jason said. 'Kudos. You're a bit young, though, aren't you?'

'We're old enough to get married,' Matthew couldn't work out what the new guy was getting at.

'But that doesn't mean you *should* get married. What if one of you gets bored? Or meets someone else?' He glanced again at Lucy. 'She's going to get plenty of offers, believe me. Being engaged isn't going to count for much.'

'She wouldn't-'

'Do you know Kathryn?' Alastair asked, raising his voice slightly to talk over his friend.

Matthew bit his lip. 'Excuse me,' he said.

He walked over to the other group and stood beside Lucy, his heart thumping against his chest. Lucy turned towards him and introduced him to Kathryn. Unlike Jason, Kathryn didn't say much and made little eye contact, but she was immediately the more likeable of the two. Matthew could hear Alastair and Jason still talking. He knew his friend had tried to steer the conversation away from Lucy, but he could see Jason still glancing towards his fiancée.

'What's Jason like?' Lucy whispered to Matthew while Vanessa described a book she'd just read.

Matthew shrugged. 'Not my type.' It took all his self-control not to add, *Or your type, either.*

———

MATTHEW HAD FOUND himself a quiet corner of the room and settled down to finish the work set for his next tutorial at college. He tapped a pencil on the pad resting on his lap as he read the question.

'What are you doing?' Kathryn lowered herself into the chair next to him.

'Number Theory.'

'I don't know what that is.'

'It's the study of the properties of integers.'

'Right.' She half-smiled. 'I guess it's an accurate title then.' She paused. 'It doesn't sound that hard, but I'm guessing it is.'

'Have you heard of Fermat's Last Theorem?'

Kathryn nodded. 'It was in the news a few years ago. I remember a teacher mentioning it at school.'

'It's a simple theorem. It states that it's impossible to find a solution where an integer, *a,* raised to the power of *n*, plus integer, *b,* also raised to the power of *n,* equals integer, *c*, raised to the power of *n.*' Kathryn shook her head. 'You can solve it when *n* is 2. Four squared, plus three squared, is twenty-five.'

'Which is five squared,' Kathryn said. 'I can do that much.'

'Right. But for any power higher than the square, it's impossible. That's what Fermat claimed. He wrote a note in a textbook to say he had an elegant proof, but there wasn't enough room in the book's margin to set it out. That was in 1637. A proof was first published in 1995.'

'Wow. Same proof?'

'I doubt it,' Matthew said. 'The proof was over 150 pages long.'

Kathryn was quiet for a while. 'You guys,' she waved her hand around the room, 'I'm guessing you're all super smart.'

Matthew scratched his chin. The honest answer was yes. 'I think a certain level of academic ability is a requirement of the scholarship,' he said.

'I'm not like that,' Kathryn said. 'I mean, I did well at school, and I'm coping fine at university, but I have to work hard. I'm not naturally bright.'

'I work hard,' Matthew said, looking at Kathryn.

'Yeah, but Lucy said you won some national Maths competition.' Matthew averted his gaze. 'And she said that the girl who was here before, the girl who left, Dylan, she said she was a computer freak.'

Matthew almost smiled at the description of Dylan. 'I'm sure you're here because Caesar sees something special in you.'

'I don't know, maybe. I'm studying History of Art at Warwick.' She shuffled in her seat. 'Can I ask you something about the scholarship?'

'Okay.' The word stuck in his throat, and Matthew coughed before repeating it. 'Okay.'

'Caesar told me I must commit to a research project once I graduate. Did he say that to you?'

Matthew nodded. 'He said it to all of us.'

'Okay.' She relaxed back into the chair. 'That makes me feel better.' She clasped her hands together. 'Has he told you what it might involve?'

'Not explicitly, but if I had to guess, I think he'll ask me to do something with linear algebra, calculus and probability.'

'Pretty specific guess,' Kathryn said.

Matthew shrugged. 'It's the core maths behind the development of AI.'

'AI?' Kathryn looked puzzled.

'Artificial Intelligence.'

'Oh, right. That sort of thing leaves me cold. Do you think that's possible?'

'I'm not sure. Machines can certainly get a lot smarter than they are.'

'Smart enough to think like us?'

'Maybe. Deep Blue beat Gary Kasparov at chess.'

'Yeah. The thing is, I can live with a computer being the best at chess,' Kathryn said. 'Cars move faster than we do, yet we still have running races—as long as the computers leave something for the rest of us to do.'

Sammy was walking over towards them.

'Caesar's asking us to join him outside,' she said.

Kathryn nodded and stood up. Matthew slipped his pencil and papers back into his bag and zipped it up. He left it next to the chair and followed the others out of the room.

'WE'RE GOING to run an exercise focusing on trust,' Caesar said. He stood in the middle of the lawn that swept down to the woodlands at the end of the garden. The sun was shining, but there was a chill in the air. Caesar handed Matthew one of the strips of black material he was holding.

'I'm giving out blindfolds,' Caesar said. 'I'd like everyone except Lucy to put one on.' He walked around the group, passing out the blindfolds. 'Lucy, please come over here with me. I want you to stand in the centre of a circle. Once everyone has covered their eyes, I want you to position everyone based on how much you trust them. Being closer to you means higher levels of trust. Everyone, Lucy's going to need to move you. Please move whichever way she guides you.'

Matthew didn't need to be able to see Lucy to know how stressful she would find this exercise. A few seconds later, he felt her hands on his shoulders. He moved a few yards under her direction and then stopped. Her hands dropped away as she went to position someone else. After a minute, Matthew couldn't hear any more movement.

'Okay, Lucy,' Caesar said. 'Are you happy with where everyone is positioned?'

'Yes.' Her voice was quiet, but Matthew could tell he was very close to her.

'Okay. Everyone, please remove your blindfolds.'

Matthew heard Lucy gasp. He slipped off the black cloth and looked around. He was closest to Lucy, less than a yard away. Sammy was next, then Vanessa and Alastair. She had placed Daniel slightly further away, with Kathryn just beyond him. Further away still, and the last man standing, was Jason.

'I'm sorry,' Lucy said, looking at Jason. 'We've only just met.'

'You only met Kathryn today, too,' Jason said, smirking. 'Don't worry. It's fine. You just need to get to know me.'

'Right,' Caesar said. 'Lucy, it's your turn to wear the blindfold. Jason, please come over here.' Matthew watched Jason saunter towards Caesar. 'Lucy, you're going to fall backwards, and Jason will catch you.'

Matthew swallowed, and Lucy looked pale. How could Caesar know that Jason would catch her?

'Sounds like a fun game,' Jason said.

'It's not a game,' Caesar said. 'You will stand close enough to catch her. Lucy will effectively fall onto you. This is about Lucy trusting you to catch her.'

'Got it,' Jason said, but he was still smirking.

'Are you sure this is a good idea?' Matthew asked.

'Don't worry,' Jason said, 'I'll take good care of your fiancée.'

'Okay, Lucy,' Caesar said. She stood with her arms crossed over her chest and her back to Jason. 'On the count of three. One, two, three.'

Lucy tipped backwards. Jason immediately took a half-step backwards, and Matthew's heart hammered against his chest. Then Jason squatted and caught Lucy.

Vanessa cheered, and Lucy laughed. Jason helped Lucy back

upright, but as far as Matthew was concerned, his hands lingered on Lucy for too long.

MATTHEW OPENED his eyes and looked around. He was in the boys' bedroom, and it was dark. Alastair was out of bed and looking out the window.

'Something's going on downstairs,' he said.

Matthew rubbed his face and swung his feet out of bed. 'What is it?' He looked at his watch. It was nearly two o'clock in the morning.

'I'm not sure.' Alastair peered into the darkness. 'I think I heard a car.' There was a thud. 'That was the front door.'

Daniel pushed himself up in bed. 'Jason's not here,' he said.

'He hasn't been here all night,' Alastair said.

'What?' Matthew looked at the fourth bed. The duvet was neatly tucked around the bed. It hadn't been slept in.

'He disappeared at the end of the evening,' Daniel said. 'I've no idea where he went.'

'Let's go and find out,' Alastair said, pulling on his jeans.

Matthew scrambled into his jeans and jumper and followed Alastair out of the room, with Daniel close behind. They immediately bumped into Vanessa and Kathryn, who were leaving the girls' bedroom.

'Do you know what's going on?' Alastair asked. 'Something's happening outside.'

'No. But Lucy and Sammy haven't made it to the bedroom.'

Matthew's stomach pitched.

'Jason's missing, too,' Daniel said. 'Come on.' He jutted his jaw as he pushed on down the stairs.

They walked down the corridor and turned the corner into the library. Lucy and Sammy huddled on a sofa, whispering to each other. There was no sign of Jason Tanner.

'Are you two okay?' Alastair asked as the group walked over.

Sammy brushed her hair away from her face and stood up. 'Yes, we're okay.' Her voice was calm.

Matthew walked over to Lucy and hugged her. She smiled at him, but there was something else, something that he couldn't immediately place.

'What's going on?' Vanessa asked. 'Where's Jason?'

Sammy replied. 'He was speaking with-' She broke off as the door at the far end of the library swung open, and Caesar walked in.

'Good evening, everyone,' he said. 'Well, we've had enough excitement for one day.'

'What's happened?' Alastair asked. 'Where's Jason?'

Caesar was smiling, but Matthew didn't think he looked happy. 'Jason Tanner has left. He is no longer part of the scholarship programme.' Matthew looked at Caesar and then at Lucy. 'I terminated the arrangement.'

'Why?' Alastair had always been happy to ask landmine questions where others feared to tread. 'What did he do?'

'That's not important. There was always some risk of imbalance, and unfortunately, that turned out to be the case.' Caesar straightened his tie. 'Now we are back to harmony. It's late, so I suggest you get some sleep. Goodnight to you all.'

He turned and left the room, closing the door behind him.

Daniel stood next to Sammy. 'Do you know what Jason did? He must have done something to upset Caesar.'

'We were talking with him,' Sammy looked at Lucy, 'the two of us. Everything seemed fine, and then he started getting upset. Not angry as such, more ... emotional. He made some comment about us not liking him, about not fitting in.'

'He got that right,' Matthew said.

'We carried on talking to him. I thought he might calm down, but he didn't. Then he walked out into the garden.' Sammy flicked a glance at Lucy.

'What happened then?' Daniel asked.

'I followed him,' Lucy said.

Matthew shuffled on the spot. He saw Alastair stiffen and knew they were thinking the same thing.

'Did he hurt you?' Matthew asked.

'No. Nothing like that. Not really,' Lucy said.

'Not *really*?' Alastair echoed.

'I found him standing amongst the trees at the end of the garden. He carried on with what he was saying before. I tried to be sympathetic.' She shook her head. 'I can't believe I fell for it.'

'Fell for what?' Matthew asked.

'He was murmuring. I moved my head closer to him so I could hear.' She swallowed. 'He kissed me.' Matthew balled his hands but said nothing. 'He'd been drinking; I could taste alcohol. I told him to stop. To leave me alone.'

'Did he?' Alastair asked.

Lucy nodded. 'Yes. I walked back to the house.' She sniffed. 'I think Caesar was watching through the window. He didn't say anything but walked past me, heading towards where I'd left Jason.'

'Then what?' Kathryn asked.

Sammy shrugged. 'We don't know. We couldn't hear anything but saw him leave about half an hour later. The doorman loaded his case into a car, Jason climbed in the back seat, and they left.'

'Good. It couldn't happen to a nicer guy,' Matthew said. 'I'm glad Caesar kicked him out.'

'He's gone now,' Lucy replied. Matthew knew she was speaking to him. 'I don't suppose any of us will ever see him again.'

'I still can't believe Caesar selected him in the first place,' Alastair said. 'I could tell from his suit he'd be trouble.'

17

NOW

TUESDAY, 18 JUNE 2019

Wimbledon Village, London

MATTHEW SHUFFLED INTO PROFESSOR HUNTER'S LIVING ROOM. HE HAD succeeded in tracking down the author of the quote in Bannister's obituary. She was alive and well and living in Wimbledon Village.

He was still trying to process everything Dylan had told him. Was she correct that Ben Caesar had a blueprint for genetic pairing—that Matthew and Lucy had been selected not for their intellect, not because Caesar judged them as worthy or promising, but because he hoped they would have a genius child? The details of Dylan's operation and her subsequent expulsion from the scholarship reverberated through his mind.

'Please, sit down,' Professor Hunter waved towards an armchair.

She was slightly built, or at least she had become that way, but she moved quickly enough to show Matthew into her sitting room. And she was living by herself despite now being well into her nineties.

Matthew lowered himself down. His nose twitched at the musky smell. The curtains were only half pulled, and the daylight outside made little impression on the room. A beige lamp shade was hanging from the ceiling, and there was a lamp on the table beside the sofa where the host was sitting, but neither light was switched on. Matthew tried to organise his thoughts. Hunter had written Henry Bannister a glowing obituary, but Matthew wanted to know the details of his life which weren't for public consumption.

'It's very good of you to see me,' he said.

'I can barely see anything these days,' she shot back. 'My memory's fine, though. You said you want to talk about Henry Bannister. Well, fire away.'

Matthew cleared his throat. 'I wondered whether you could tell me about him.' It was an open-ended prompt, but he wanted to see where Professor Hunter would start.

'Did you know Henry?' she asked. Pulling a shawl around her shoulders, she shifted her position on the sofa while she waited for his reply. Perhaps she also wanted to see where the conversation would start.

'No.' She looked at him, waiting for him to continue. 'Not well.' He hadn't wanted to talk about Lucy, but it seemed he must. 'My wife,' he paused and then pushed on, 'Lucy, she was treated by him.'

'I see.' Professor Hunter adjusted her glasses. 'What for?' she hesitated, 'if you don't mind me asking.'

'I'm not sure.' Matthew laughed nervously. 'It sounds silly, I know, but she didn't tell me.'

'You haven't asked her?'

'That's difficult.' He swallowed, sandpaper scratching his throat. 'She's ... she'd dead.' Matthew's head jerked down towards the floor.

'I'm sorry.' There was another pause. 'Why are you interested in him? I hope you don't mind my being direct, but it seems strange that you should seek me out to ask me about a dead man who used to be your wife's doctor.'

Matthew hesitated. 'My wife and I were part of a scholarship programme. That's how we met. We were introduced to Doctor Bannister through the scholarship. He was a friend of our patron.'

'And who was that?'

'He's called Benjamin Caesar.'

'I remember that name.' She touched Matthew's arm. 'A name

made for greatness, if ever there was one, wouldn't you say?' She smiled as if she was about to share a secret. 'Perhaps you would be kind enough to pass me the photograph album from the sideboard?' Professor Hunter tilted her head towards the far side of the room.

Matthew was grateful for the opportunity to move and deflect his thoughts from Lucy. The album cover was brown with a gold diamond pattern embossed on the front. He handed it to the professor.

'Sit here.' She patted the sofa next to her. 'I don't know whether these photographs will be of any interest.' She switched on the lamp and started to leaf through the album. 'I haven't got many, but there are a couple with Henry in them. One of them should be ... oh yes, here it is.'

Matthew studied the photograph of the three men and a woman. The professor pointed to the man on the far left. 'That's Henry.'

He wouldn't have recognised Bannister with his dark hair reaching his shoulders except for his height—the doctor towered over the others. 'Are they his friends?' Matthew asked, pointing to the others. He didn't recognise any of them.

'Oh goodness me, no. Henry couldn't abide my other students. He thought they were all stupid. He was only in this picture because I insisted.'

Matthew leaned forward. 'In his obituary, the one I read anyway, you said he was radical and liked to push medical boundaries and challenge conventional thinking. What did you mean?'

The professor's hesitation stretched into silence, and her breathing quickened. After a few seconds, she turned the album pages, stopped, and tapped on a photograph. Henry Bannister stood in front of a wooden door leading off a hallway. The door was open, and there were steps leading down. An eerie light shone up from the room below.

'What...' Matthew stopped. 'I don't understand what I'm looking at.'

'Look at the sign on the door.'

Matthew peered at the picture. A piece of paper with black writing was stuck to the centre of the door.

Genius Club.

'What the hell?' he said under his breath. Alastair had been the first to gloss the scholars with the Genius Club name. Caesar rarely used it, and he had never mentioned a precursor club. He had also never referenced anyone else in connection with the scholarship—it had always been one hundred percent Caesar's programme.

'Yes, that's what I thought, too,' she said. 'Henry and his friends, what shall I say? Well, they didn't lack confidence.' She laughed. 'There was no room for modesty with Henry. This Genius Club was a debating society. Well, I say society, but there were only three of them. I guess no one else was clever enough to be invited.' She winked at him.

Matthew had so many questions, but Professor Hunter was still talking. Her eyes were unfocused as if she were searching back in the past. 'I don't know what they did. Most of the time, they were probably drinking and taking drugs.' She laughed again. 'Don't look so shocked, Professor Stanford. Most of the stories about students in the seventies are true.'

'Did he ever talk to you about methods of boosting people's intelligence?' Matthew asked.

'He most certainly did. It was practically an obsession with him. That's what their society was all about. The three of them endlessly debated different methods of doing that.'

A space opened inside Matthew's stomach. 'What methods?'

'He talked about all sorts, but Henry's focus was the genetics of intelligence.' Matthew felt the air leave his body. Professor Hunter shuffled on the sofa. 'Last year, there were media reports that twin girls had been born in China with modified genes to make them HIV immune. Henry would have loved that.'

'Modified, how?' Matthew's mouth was dry.

'Gene-editing. They used a technique that's been discussed for nearly thirty years, but it's not simply the gene editing that would have excited Henry; it's the particular gene they targeted. The CCR5 gene that enables HIV infection is also known for something else.' She smiled. 'Brain function.'

Matthew massaged his forehead. 'Do you think Henry ever-'

'Oh no. He was involved in the research, but he didn't ever do anything like that.' She closed the photograph album. 'But, if he were still alive today…'

She didn't finish the sentence, and Matthew didn't need her to. 'How about the use of transcranial direct-current stimulation?' He had to force out the words.

She shrugged. 'I don't recall him talking about that, but I suppose it's possible.'

Matthew did his best to plaster a smile on his face as the recent revelations began to crowd in on him. The history of the scholars' doctor had cast a red warning light over the treatment he'd given them.

Matthew had stopped taking the pills Bannister had prescribed him after a year because he was suffering frequent pins and needles and headaches. The pills hadn't helped his asthma, but he had noticed that he felt sharper and could concentrate for longer when he took them. Was it possible that Bannister had prescribed him smart pills? Unethical, sure. Illegal, probably, but still possible.

Then, there was Lucy's use of the tDCS device. Could that have been an intelligence enhancement programme suggested by a maverick doctor who was deeply interested in genetic editing techniques? He shuddered.

'You said there were three of them in the club?' Matthew said.

'Yes, that's right. Henry gave me that photograph after he graduated, and he said the oddest thing to me.' She rested her hand on Matthew's arm and spoke in a deep voice. 'You should keep this, Prof Hunter, because one day you'll be able to say that you knew the men that changed the course of humanity.'

'One of the three was Benjamin Caesar?'

'Oh yes, I'm sure of that. I can't recall the other man's name, but I have a hunch he became a banker.' Her face lit up. 'I do remember Henry being somewhat disparaging about the girlfriend.

She clearly wasn't genius material.' Professor Hunter rolled her eyes.

Questions looped around in Matthew's head as he stood to make his departure, but they all came back to the same thought.

He'd believed that he knew Caesar, but the deeper he dug, the less sure he was. He was facing an increasingly unavoidable conclusion.

They had been selected not for patronage but for experimentation.

MATTHEW WALKED DOWN THE DRIVE, his mind still spinning with possibilities. He pulled out his phone, selected Sammy's contact details and hit the call button. She answered immediately.

'Oh, hi, Sammy. Yes, I'm okay. I wanted to get everyone together before the meeting with Caesar.'

'That sounds like a great idea.' He could hear the surprise in Sammy's voice. He'd never been one to suggest a get-together. She'd no doubt be thinking that he was feeling lonely. 'I think it will help ... it'll be ... perhaps the weekend-'

'How about tomorrow?' Matthew asked.

'Tomorrow? Does it need to be ... well, I can see if everyone's free. Leave it with me, and I'll arrange it. I'll book somewhere for us all. My treat.'

'I'd like to do it tomorrow.' He knew he was pushing it.

'Sure. I'll crack the whip and get everyone to attend. Daniel and I can certainly make it.'

'Great,' Matthew said and ended the call. He bit his lip and then hit the redial button. 'Was I rude just then?'

'No, not at all.'

'Sorry.' He paused. 'I'd usually check with Lucy.'

'I know, Matthew. You're fine. I'll see you tomorrow.'

He knew words didn't always tell the whole story, but his friends had always been straightforward with him. 'Okay. Well, thanks. Bye.'

He hung up for the second time.

Raynes Park, London

MATTHEW DIDN'T RECOGNISE the persistent, dull vibration coming from his bedroom. After some searching, he realised that it was the mobile phone Dylan had given him. He flicked open the clamshell—three missed calls. He selected one of the missed calls and hit the dial button.

'About time,' Dylan said by way of a hello.

'Sorry. I forgot about it. I couldn't work out what the noise was in my bedroom.'

'Keep it on you from now on.'

Matthew brushed the implied criticism aside. 'What do you want?'

'I've found a connection to Caesar that confirms his interest in medical research,' Dylan said. 'And I've found someone we might be able to speak to.'

'A friend of Caesar's from college?' Matthew asked.

'He works with him,' Dylan replied. 'I don't know how they met.'

'Is it Doctor Henry Bannister?' Matthew removed the phone from his ear and looked at it to check the call was still connected. He caught himself before he said her name. 'Are you still there?'

'Doctor Henry Bannister was at college with Caesar?' she asked. There was tension in her voice.

Matthew's heart rate kicked up a level. 'Yes. I thought that's who you meant.'

'Bannister was the doctor who recommended my surgery.' Dylan's voice was emotionless.

Matthew's mouth was dry. 'I thought you said your doctor was Sharon Callaway.' Even as he said it, he realised the confusion.

'Sharon Callaway was the surgeon. Bannister was the GP who

referred me. He was Lucy's doctor. I didn't know he was connected to Caesar.'

A shiver ran down Matthew's back. 'They were at college together,' he said. 'Bannister died in 2011.' He swallowed. 'I spoke with one of his professors. She told me Bannister was obsessed with the possibility of genetically engineering intelligence. I thought he was who you found.'

'No. I found a man called Christopher Goldman.'

Matthew didn't recognise the name, but Hunter's words floated back into his head. Her hunch had been that the third man was a banker. A banker by name, or banker by nature, he wondered. 'What's his connection to Caesar? You said they worked together.'

'They're both directors of a private company,' she said. 'It's called Cerebrum Limited.'

Matthew froze. Cerebrum was Caesar's research project. Matthew had signed a non-disclosure agreement when he'd agreed to start working on the Cerebrum programme. They all had. He hadn't even bothered to ask Daniel to look at it before he signed because he'd never imagined he would need to discuss it with anyone other than Caesar or the other scholars. He certainly hadn't foreseen it being linked in any way to the death of his wife. As memories of Lucy flooded his brain, he decided he didn't want to get into a debate with Dylan about Cerebrum right then.

'What's the significance of Goldman being a company director?' he asked.

'I'm not sure yet. Caesar is the sole shareholder, but as a director, Goldman will be involved and know what the company is doing. There's not much publicly available information. There's no website, and the company accounts just says it performs medical research.'

Matthew closed his eyes. He had to decide whether or not to trust her. He may not have been prepared to get into Cerebrum, but if he wanted to find the truth, his best chance was to work with Dylan. He raked his hand through his hair.

'The professor I spoke with said that Bannister, Caesar and one other man formed a select group to debate the nature of intelligence and ways of enhancing it. They called themselves the Genius Club.' Dylan said nothing, but her breathing quickened. 'Goldman must be the third member, which means he knew Bannister, too.'

'You need to speak with him,' Dylan said.

Visiting him was the right starting point. Matthew rubbed his forehead. 'I was thinking I could ask one of the others,' he said. 'Alastair's good at that sort of thing.'

'No.' Dylan paused before continuing. 'I have no idea whether any of this is in any way linked to Lucy's death, but until we know for sure, you can't trust anyone.'

Matthew couldn't believe that Alastair was involved in Lucy's death. He couldn't believe it of any of his friends, and that included Caesar. Yet, after all these years, he was learning things about Caesar that gave him plenty of pause for thought.

'Okay. I'll do it.' Matthew was prepared to approach Goldman but wanted to speak with Caesar first. He still hadn't been able to reach him, and as far as he knew, neither had the others. It had been over a week now. Just then, the phone beeped in his hand.

'I've texted you Goldman's address from the filing with Companies House,' Dylan said. 'Let me know how it goes.' The line went dead.

18

NOW

WEDNESDAY, 19 JUNE 2019

East Dulwich, London

It took Matthew over an hour on the tube and bus to reach Christopher Goldman's home. The building was squeezed into a row of terraced houses that looked like they were resolutely holding in the tension like a compressed accordion. The whole house could have stood more comfortably inside Caesar's reception room than in its actual location. The building was smartly presented and stood behind an orange and yellow flagstone chessboard driveway, with the roofed porch held up by two white metal poles. Matthew was walking up the drive when his mobile rang.

'This is Matthew.'

'Hello, Professor Stanford, this is Sheila Ryan.'

He recognised her as the secretary to the headmaster at Alfie's school. 'Yes, hello.'

'Mr Logan would like to meet with you, if possible, to discuss Alfie. Would you be able to meet at ten o'clock on Friday morning?'

Matthew swallowed. 'No, I'm sorry. I can't.'

'It's important, Professor Stanford.'

'I understand.' He took a breath. 'But Friday is the day of my wife's funeral.'

'Oh, I'm so sorry, Professor Stanford.'

He hadn't meant to be pointed, but he didn't know how else to say it. Friday was Lucy's funeral. It was an inescapable fact. 'I could come in on Monday if that's possible.'

Miss Ryan had recovered her poise. 'Yes, ten o'clock? That would work for Mr Logan.'

'Okay.'

'Thank you, Professor Stanford. And I hope the funeral ... well, I hope it goes as well as these things can.'

'Thank you.'

Matthew heard her take a deep breath just before the call disconnected. He pushed thoughts of Alfie's school away and tried to focus on what he needed to do right then.

Christopher Goldman might be the only living person, other than Caesar himself, who knew the truth about the original plan for the scholars.

He knocked on the door, and for a while, he thought there wouldn't be any answer, but after a few seconds, the door opened. He guessed the woman opposite him was a little over five feet tall. Her hair was white and short, and her face was creased with years of experience. Her eyes were dull, but he saw them flicker as she decided to shut out the stranger on her doorstep.

'Please, Mrs Goldman, I need to talk to Christopher.' The door stopped moving, and he leant towards the gap. 'Sorry, I made an assumption. I'm looking for Christopher Goldman.' The door didn't move. His mouth was dry. He'd started in the wrong place. 'My name's Matthew Stanford. I want to talk to him about Benjamin Caesar.' The gap opened slightly.

'Ben Caesar.' She said the name matter-of-factly. 'I haven't heard that name for many years.' Her strong northern accent floated around the door. Matthew thought he caught a quiet sigh. 'Well, you'd better come in, but Christopher doesn't live here. He lives in the States.' She stepped back to allow him into her house.

Matthew absorbed the news. He wouldn't be speaking to Goldman face to face, but surely he'd be able to get a number to call him.

'Can I interest you in a drink?' she asked.

'No, thank you.'

'Very well. This way, then.' She shuffled into her lounge and lowered herself into an armchair, indicating a wooden chair for him to sit on. 'Is Ben dead?' she asked. 'Is that why you're here?'

'No.' Matthew bit down on the desire to add, *not as far as I know.* He'd decided to share as little as possible and stay focused on discovering what he wanted to know. 'It's nothing like that. I wanted to ask about Christopher's friendship with Caesar back at university.'

'I try to leave the past where it belongs, especially where my ex-husband is concerned.' She pursed her lips.

Matthew frowned. 'I apologise. Someone gave me this address for Christopher.' He stared at the floor.

Mrs Goldman shrugged.

'There's no easy way to say this.' Matthew cleared his throat. 'My wife was killed a few weeks ago...' and, as if to prove his point, he was suddenly unable to finish the sentence. He sucked in some air and swallowed his rising pain.

'I'm sorry,' Mrs Goldman said, bowing her head. 'Does your wife's death have something to do with Ben Caesar? Or my ex-husband?' she asked.

'I don't know. Maybe. There's a lot I don't know.' He blew out a sharp breath. 'I'm sorry just to spring this on you. I'm trying to find out what happened when...' He trailed off again and shook his head. He focused on the wall slightly behind her. Lucy had always encouraged him to maintain eye contact, but he needed to get through this however he could. There were three framed wildlife photographs hanging on the off-white painted walls. He stared at the picture of the Kingfisher as he spoke. 'Nearly two decades ago, Benjamin Caesar selected a bunch of school children for college scholarships.'

'And you're one of them?' Her words were clipped.

'I am, yes. He still provides us with a scholarship to this day.'

'I see.' She clasped her hands together. Something told Matthew that this wasn't news to her. She cocked her head. 'I'm not sure how I can help you.'

'Your ex-husband, Ben Caesar and a third man, Henry Bannister, knew each other at college.' Matthew paused. 'They referred to themselves as the Genius Club.'

He forced his gaze away from the Kingfisher to watch her. He would have missed it if he hadn't been looking specifically for it. Lucy had taught him how to focus on particular moments and to be ready to try to read people. He saw a slight flinch, a tightening of her body, and a pinch of her lips. She knew something. He waited for a few seconds, but she said nothing.

'I wondered if you knew anything about their club?' he asked. Now, he couldn't read her expression at all. So, he waited, saying nothing this time.

Slowly, she pushed herself out of the chair. Was she going to ask him to leave? She walked over to look out the window and started to speak.

'Christopher and I married young. Too young, probably. Immediately after university, he was offered a job with a US investment bank, and we moved to America. I was glad of the fresh start. There was something about his friendship with Ben and Henry, something about their club, that unsettled me. It had a fanatical edge that I didn't like. I hoped that the Atlantic would insulate us.' She smiled, but not with any joy. 'I was wrong. Four years after we married, we divorced, and later that same year, I moved back here.' She waved around the room. 'The house is still registered in his name.'

'What do you mean about a fanatical edge?' Matthew's mouth was dry.

For a moment, he didn't think she would answer, but after a long silence, she turned to face him. A shadow passed over her face. 'Christopher had this solid walnut filing cabinet which he kept locked. I was sure it had to do with that club.' Matthew tried to keep his expression neutral. Where was she going with this? 'One day, he left it unlocked while he went to the toilet, and I took my chance. I didn't have long. I looked at as many files as possible until I heard the toilet flush.'

Matthew shuffled forward on his chair. 'What did you find?'

'Each file had information about a specific woman - medical details, photographs, and academic results. In those few minutes, I skimmed through the details of five different women. There were maybe twenty files—twenty different women.' She shook her head before continuing. 'He must have had any number of affairs, but throughout our divorce proceedings, he denied he slept with any of them.' She smiled, but her eyes were brimming with tears.

'I'm sorry,' Matthew said.

'Despite all his denials, I still think Caesar and Bannister were somehow involved with those files. It was like their own dating agency database.' She shuddered. 'But this long pre-dates your university scholarship,' Mrs Goldman said. 'I can't see how it would relate to your wife.' Matthew looked down at the floor. 'I do have a telephone number for Christopher, but I haven't had any contact with him for years,' Mrs Goldman said. 'I'll get the number for you.'

Matthew swallowed. 'Thank you.'

A few minutes later, she returned and handed him a piece of paper. He stood up and cleared his throat.

'Does the name Cerebrum mean anything to you?' he asked, studying her face. 'Christopher is a director. This house is recorded as its registered office.'

There wasn't so much as a flicker of recognition. She shook her head. 'No, I'm sorry.' Then she indicated towards the front door. It was clear she thought it was time for him to go.

'Thank you for your time.' He stepped out onto the front step.

'Good luck, Matthew.' The door closed behind him.

Raynes Park, London

Matthew picked up his phone, holding the number from Mrs Goldman in his other hand. He rehearsed his pitch again. He needed to get it right. He chewed his lip as he tapped in the number. There was a second of silence before he heard the ringtone. Without thinking, he counted the number of rings. By the time it reached seven, he began to think there wouldn't be an answer, but then there was a click, and a man spoke.

'Yes?' Short and to the point.

'Hello, Mr Goldman, Christopher Goldman?'

There was a hesitation before the man spoke again. 'You don't sound very sure who you've called.'

Matthew closed his eyes. 'I wasn't sure you would still be living there. The person who gave me your number wasn't sure themselves.'

'I see.' There was a hint of steel in his voice. 'You're a friend of Eleanor, I take it.'

'No, not a friend, exactly.'

'Hmm. Well, friend or not, I've got a game of golf to get to.'

Matthew flicked his focus back to the script. 'I wanted to ask you about Benjamin Caesar and Henry Bannister.'

The man's breathing quickened. 'Who are you?' His tone was harsh.

'Professor Matthew Stanford.'

'Well, Professor Matthew Stanford,' he replied, emphasising the title, 'let me help you out. I am not Christopher Goldman. Christopher died two years ago.'

Matthew's heart rate kicked up. Christopher Goldman was dead. Caesar was the only remaining member of their club, and he was practically incommunicado. 'I need to speak-'

The man's voice cut in. 'Christopher was a good friend of mine, and if there's one thing I knew about Christopher, it is that he wanted nothing to do with his ex-wife.'

'But it isn't his ex-wife that I want-'

'Goodbye, Professor Stanford,' the man said. 'Don't call again.'

Eleanor Goldman may not have given Matthew all the answers he had hoped for, but he knew where to look next. He waited until he heard Alfie's bedroom door click shut before he started to search for the details of the Goldman's divorce.

Eleanor Goldman had filed the petition on the grounds of her husband's unreasonable behaviour - and because he had chosen to defend himself against the petition, the full details were available for anyone to read. Christopher denied any inappropriate behaviour with a woman called Rebecca Grey. Still, he was unwilling to fully explain why his wife had found a photograph of the woman in his wallet and claimed to have seen a cache of information he kept on numerous other women stored in a locked cabinet.

Matthew tapped his fingers against his mouth. What was the reason Goldman kept another woman's photograph? He shivered. What word had Mrs Goldman used? *Obsessed.* Matthew carried on reading.

Rebecca Grey was twenty-five years older than Matthew, making her about the same age as Caesar. The case report also stated that Rebecca Gray had worked for a bank. According to the court, Christopher Goldman had been a highly successful banker, but the court filing confirmed that Rebecca and Christopher didn't work for the same bank.

Matthew typed her name into Google. There were 123 million results in 0.46 seconds. If he read one a second, it would take eleven solid days to make his way through only the first million results. On a whim, he added *genius* to his search but found the first few hits were homages to the brilliance of Daphne du Maurier.

He sighed as he typed in Rebcca Grey, the word divorce, and the hearing date. The second hit was a blog post. *The mystery woman at the heart of a divorce.* He clicked into it and studied the photograph of Rebecca Grey. The report claimed the picture was the same one Christopher had treasured, but the article was mostly innuendo, with no meaningful information about why Rebecca Grey was important to Goldman.

Matthew printed copies of the divorce proceedings and the blog.

Instinctively, he wanted to ask the other scholars about what he'd discovered. He had no concrete evidence to support Dylan's suggestion that not only had they been selected but that they had been groomed for parenting, and certainly nothing that conclusively linked Lucy's death to the scholarship. All he knew for sure was they'd each been selected in their final year of school and identified as having faced adversity early in their lives. But then what—nurtured, encouraged, and supported? Or manipulated? Or even worse, exploited?

Matthew looked at the neat stack of printed paper. Was Rebecca Grey simply a woman that Goldman was interested in, or was she their first scholar? Matthew felt bile rise in his throat. What was the reason for Goldman's interest in Rebecca Grey, and why keep it a secret if it wasn't an affair? He buried his head in his hands. There was no good answer to those questions that he could think of.

19

THEN

JANUARY 2003

Christ Church Meadow, Oxford

MATTHEW KNEW ALASTAIR WAS DRUNK WHEN HE CLAIMED HE COULD hear the stars talking to each other. They were in the meadow, lying on their backs and staring at the night sky.

It had been a cold, crisp day, and Matthew was glad of the thick jumper underneath his coat. He was also glad of the company of his best friend, who had forsaken yet another house party to spend the evening with him. Alastair had, however, been drinking from the moment his parents had left that afternoon.

'I don't think stars can talk,' Matthew said by way of a rebuttal.

Alastair shrugged before fighting to roll over and prop himself up on his elbows. 'Hey, thanks for meeting my parents. I think you made a good impression.' His speech was slurring.

'Water to drink, and no bad language. God put me on this earth to impress people like your parents,' Matthew said.

Alastair hung his head. 'I feel such a fake with my parents.'

Matthew knew his friend's parents were Presbyterian and had been regular churchgoers when Alastair was young. They had stopped going for some reason, but their values hadn't changed. They were proud of their son, although they knew he didn't have quite the work ethic they'd have wished for him. Alastair's academic achievements implied, mistakenly as it happened, a reasonably solid level of effort.

In effect, turning up to school had been translated into putting in a decent shift, so everyone was happy—until Alastair hit puberty, looked out at the world with wide teenage eyes, and developed his false idol status by tilting at the Ten Commandments.

'Surely they know you're not a saint?' Matthew asked.

'God, I hope not. If they do, they know I'm lying whenever I see them.' He pushed himself up so he was sitting. 'Perhaps I *should* tell them?'

'What do you think they'd do if you did?'

Alastair pulled out a packet of cigarettes and eased one out with his fingers. He lit it and blew out smoke before answering. Matthew pulled the zip up on his coat as far as it would go and watched his cold breath frost like fake smoke in the night air.

'I don't know. They might forgive me if I told them and did the whole mea culpa thing.' He took another drag. 'I mean, they'd want me to do rehab, or penance, or something. But it might be okay.' He was silent again. Perhaps he was waiting for the stars to give him an answer. 'The worst possible thing would be for them to find out from someone else.'

Matthew could see that—the double blow of discreditable behaviour and dishonesty. 'Well, your secret's safe with me,' he said.

'Talking of secrets,' Alastair said, 'Vanessa's coming to stay with me next weekend.'

'You need to keep that a secret from Caesar and your parents.'

'You think?' His words were slurred. 'You and Lucy got a pass. I'm pretty sure he must know about Daniel and Sammy. Why do you think he'd have a problem with me and V?'

'I can't speak for Caesar.'

'What does that mean?' Alastair asked.

'You'll get upset with me,' Matthew said.

Alastair rolled his head to stretch his neck. 'I'm not going to get upset with you,' he said.

'Okay. Lucy and I are engaged, and Daniel and Sammy are steady. Maybe Caesar's happy with that. It fits with his *no drama* philosophy.'

'And what? Vanessa and I are drama?'

'You're ... I don't know ... up and down, I guess.'

Alastair started to laugh. 'There is some of that going on.'

Matthew shook his head. 'You know what I mean.'

'Yeah.' He was still laughing. 'I know what you mean.'

20

THEN

SEPTEMBER 2003

Cambridge

BEN HAD THE DATE CIRCLED IN HIS DIARY. HENRY WAS WITH HIM IN THE room, and Christopher was on the line from his new home in Naples, Florida. They had allowed themselves two hours to work through their agenda.

Ben wetted his lips. He was ready to push forward and felt the others were ready, too.

'Have you read the paper?' he asked.

'Which one, Ben?' Christopher's telephone line had a faint echo. 'You sent several.'

That was true, but Christopher would have read them all before the meeting. 'You know very well which one,' he said, sensing his friend's smile.

'Well, the paper on the moral distinction between forcing something and not acting to stop it was *most* interesting. It would certainly be helpful if we could settle on our collective position.' Christopher's voice echoed around the room.

'I agree, but we'll get to that later,' Henry said. 'Unless anyone wants to debate anything more at this stage, shall we turn to the formal proceedings?'

The protocol had been agreed upon at the outset: one vote per founder. Some votes required a simple majority of the three, but any action directly involving the scholars needed a unanimous decision. The early votes had all been carried, but as their plans evolved, Ben was finding himself to be more cautious than the others.

Very well, Ben thought, let's find out what everyone thinks. Even if it wouldn't ultimately change his course, he would at least know who was with him and who wasn't. He started to read from the minutes.

'Red Vote six, proposed by me.' Ben took a sip of his iced water. 'The proposal requires the scholars to complete a morality test to assess their likely response to future plans and research.'

'I vote in favour.' Christopher and Henry spoke at the same time.

'For the record, I, too, am in favour,' Ben said. 'Red Vote six is carried, and we move to Red Vote seven, to be carried by a unanimous vote only. Again, this vote is proposed by me, and it invites the scholars to join the Cerebrum project. Henry?'

'I vote in favour.'

'Noted. I, too, vote in favour.' Ben turned towards the speakerphone. 'Christopher?'

'I vote in favour.

'Excellent,' Ben said. 'Let the minutes show that Red Vote seven was carried.' He took another sip of water and bit a small chunk of ice between his teeth. 'Henry, as the proposer for Red Vote eight, you can talk us through this before we vote.'

Henry cleared his throat before he began speaking. 'A team of Dutch scientists at Utrecht University have shared their interesting work on so-called Cas genes. In short, we may be able to harness this technology as a tool to edit genomes in human cells over the next decade. Together with our research, the future looks very promising indeed.' He looked at Ben and nodded. 'The specific motion is to harvest genetic material from the scholars through an annual medical. The material will be stored to allow future gene editing research.'

'Have you considered the points I raised?' Ben asked. 'Principally around the need to secure the patient's consent.'

'I have some proposed wording which will be included in the contractual terms for their annual medical.' He cleared his throat and began to read. '*The patient consents to allow the facility to keep any excess samples collected as part of any procedure or annual medical, and to use the material for research purposes.*'

Ben tapped his fingers on the table. 'It's hardly explicit,' he said.

'I believe it's clear enough,' Henry said, 'and as the proposer, I vote in support of the motion.'

'I also vote in favour.' Christopher's voice carried across the room.

Could the wording Henry was proposing constitute freely given consent? He stopped tapping his fingers. Henry was looking at him. It was time for him to vote.

'I want the consent wording to be explicitly drawn to the scholars' attention before they undergo their medical,' he said.

'I can live with that,' Henry replied.

'Very well,' Ben said. 'I vote in favour of the motion.'

21

THEN

OCTOBER 2003

Oxford

MATTHEW WAS SITTING IN A SMALL BOX ROOM IN A RENTED OFFICE WITH the door closed. He was facing a computer screen, wearing headphones and listening to a series of questions. The test itself differed from any Matthew had sat before because there were no right or wrong answers, yet he felt as if he was being evaluated in a profound way.

Caesar had explained that Harvard had devised the test he had asked Matthew and the other scholars to sit, and their answers would be used to compile the user's 'morality profile.'

The voice announced that the test was over. Matthew slipped off the headphones and placed them on the desk beside the keyboard. The sequence of tests had been short, about ten minutes each to complete. The last one had been entitled *Disgust*. He'd already completed *Empathy, Morality, Judge* and *Psycho*. *Disgust* consisted of twenty-seven predetermined but randomly selected questions, all requiring him to imagine he was at the centre of a stressful situation.

Leading a mountaineering expedition that is stranded in the wilderness.

Negotiating with a terrorist.

Watching a runaway trolly heading down a track.

They all offered a trade-off, such as one life for many or causing someone pain to save others.

All the questions had to be answered on a scale from *Forbidden* to *Permissible* to *Obligatory*. There were also halfway points between *Permissible* and the two most extreme answers. According to Caesar, over five thousand responses had already been received to the Harvard-designed questionnaire.

Matthew clicked on the spacebar to see his results. He scored four on a scale from one to five, tending towards the logical pathway to minimising the total number of deaths and the overall amount of pain, or maximising the quality of life for the most people.

Lucy had already taken the test. She didn't tell him what it was about, but she did tell him she'd scored one and a half. It was probably the lowest score she'd ever recorded in a test, but in this particular case, a higher score wasn't objectively better. Matthew sighed as he logged off. He knew there wasn't a right or wrong answer, but he couldn't help but feel slightly guilty for some of the answers he'd selected. After all, notwithstanding that all the questions were entirely hypothetical, he had just suggested it would be acceptable to kill another human in certain situations. He thought he'd feel better if he focused on how many hypothetical lives he'd saved rather than taken. He shuddered, slipped on his coat and walked outside.

It was raining, and he fastened his coat and pulled out his phone. The moment he switched it on, it beeped with a missed call from Lucy. He called her back.

'So, how was the test?' Lucy asked.

'Disquieting,' he said. 'I'm glad it's done.'

'I know what you mean. I couldn't stop thinking about it afterwards. Anyway, I have some news.' Matthew waited. 'Kathryn's quit.'

'Why? What happened?' Matthew wasn't sure what to expect after the drama of Dylan and then Jason.

'She came to find me earlier today. She'd just met with Caesar and told him she didn't want to continue. She didn't feel she was on the same level as the rest of the group.'

Matthew thought back to his first proper conversation with Kathryn. She hadn't said anything more to him about her concerns since then, but it seemed the self-doubt had lingered. 'That's a shame,' he said.

'Yeah. She's quiet, but I like her. We sort of click in a funny way. She told me her grandparents gave her enough money to get her through university without her needing to rely on the scholarship. She said something odd, though.

'What?'

'She said that she'd had a message from Jason Tanner.' Matthew swallowed. He'd be happy never to hear that name. 'He wanted to meet up with her.'

'I can't think why he'd think any of us would want to see him.'

'I know,' Lucy said. 'He told her that he wanted to talk about us. To have the opportunity to put forward his side of the story.' Matthew wiped the raindrops off his face and said nothing. 'But that wasn't the odd bit. He sent her a final reply when she said no to meeting up. Matthew waited. 'He told her not to get on the wrong side of her because he was joining the army.'

'He's what Vanessa would call a *drama queen*.'

Lucy laughed. 'I guess so. It's a shame he enjoys making people feel uncomfortable.'

Matthew remembered the day Jason Tanner had joined and left the scholarship and his comments about Lucy. He hadn't adjusted his behaviour when he learnt that Lucy and Matthew were engaged, and Matthew thought it showed a distinct lack of class. 'Will we see Kathryn before she leaves?' he asked, keen to move the conversation away from Jason Tanner.

'I don't think so,' Lucy said. 'She asked me to let everyone know. I think she wants to slip away without any fuss.'

'Fair enough,' Matthew said. He wondered what he would do if he ever decided to leave, but his brain couldn't wrap itself around that idea.

'I've got a lecture now, but I can't wait to see you tomorrow,' Lucy said. 'Love you.'

'Love you, too.'

22

NOW

WEDNESDAY, 19 JUNE 2019

Mayfair, London

MÖBIUS, AN EXCLUSIVE RESTAURANT IN THE WEST END, HAD THE TYPE of discrete front door that tipped its hat to the Tardis and an interior that held out a neon candle in homage to an Ibiza nightclub. It was only when he was inside, standing with the others and clutching his bag, that Matthew wondered whether there was a dress code. Sammy hadn't said anything to him, but the others were smartly dressed.

Matthew shuffled on the spot, hoping the others' suits and sparkles would hide his jeans and hoodie combination. The maître d' checked the reservation list and nodded to his colleague hovering behind him. The waiter clasped his hands together and greeted the group with a smile. The knot that had been forming in Matthew's stomach started to loosen.

'We have one more guest coming, Vanessa Wordsworth,' Sammy said.

'Yes, of course. We'll show her through as soon as she arrives. If you'd all like to, please follow me.' The waiter extended his arm towards a private dining room at the back of the restaurant, glancing at Matthew but making no comment.

Matthew looked down at the floor as he followed the others into the room. Sammy had thought about the dress code. Money fixed so many problems.

The room was decorated in purple and pink with a rectangular table covered with a white tablecloth, standing on a carpet that zigged and zagged its way across the room. There were three upholstered chairs on one side, facing off against two chairs which guarded an open fireplace on the other. The places were generously spaced, unable to hide that the room would have been a better fit for six than five. Matthew bit down on his lip. Sammy moved towards a seat on the far side of the table. She was wearing a trouser suit and looked immaculate. Daniel, his navy suit twinned with a purple tie, pulled back the chair for her, and Matthew saw him rest his hand on his wife's shoulder and gently squeeze it. Matthew caught Daniel's eye. His friend nodded at him and withdrew his hand, glancing at his wife as he did so. He seemed to freeze briefly as if forgetting that anyone else was in the room. Vanessa chose that moment to sweep into the room.

'Hi, V. It's Great to see you,' Daniel said. She tilted her head so he could kiss her on each cheek.

She walked over to Matthew and pulled him into an embrace. She held him close for a few seconds before releasing him. She looked like she was about to say something but settled instead for rubbing his arm. Matthew swallowed and tried a smile.

Alastair held Vanessa's chair before sitting next to her. 'I listened to your company's AGM call the other night,' he said.

'Ah, that's sweet. You lead such an exciting life.'

'Oh, don't worry. It was only on in the background. My girlfriend kept begging me to turn it off.' Alastair spoke easily and with a smile.

Vanessa and Alastair had an on-and-off relationship, although Matthew never knew which way the switch was flicked.

'I know how hard you find it to do two things at once.' Vanessa's eyes glinted.

'Vanessa! Please. They are women, not things,' Alastair said. Daniel laughed whilst Vanessa rolled her eyes. 'Seriously though, don't the company scientists get annoyed with you answering all the genetics questions? You're the CEO, not the technical guru.'

'Well, I knew the answers to some of the questions.' Vanessa's face was impassive.

'You answered *all* of them,' Alastair said.

She grinned at him.

'I'm sorry I missed it,' Sammy said. 'I normally dial in, but I was out that night.'

Daniel leant forward to address the table. 'Sammy was at the Fund Manager of the Year Awards at the Grosvenor. She was up for an award.' Then he sat back and waited.

Alastair nodded. 'Of course. So, the obvious question.' He kept his tone neutral and then paused for a second. 'Has anyone else noticed that duffel coats seem to be making a comeback?'

'Al!' Vanessa gently slapped him on the arm. 'Come on then, Sammy. Did you win?'

Matthew saw Sammy look down at the table before glancing at her husband.

'She was given an outstanding contribution award.' Daniel led the group in a round of applause whilst Sammy studied the tablecloth again. 'And Angel Capital also won the Absolute Return - Equity Fund award.'

Sammy's hands were tightly balled. Daniel rested his arm on his wife's shoulder, and Matthew saw her flinch. What was that about?

Daniel turned to face Matthew. 'So, how are you, Matt?'

Matthew jerked at hearing his name. 'I'm okay.' Everyone was looking at him as if eyes could hug.

'It's so awful.' Vanessa reached out and squeezed his hand.

There was a pause. Matthew picked up his glass of water and took a sip.

'Can we...' he swallowed. 'I know how much you all care; it means a great deal to me. But I'd find it easier if we could talk about something else, please?' His voice cracked as he finished the sentence.

Sammy moved forward on her seat and spoke. 'So, who's looking forward to seeing Caesar next week?'

'I am.' Vanessa cleared her throat. 'We're making good progress with Cerebrum. We've been developing an improved wireless design for the brain interface. We're getting close to our first human trials.'

Matthew sipped his water and tuned out. He'd wait for a better time, but for now, he'd enjoy listening to his friends, and if he tried hard enough, he might even be able to forget that Lucy wasn't there, just for a moment.

MATTHEW PUSHED HIS PLATE AWAY. He was no longer hungry. There was a click of spoons as everyone else ate their dessert. Matthew paused to see whether anyone else would pick up the conversation before speaking himself.

'I've got an update too.' Everyone turned to look at him, and the atmosphere seemed to shift as if resetting to a different scene. 'It's not about my Cerebrum AI research, though.' He cleared his throat. 'I've discovered some things about Caesar I think you should all know.'

'Did you say *about* Caesar?' Alastair raised his eyebrows.

'Yes. He had two friends at university.'

'Two friends?' Alastair deadpanned.

'Yes. The three of them were known as the Genius Club.'

Vanessa laughed. 'I think that's quite sweet.'

Matthew felt a flicker of irritation. 'It was the name they gave to their debating society. One of the friends was Henry Bannister.'

'Doctor Bannister?' Vanessa said. 'I didn't know the two of them were friends from college, ' she shrugged. 'Why does it matter?'

Matthew stared at her before ducking under the table to remove the folder from his bag. He started to pass around printouts of the divorce hearing and the blog post about Rebecca Grey. 'The third man was called Christopher Goldman. I've found some details about him, too. He's a director of Cerebrum.'

'What?' Daniel stared at Matthew. 'Caesar has never mentioned anyone else being involved with Cerebrum, let alone another company director. Are you sure?'

'Yes,' Matthew said. 'He's listed as a director on Companies House.'

Daniel was tapping on his phone. After a few seconds, he nodded. 'He's been a director since the company was incorporated. That's strange.'

'What's this all about, Matt?' Alastair was leafing through the pages of paper. 'This is a divorce case. Is there some connection to Cerebrum?'

Matthew barely heard what Alastair had said because he was looking at Daniel, who was frowning at the photograph of Rebecca Grey in his hand. Daniel touched his wife on the arm.

'What the hell?' Sammy took her glasses off and studied the picture. After a few seconds, she levelled her gaze at Matthew. 'Why have you got a photo of my mother?'

For a moment, the room was silent. Matthew stared at Sammy. Her mother had died five years ago, but he'd never met her, and he couldn't recall ever seeing a picture of her either.

'I didn't know that woman was your mother,' he said, clasping his hands together and squeezing them. 'I found the photo when I searched for information about Goldman's divorce. He also kept a locked filing cabinet with details on many different women.'

'Sorry,' Sammy said, slipping her glasses back on, 'this guy, Christopher Goldman, had this photograph of my mother and kept secret personal records on specific women?'

Matthew nodded. 'I think so. His wife found the photo in his wallet and saw some of the papers in his private files.' He scratched his temple and shuffled on his seat. 'He was a banker.' Which he knew didn't explain anything but was nonetheless a fact.

Sammy pursed her lips. 'My mother worked at a bank.'

'Perhaps they knew each other through work,' Daniel said.

'According to the divorce proceedings, they didn't work at the same firm,' Matthew said.

Sammy put the photograph on the table. 'Why would he—why would anyone keep her photo in their wallet?' She looked at Matthew again. 'She looks young in the photo. I'd guess it was taken before I was born.' She picked up the photograph and looked at it again. 'I've never heard the name Christopher Goldman before.' Matthew could see tears in her eyes now. 'I'm sorry. Seeing it out of the blue, it's...' She brushed her cheek with her hand.

Matthew wasn't sure what to do. He hadn't meant to upset anyone, and he'd certainly had no idea that Rebecca Grey was Sammy's mother. He'd wanted to talk about Bannister and any medication or treatment that the doctor may have prescribed to any of them. He'd wanted to find out whether Caesar had recruited any of them into an experiment, but the revelation that Rebecca Grey was Sammy's mother had thrown him.

'Perhaps we should ask the man himself?' Daniel said.

'We can't do that,' Matthew said. 'He's dead.'

'He's still shown as a director at Companies House,' Daniel said. 'I guess Caesar could have forgotten to notify them.'

There was a moment's silence before Alastair spoke. 'I'm still confused about where you're going with this, Matt.'

Matthew scanned his friends' faces. Everyone was looking at him and waiting. He took a deep breath. 'I think Caesar might be using us in an experiment,' he said.

'What?' Vanessa replied, shaking her head. 'I mean, *what* did you just say?'

'Lucy was using a transcranial direct current stimulation device.' Matthew saw the glances flick around the table.

Alastair's expression softened. 'Some people find them helpful in treating depression.' He said it without judgment, and Matthew was grateful for it.

'I know, but I don't think she was depressed. I found lots of research suggesting it as a method to boost intelligence. I think Bannister advised her to use it.' Matthew shuffled in his chair. 'Bannister prescribed me some medicine.' He lowered his gaze before pushing on. He wanted to tell them about Dylan's operation, too, but he'd made a promise, and even though he didn't believe in the afterlife, there was no way he was breaking that promise with Lucy looking over his shoulder.

'There's nothing odd about that,' Vanessa said. 'We all had annual medicals through Cerebrum, and Caesar was happy to cover the costs of our private treatment. He wanted the best for us all. What does that have to do with this guy, Goldman?' She pointed to the pile of paper next to her plate.

'Yes, I'm still unsure what you're suggesting,' Daniel said, glancing at his wife. Sammy was twisting a strand of her hair around her finger.

Matthew sucked in a breath. 'I never checked the tablets Bannister gave me. I just assumed they were for my asthma, as he said.' He could hear the sullen note in his voice.

'Well, of course you would. We all would.' Vanessa sounded dismissive. 'The doctor writes the prescription, but the pharmacy dispenses it.'

'What if they were something else?' Matthew asked.

'Like what?' Vanessa asked.

'Cognitive enhancers.' He spoke quietly. He looked down at the table. 'Smart pills. What if he was trying to boost intelligence through medication? What if the Genius Club was more about experimentation than support?' Everyone was staring at him. 'I spoke with a professor who taught Bannister at college. She told me he was obsessed with using gene editing to enhance intelligence. What if he-'

He trailed off. He felt off-balance. He'd spent so many hours running over the hypothesis that he'd lost any sense of what was reasonable.

'That's a hell of a stretch, Matt,' Vanessa said.

'Maybe,' he said, 'but there's something else.'

'Go on,' Alastair said.

'I think Caesar wanted us to procreate. I think it was his plan all along.' Matthew was struggling to read the room. They were his friends; they cared for him, and they wanted to protect him and help him deal with Lucy's death, but their expressions were somewhere between confusion and scepticism. Did they think he was lurching into conspiracy theory territory?

'But Caesar was totally against any sexual activity between us from the outset. That's why that guy...' Vanessa looked around the table.

'Jason Tanner,' Matthew said.

'Yes, Jason Tanner. That's why Caesar kicked him out.' She paused and lowered her gaze. 'I know some relationships came out of the scholarship, but I don't believe Caesar planned it that way; quite the opposite.'

'I agree,' Sammy said. 'Whatever you think about Bannister, I never felt that Caesar tried to interfere in our relationship.' She glanced at her husband as she spoke.

There was a silence that lasted for a few seconds. Matthew chewed his lip. 'So, none of you ... Bannister didn't ... you weren't asked to do anything you didn't want to do? Anything out of the ordinary.'

Daniel and Sammy exchanged another look, but it was Alastair who spoke.

'Well, there was this girl in Edinburgh one summer,' he said. He took a sip of wine. 'Although she turned out to be extremely persuasive.'

Matthew could understand their scepticism. He didn't have any hard evidence. The reason for Dylan's expulsion was the strongest, but he wasn't going to share that with them, and even if he had, he wasn't sure they'd believe it. They thought he was reaching for something that wasn't there, an explanation that might somehow explain Lucy's death and permit him not to have to accept that she had been battling with secret depression.

He picked up his glass of water and took a sip. Perhaps what was obvious was also the truth. All his friends around the table believed that Lucy had taken her own life. Usually, that would carry significant weight. He tried to let the thought settle, but it wouldn't. He just knew as an *a priori* truth that despite whatever Caesar, Goldman and Bannister had or hadn't done, Lucy had not killed herself.

'Sorry, please excuse me.' He pushed back his chair and stood up.

'Are you okay, Matt?' Sammy was half out of her seat, too.

'Yes. I need to use the bathroom.'

Without waiting for any response, he walked out of the room. A waiter directed him towards the men's bathroom. Matthew pushed the door open and walked in, stopping in front of the washbasin. There was no one else around. He glanced at the neatly arranged white hand towels and the bottles of lotion standing on the marble top. He unfolded one of the towels before wetting it under the tap. He waited for the water to run cold before turning off the tap and pressing the damp cloth against his face. His skin tingled as the water soaked into his stubble. He closed his eyes and pressed the material around the edge of his eye sockets.

He'd been wrong to come. He carefully wiped his cheeks and his chin before dropping the towel in the basket by the door and walking back out, heading for the exit.

'HEY.' Sammy was leaning against the wall next to the restaurant exit.

'Hello.' Matthew stopped, not sure what to do.

'Come outside with me.' Sammy held out her hand and waited for Matthew to take it. 'I need to tell you something.'

They stepped outside, and the cool night air caught him by surprise. He'd had his hood up on the way over, which had kept off the worst of the chill. Sammy wrapped her arms around her torso. She'd come out without her jacket, which suggested she would go back in.

'I need to talk to someone.' She was looking away from him as if searching for someone, anyone, who would listen.

'Can't you talk to Daniel?'

'It's Daniel I want to talk about.'

Matthew waited, unsure what to say next, but he felt that shouldn't be a problem. After all, Sammy had told him she had something to say. His role was to wait and listen, and he could do that.

'Christ. At times like this, I really wished I smoked.' Sammy laughed. Short and full of sadness. 'Something's going on with Daniel at work. He's been-' She broke off and looked away with a slight shake of her head. She turned back to face her friend. 'He's been accused of sexual harassment. It's ridiculous. I can't believe it's true, but they've already interviewed him. Now they're undertaking a formal investigation.'

Matthew rubbed his temple. 'What does Daniel say about it?' he asked.

Sammy glanced towards the door. 'He's angry. He swears he hasn't done anything wrong. He can't understand why his firm doesn't believe him. He's a founding partner,' she brushed a strand of hair behind her ear, 'but of course, they have to investigate any claims.'

'Well, hopefully, the investigation will clear him.'

'I know,' Sammy said, nodding. 'I guess all I can do is wait.' She hesitated and brushed her fingers across her eyes before continuing. 'The photograph of my mother, I know it's unrelated, but it's unsettling.' Sammy jumped as the front door opened, and a young couple staggered out, laughing at everything and anything. 'I don't need you to say anything, Matt. I just wanted someone else to know.'

Matthew nodded. He didn't have any answers. There was nothing he could say. Outwardly, Sammy and Daniel seemed to have it all. He recalled Daniel's hand on Sammy's shoulder earlier that evening. Now he knew what Daniel was reaching for. He was trying to find an answer to one of the problems money alone couldn't solve.

23

NOW

THURSDAY, 20 JUNE 2019

Putney, London

MATTHEW WAS SITTING AT DYLAN'S KITCHEN TABLE. RELATIONS HAD improved sufficiently for Matthew to be cradling a glass of water. He wasn't sure whether Dylan didn't allow any caffeine in her house or whether she just didn't feel inclined to offer anything more exotic than water.

'I came to show you something.' He pulled out a copy of the documents he'd shared with the others the night before and handed it to her. 'This is the report of the Goldmans' divorce and an article about the woman named in the proceedings.'

Dylan said nothing as she leafed through the papers. There was nothing Matthew could do to short-circuit the process, and in any event, he wanted her unvarnished reaction. When she had finished, she slid the page with the picture of Rebecca Grey into the centre of the table.

'She looks like Sammy,' Dylan said, which Matthew had to admit was one hell of a shout.

'It's her mother,' Matthew confirmed. 'So why would Christopher Goldman have a photo of Sammy's mother in his file?'

'One explanation would be that he, that the three of them, kept files on all of us, and the information included details of our parents, but...' she trailed off.

'But what?'

'He had this photograph when he was still married. That's before Sammy was born.'

'You think it's possible that our parents were selected for the scholarship programme *before* we were born?' he asked.

'It's possible.' Dylan was sifting through the papers. 'Parents sign their unborn children up for all sorts of things. Nursery and school places, for a start. Although that does make an important assumption.'

He nodded. 'That our parents knew about the scholarship.' A memory scratched in Matthew's brain. 'When you got your letter from Caesar, did it include a line about confidentiality?'

'Mine was an email.'

'Sorry?'

'My invitation was sent by email. I think he was trying to impress me.' She paused before continuing in a monotone as she quoted from his message. 'Acceptance of the scholarship is conditional on confidentiality although, of course, you may share the details with your parents or guardian.'

Matthew stared at her. He'd put money on her recollection being word-perfect twenty years later.

'I'm positive that my dad didn't know anything about it until I told him,' he said. He knew that Dylan had been brought up by her mother, but that was the full extent of what he knew about her family, and she didn't look as though she was about to sketch him her family tree. Matthew's neck was tingling. Everything pointed towards the conclusion that Caesar, Bannister, and Goldman had groomed them all from an early age, possibly even before birth.

'Wait here,' Dylan said, 'I've got something you should see.'

Matthew looked up. 'What is it?'

'A list of all the children that Caesar screened for the scholarship.'

Matthew's mouth was dry. He knew they'd all been through a

selection process, and he'd assumed there may have been others who weren't offered the scholarship or even invited to interview. But the existence of a record of all the candidates hit him like a cold wave in the sea, smacking him in the chest with the undertow dragging him off his feet.

'You hacked into his computer?' he asked.

Dylan tilted her head. 'No. Although maybe I should have tried that. This was old school. I took it off his printer on the day I quit. I was angry. I didn't even know what it was until I looked at it later. Wait here.'

DYLAN WALKED BACK IN, clutching a couple of sheets of paper, and handed them to Matthew. He could feel her studying him as he looked at the printouts; their roles reversed from just a few moments ago. He tried to block out her presence and focus on the information before him.

The data was displayed in a grid. The left-hand column was a list of names; the top six were the familiar names he had expected. The names continued across two pages. Eighteen children formed the longlist for Caesar's scholarship programme. Matthew glanced through the names.

'You're not on here,' he said, revising the number to nineteen.

'I know. When he decided to kick me out, he must have deleted me.'

Matthew didn't say anything but looked again at the other names. After each name was a digit between three and twenty-two, but there was no key to explain the significance. Maybe it was some sort of grading. Matthew was a seventeen, as was Daniel and a woman he didn't know. Sammy had the lowest number, a three. Lucy was a four, Alastair eleven, and Vanessa twenty- two.

If it was a grading, it made no sense. No disrespect to the others, but Dylan and Alastair had an intelligence that outshone them all. Only four other names were awarded single figures, and the only one he recognised was Kathryn Farthing. Matthew shook his head. At the other extreme, with the maximum score of twenty-two, were Vanessa and another unknown name. Jason Tanner had been allocated the number eighteen.

The following few columns recorded percentages. Instinctively, Matthew knew they were test scores, though the nature of each test was unclear. The scholars' marks were the highest, with Alastair recording one hundred percent in three cases. Lucy had one perfect score, whereas for Vanessa, Sammy, Daniel, and Matthew, their highest scores were in the low nineties. Beyond those that had made the cut, there were barely any scores higher than eighty.

The final columns recorded what Matthew guessed was the status of each child as they moved through the selection process. The four column headings were *Gate 1* through to *Gate 4*. Whatever each test was, it was clear that if the child hadn't met the grade, the gate remained shut. A handful of hopefuls had made it through the first three, but only the club members had made it through all four. Whether the last assessment was the scholarship interview or an earlier stage was impossible to know just from the chart.

'Feels strange to see our early lives reduced to numbers on a piece of paper,' Matthew said, eventually.

Dylan didn't reply.

It felt like an important piece of the puzzle. He now had concrete evidence that there was a selection system, and the fact that all the children, even those who didn't make it through *Gate 1*, had a complete set of test scores showed that some information had been recorded before the invitations for interview were sent out. How early in their lives had the monitoring begun?

'Do you mind if I take a photo of these?' He nodded to the pages he had placed on her kitchen table.

'Knock yourself out.'

Matthew blinked at hearing Dylan using the exact phrase Alfie used in his voicemail message. 'I'm going to look into some of these other people.' Matthew pulled out his iPhone and snapped the pictures, checking that the resolution was high enough to allow him to read the details. 'I'll message you if I find anything out. Right, I'd better get back to Alfie.'

He stood up but hesitated as he walked towards the door. 'Hey, did you get an invite to Caesar's meeting? It's on Wednesday.'

Dylan shook her head. 'He's never invited me.'

'Okay, well, I guess I'll let you know how it goes.' He paused, uncertain how to phrase his next question. 'It's Lucy's funeral tomorrow.' He let it hang in the air.

'I don't want to come,' Dylan said.

Some of the tension eased in Matthew's shoulders. 'You should come. She'd have liked you to be there,' he said.

Dylan shook her head. 'She'd have liked the fact that you invited me more.'

24

THEN

AUGUST 2004

St Stephen's Cathedral, Vienna

MATTHEW'S CHEST TIGHTENED AS HE FOLLOWED THE OTHERS THROUGH the catacombs deep beneath Vienna. They walked in single file through the door at the end of the passageway into a room. The walls were white - stark under the bright lights. A dining table set for six dominated the room, and he could see names neatly printed on folded white cards, marking everyone's place. Matthew exchanged a glance with Lucy. Tonight was a celebration, the culmination of the last few years, and a look forward to their future.

The lights dimmed, and music started pumping out from the sleek floor speakers. A drumbeat segued into a dirty guitar riff. Matthew smiled as he listened to the vocalist almost screaming, 'Highly evolved.' The song ended suddenly after little more than a minute. There was a subtle click from the ceiling-mounted projector, and the wall at the end of the room sprang into life.

Images of people flashed onto the wall: Rosalind Franklin, Alan Turing, Kurt Gödel, and Simone de Beauvoir—geniuses, one and all. The last picture faded with the music, but the lights stayed off. They waited, and then Benjamin Caesar's disembodied voice filled the room.

'Welcome, scholars. Today is your graduation, the end of one phase of your life but the beginning of another. The meal you are about to share is your opportunity to look back, to congratulate yourselves on all that you have achieved since you accepted your scholarship.'

Matthew bit his lip. Caesar wasn't going to be joining them for the meal. He tuned back into Caesar's words.

'...meeting of The Vienna Circle. Many of the finest minds in philosophy, science and mathematics met here in the nineteen twenties and thirties. A meeting of some of the greatest thinkers of their generation, with the capacity to have an immense influence on the world.'

Matthew could see Alastair trying and failing to suppress a grin.

'I have spent three years getting to know you. I will meet with you individually tomorrow to discuss what you want to do after graduation. I will shortly share a new opportunity I believe you'll find exciting. I sincerely hope that you will join me in my next venture. Dream long and work hard, and you can achieve whatever you want. Enjoy the evening, and I look forward to seeing you tomorrow.'

Matthew and Lucy had already talked about what was next. University had been a clear path, three years mapped out, but beyond that, the whole world awaited. They both knew Caesar would have a plan; he'd want to drive them forward, push them hard, and offer his support. He had mentored them for three years and made it clear he would continue doing so for as long as they wanted, provided they committed to supporting his research.

Matthew reached for Lucy's hand, and she instinctively squeezed as their fingers linked. Being selected for the scholarship had changed his life forever—not because of Benjamin Caesar, but because of Lucy. A shiver pulsed through Matthew as the music started up again. A guitar looped over a drumbeat, with waves of fade-out swamping the melody. Text appeared on the wall, each word seemingly etched by a cold blue laser.

genius (n.)

late 14c., "tutelary or moral spirit" who guides and governs an individual through life, from Latin genius "guardian deity or spirit which watches over each person from birth.

*from root *gene*

Meanings "person of natural intelligence or talent" and that of "exalted natural mental ability" are first recorded 1640s.

Suddenly, the wall was filled with some of the world's most famous works of art. Matthew gazed at Van Gogh's The Starry Night before his attention was drawn upwards by what appeared to be the ceiling of the Sistine Chapel. Classical music floated through the room. He identified a Jackson Pollock painting. Number 5, 1948. Also known for another number. One hundred and forty, the millions of dollars it had sold for. Snatches of literature were being read aloud - extracts of James Joyce, Sylvia Plath and Lewis Carroll, vying with the music.

Caesar was speaking once more. 'Our history is blessed with great men and women whose genius has written our future. Imagine creating genius at will, whether from birth or through transformation in adult life. Think about what we could do, what we could achieve. Consider what it would mean for the world, humanity, and our future. For decades, I have dreamed of a time when we can enhance human intelligence and cultivate genius. A perpetual golden age awaits. Today, we are on the threshold of achieving this vision. The time has come.'

The works of art dissolved, and an image of Caesar appeared, standing on a blazing sun with the planets orbiting around him.

'There's a significant body of research pointing to intelligence peaking in middle age. Statistically, you are at your most intelligent right now and for the next decade, but for you to continue to produce at the same level as currently or even to improve upon your current production, something will need to change. Otherwise, your intelligence will dim.'

The planets faded, and Matthew stepped back as a spiralling column—a twisting double helix — grew up from the ground.

'For years, I have researched cognitive enhancement and augmented intelligence. I have concluded that now is the time to focus on innovations, allowing us to build a new generation of highly intelligent beings. We stand at the gates of history.' Caesar snapped his fingers, and a large brain descended towards him, spinning slowly around. 'We can define our future. We can shape humanity. Together, we have the expertise to build a new future.'

'So today, I am launching Cerebrum, an enterprise focused on improving human intelligence. Until now, no one has risen to meet this challenge. The moral debate has stifled innovation, but we will change that. This will require all your ability and character, but we will change the world together.'

'Tomorrow morning, you will each receive my detailed paper. Until then, enjoy your evening.'

Matthew was stunned. He looked at his friends. Lucy's face gave nothing away. Daniel was stroking his chin, and Sammy was twirling a strand of hair repeatedly around her finger. Matthew turned his head. Vanessa was tapping her hands on the table, her eyes shining brightly.

Finally, Matthew's gaze fell on Alastair. His friend had his eyes closed. Alastair wasn't religious, but it looked for all the world like he was praying.

Hotel Imperial, Vienna – breakfast room

SAMMY SWALLOWED a mouthful of coffee and started speaking. 'I still can't believe it.' She was holding her copy of Caesar's paper. 'I mean, designing a neural implant to merge the brain with AI is crazy.'

'It does sound mad when you say it out loud.' Vanessa paused. 'The pathway he's set out is credible, though.'

Lucy shivered.

'What's wrong?' Sammy asked.

'I can't get over the idea that he always had this in mind, even when he first interviewed everyone. The specific roles he needs map perfectly to you all.'

'It sounds like you don't see a role for a Cerebrum poet,' Alastair said, picking up a croissant. 'But I, for one, would love to read your Ode to a Cyborg.'

Lucy hit him on the arm. 'Very funny.'

'I'm still stuck on the ethics of him wanting us to set up a genius factory,' Daniel said.

'I think it sounds like a lot of fun,' Alastair pushed back on his chair. 'We'll get our own monkeys and rig them up to a computer by glueing on a cap with microwires that stick into their motor cortex. Then we try to get them to play pong just by thinking. What's not to love?'

'Someone's going to do it one day,' Matthew said.

'Only if it's legal,' Daniel said.

'Whether it's legal or not,' Alastair said. 'Someone will do it. Or they'll claim they can,'

'Scientists are already trying this stuff. It's only a question of time before the first human trials.' Vanessa leant forward and glanced around the group. 'We're late starting, but if we work together, we could be at the forefront of this.'

'It raises an interesting question, though,' Daniel said. 'Where does enhancement stop and a new being start? Steroid injections? Amniocentesis?'

'Gender selection at birth? Removing a defective gene?' Vanessa offered. 'Or editing an intelligence gene? There's already a Chinese organisation conducting gene-trait association studies of general intelligence.'

'I'm still not sure,' Sammy said.

'Well, you'll only need to worry about raising the money.' Alastair smiled at her. 'But if someone's going to do it, perhaps it's better that it's us. We could build responsible safeguards around it. Society already accepts all sorts of enhancement: implants, laser eye surgery, pacemakers, teeth whitening.'

'Maybe. It's just that if we stop caring about where humanity starts and finishes, then...' Sammy trailed off, unable to find the words for the future she foresaw.

'We'll be facing the tyranny of choice,' Matthew said. He hadn't meant to speak. The others were all staring at him. He shrugged. 'Logic suggests that being able to make your own choices about too many things results in misery.'

Daniel sighed. 'It's an important point. This needs to be democratic, with access for all. We don't want to help create an intellectual elite.'

'Everybody's clever nowadays,' Alastair said. 'That's our tagline.'

Lucy laughed. 'Now that I know. That's Oscar Wilde.'

'I was hoping you'd think it was an Alastair Niven original,' he grinned.

'There's no such thing,' Vanessa shot back.

'Well, it's still a good strapline. I'm going to celebrate with another croissant,' Alastair said, already reaching towards the breadbasket. 'My work here is done.'

25

NOW

FRIDAY, 21 JUNE 2019

St Mary's Church, Wimbledon

IT TOOK ALL MATTHEW'S ENERGY TO STAND AND SHAKE HANDS WITH the guests. He briefly closed his eyes in the hope that it would ease the pain in his head, but today, he had no choice other than to push on. Any funeral was an ordeal, but the coroner's verdict that Lucy had taken her own life painted another emotional layer over the immediate shock of her being gone, especially when Matthew couldn't accept the verdict.

He didn't speak, preferring simply to nod as a procession of faces mumbled their condolences. He would have felt sorry for them, having to deal with the awkward conventions of a burial service, if he had been able to feel anything. But he was hollow whilst his thoughts churned, tripping over themselves in the search for answers.

Sammy's hand was rubbing his back, encouraging him to move. He turned to face her and saw the compassion in her eyes. Her large, dark-rimmed glasses covered the top half of her face, and her slightly crimped, brown hair flopped forward to offer extra protection. Matthew allowed himself to be guided away from the church entrance. As soon as they started to walk, she linked her arm with his, saying nothing but leading him down the cobbled path. The stones were shining, and small pools of water had gathered where the grass ran up to the border.

Matthew was starting to accept that people, that the world, would return to mystifying him. Lucy had been his guide for the last twenty years, and he'd seen life more clearly than ever before. They had talked for hours sometimes about ideas and philosophies, whims, music, or writing, but he'd never been in the habit of asking her what she was doing, where she'd been, or what she was planning. He'd never seen the need and believed that Lucy felt the same way as he did, but today and every day since her death, he wished he had. Because now he knew that by not asking, he'd missed something, a sign or a tell that she was in danger.

'We can take you home now if that's what you want?' Sammy said. 'Daniel's waiting in the car.'

'Thanks.' The word came out as a shrug.

Matthew knew nothing about cars, but whatever vehicle Daniel and Sammy owned gleamed in the rain. The rear door swung open as he approached, and Daniel stepped out, holding the door and waiting for Matthew to climb inside.

'I won't be a minute,' Daniel said after helping Sammy into the front passenger seat.

Matthew momentarily closed his eyes. Everything seemed easier that way. He touched his face and felt that it was wet from what could only be his tears. He hadn't realised he was crying. He wasn't sure what to do next, so he just waited.

'Let's get you home to Alfie,' Sammy said.

Matthew opened his eyes. His vision was blurred. He wiped his eyes with his hand. *Alfie.* They'd discussed the funeral, and eventually, Alfie decided he wouldn't attend. Alastair had agreed to stay with him, and Matthew knew that his friend would be doing his best to take Alfie's mind off what was happening, even though he might as well have been trying to stop the sun from rising.

'Thank you.' The words sounded detached. Had he even spoken? He wasn't sure. Matthew could hear the rain pounding on the car roof. He tightened his focus, trying to discern a pattern in the dance of the raindrops. He had to find some meaning somewhere. 'At the dinner, when I mentioned Doctor Bannister, I thought you and Daniel ... I thought you were going to say something.' He lifted his head to look at her in the rear-view mirror. She had coiled a strand of hair tightly around her finger. 'Maybe I was seeing something that wasn't there, I don't know, but if there's anything...' He massaged his forehead. 'Please.'

'Okay.' She twisted round and reached out to take his hand. She sighed before starting to talk. 'As you know, Daniel and I tried unsuccessfully for a baby for a long time. A year after we started trying, we had some fertility tests.' She let her hair fall over her eyes. 'We also tried a couple of rounds of IVF.' Matthew swallowed. He knew what he would hear next. 'Our doctor was Henry Bannister.' Sammy pushed her hair behind her ear. 'When we finally accepted we weren't going to be able to have children, he tried to persuade me to freeze my eggs. He was a great believer in advancements in medicine and technology giving us a chance to have children in the future. We decided not to and told him our answer was no. We wanted to live in the present. We didn't hear anything more from him for a while. Then, a few months before he died, he got in touch.'

Matthew looked at the floor of the car. 'What did he say?'

'He told us that there was a new technology. Something that allowed DNA to be manipulated. He referred to the technology as *genetic scissors*.'

A cold wave rolled down Matthew's back. 'Professor Hunter, the woman who taught Bannister, told me that twins were born in China recently, and there's speculation their DNA was altered to eliminate the risk of HIV. She also told me that the same gene affects brain function.' He paused. 'Apparently, Bannister was researching similar ideas.'

Sammy nodded. 'He told us we were still young—we were on the verge of turning thirty. He said there was still hope, not just for us to have children, but for us to have *remarkable* children.' Matthew said nothing, and after a moment, Sammy continued. 'We didn't really think about it. We were irritated he was still pressuring us to try for children when we'd already told him that we'd decided to put that behind us. But what you told us...'

'...you think there could be something more to it.'

'I don't know, maybe.' Sammy shrugged. 'I guess we ask Caesar on Wednesday.'

'If he turns up,' Matthew said.

Sammy wrapped her arms around her torso. 'Surely, he would have told us by now if he wasn't going to be there.'

'I don't know.' Matthew massaged his hands. 'He wasn't well enough to come today.'

Since that one email, he hadn't heard from Caesar again, but Matthew had still hoped their patron would make the funeral—not just because he needed to speak with him but because he'd wanted him to come for Lucy.

'Do you ever wonder about how he found us all?' Matthew asked.

'He selected kids who had challenging upbringings,' Sammy said. 'It was one of the reasons I accepted the scholarship in the first place—that and the money.' She grinned at Matthew. 'Seriously, though, there are so many routes for kids with a comfortable upbringing to get support that they often don't need. I've always thought of him as a class warrior. Even Cerebrum, he's not doing it for the money.'

'I guess so.'

It was true that collectively, they had faced more than their fair share of challenges. Adoption, lost parents, divorced parents, and even the death of a sibling. And they were only the things he knew about. He didn't often talk about personal experiences with the others, but he was sure that Lucy would have been able to provide a complete list. Everyone used to confide in Lucy.

Thoughts were spinning around in his head. If Sammy were right, on Wednesday, he'd have the chance to look Ben Caesar in the eye and ask him for the truth, but he had an uneasy sense about the upcoming meeting—a feeling that things were going to change and not for the better.

Daniel was walking back to the car, and Sammy twisted back to face forward. 'How's Alfie doing?' she asked over her shoulder.

'He's not saying much. He doesn't respond well if I try to push him.' He hesitated as Daniel opened the door and climbed into the driver's seat. His thoughts turned to the meeting at Alfie's school. 'I've got a meeting with his headmaster on Monday,' he said.

'Did you arrange that?' Sammy asked.

'No. The school did. I don't know what to expect.'

Daniel started the engine.

'I'm sure it'll be fine,' Sammy said.

Matthew didn't feel any better about the meeting with the headmaster than he did about the meeting with Caesar. At times like these, he'd always turned to Lucy. Looking out the window, he saw the last few mourners heading towards their cars. He didn't have that choice anymore. He balled his hands. He had to face the world alone.

26

NOW

MONDAY, 24 JUNE 2019

Fulham Broadway, London

MATTHEW SAT ON THE PLASTIC CHAIR AND WAITED. HE'D BARELY SLEPT the night before, and when he'd finally fallen asleep, his concern about the discussion with the headmaster had manifested itself in dreams of Alfie taking smart pills and blasting his brain with electricity.

Matthew needed to focus on Alfie right now. Everything else could wait. The headmaster's secretary sat quietly behind her desk, tapping away on her computer keyboard, having already explained that the headmaster was running late. Meanwhile, Alfie was in his lesson somewhere nearby. Matthew wished Lucy was with him. He always did, but right then, he needed her because she was much better than him at talking to people and advocating for Alfie. He'd just have to do his best.

Alfie was in year seven and had settled quickly. He didn't have close friends, but the other kids didn't seem to dislike him, and he found the schoolwork easy.

'The headmaster will see you now, Professor Stanford,' the secretary said.

Matthew nodded as he stood up, the chair's metal legs scraping against the wooden floor. He pulled himself out of the imaginary conversation and prepared himself for the real one. The secretary motioned towards the door she had just opened, and Matthew walked through.

'Professor Stanford, thank you for coming in. Firstly, let me say how sorry I was, that we all were, to hear the tragic news about your wife.'

Mr Logan looked exhausted. He was stocky, slightly ruddy-faced, and had grey, thinning hair. He sat behind his desk and waited for Matthew to settle into another standard-issue school chair.

'Well, I'm afraid to say that this is a serious discussion—a difficult one in many ways.' That was all he needed to say for Matthew to understand what was coming. Explaining why it was coming would take longer, but at that moment, he knew that his son was in trouble.

'There have been a series of incidents recently–'

'Has been, not have been.' Matthew stared at the headmaster. 'A series is singular.'

'What? Okay. There *has* been a series of incidents recently involving Alfie.'

Matthew clenched his fists. 'What does that mean?'

The headmaster blinked. 'Alfie has been in several fights recently, which is why we arranged this meeting. Unfortunately, there has been another fight this morning. I interviewed the children involved, and it seems clear that Alfie attacked one of the other pupils.'

'Seems clear, is not the same as clear.' Matthew could hear himself, but he was disoriented. Why would Alfie have attacked a classmate?

'It's clear enough to me, Professor Stanford,' Mr Logan replied with a subtle shake of the head. He tapped his pencil on his table. 'Professor Stanford, it is my duty as the headmaster of this school to ensure that the highest standards are upheld. Based on all the evidence I've heard today, I have recommended that Alfie be excluded for two weeks starting from the end of classes today. That will take him to the end of the Summer term.' Exclusion. Matthew balled his hands. 'I'm required to tell you that for the first five days of the exclusion, it's your legal responsibility to ensure that Alfie is not in a public place during normal school hours. Indeed, you might be prosecuted if your son is found in a public place when he's not supposed to be.'

Matthew tried to steady his breathing. 'Do you know my son, Mr Logan?'

'I assure you I've given the matter due consideration, Professor Stanford. I will follow up this discussion with a letter setting out the terms of the exclusion and the reason. The letter will also explain how you can challenge the exclusion.'

Matthew shuffled forward on the chair. 'Alfie's almost certainly one of the brightest kids in your school. He only has me to look after him, and I work full-time. His mother died thirteen days ago yesterday. Thirteen days, that will feel like two seconds to him. Some kids claim that Alfie hit someone, and you exclude him? That just isn't fair. Why take their word over Alfie's?'

'I haven't,' Mr Logan said.

'Then why are you excluding him?'

Mr Logan cleared his throat. 'It was Alfie who told me. None of the others would say anything. But it's not just that. In many ways, I admire him for being honest. The complication is what he said when I asked him why.' The headmaster bowed his head.

'What did he say?'

'He said, *I don't like Mondays*.'

Matthew turned to stare out of the window. *I don't like Mondays.* He couldn't believe that of Alfie. He wouldn't hurt anyone, let alone source a gun to shoot them. Even with everything he was going through.

'Professor Stanford,' the headmaster's voice was momentarily soft, 'is Alfie receiving counselling?' Matthew shook his head. 'I'm sorry. I know this must be very difficult.'

'I believe you are sorry, Mr Logan, I do,' Matthew stood up. 'But you can't know what this is like. I will pick up Alfie at the end of school today. He'll be back at the start of next year.'

The headmaster stood up and offered his hand. Matthew fought against his natural inclination and shook his hand before leaving. He walked through the school gate and headed towards the nearest pub. He wasn't a drinker, but he knew someone who was. He dialled Alastair's number. He would avoid the subject of Caesar, Lucy, and the scholarship, but he needed advice about his son.

'Hi Matt, what's up?' Alastair sounded as though he was struggling to speak.

'I need to talk. Are you free for a drink?' Matthew turned into the pub car park.

'I'm always happy to drink, although it's 2:30 in the morning.

'What?' Matthew frowned.

'I'm in Vegas. Are you okay?' Alastair asked.

Matthew stretched his mind around his friend being in the gambling capital of the world. He'd forgotten that Alastair was flying out straight after Lucy's funeral for the weekend. 'No. Can you speak for a few minutes?'

'Sure. What's wrong?'

'Alfie's been suspended from school.' His voice cracked as he spoke.

'Okay. I wasn't expecting that. Why?'

'Apparently, he punched a kid, confessed to it and when asked why, he said, I don't like Mondays.' He heard Alastair let out a large breath. 'I guess they had no choice,' Matthew said.

'I'll say. Confessing to being a Boomtown Rats fan. Definite exclusion. At least a week.'

'That's not funny, Alastair.' Matthew paused. 'Two weeks. Why do you think he'd say that?'

'Your son is twelve. He lost his mum less than a fortnight ago. So, he punched a kid. I bet the kid deserved it. And when the headmaster asks him why, he quotes a US elementary school shooter—a quote I'd imagine across the whole school only the headmaster and possibly a few of the other teachers would recognise. He's a smart kid. And he's playing with the headmaster. Because he's angry, well, he should blow it off for a bit. It'll do him good.'

Matthew's eyes were wet. 'I don't know how to help him.'

'All you can do is talk with him, Matt. Listen to him.' There was a pause. His voice was soft. 'Is he seeing the counsellor I recommended?'

Matthew said nothing for a while. He didn't want to answer that question. 'Thanks, Alastair. Perhaps we can talk when you're back.'

'Sure. Good luck, mate. Give my love to Alfie.' Alastair clicked off.

Raynes Park, London

ALFIE DIDN'T SAY a word in the car. He'd been told about the suspension but was in no mood to talk about it. Matthew had refused to let Alfie visit Dylan. He could go the following week, but he'd decided his son needed to be home on the day he received his suspension.

Matthew brought the car to a stop, and the red light was a sarcastic echo of his ability to communicate with his son. Still, it also gave him the answer. He had to wait. It took the twenty-minute drive home and another ten sitting on the sofa before Alfie's green light flicked on.

'I'm sorry, Dad.'

'You want to tell me about it?' Matthew had had to learn this role in the last couple of weeks because Lucy had always done it before. She and Alfie would chat away for hours.

'I hit one of the kids in my class during registration.' His son's voice was monotonal. Matthew waited to see if he would continue. 'He was saying things about Mum. They were all lies, but he shouldn't have said them.' Alfie stared straight ahead. 'So, I hit him.'

'Okay.' Matthew rubbed his son's arm, feeling a slight tremor in his own. He could feel his blood pounding. Why would a kid say something to Alfie about Lucy? He knew kids could be cruel, but...

'And you didn't say anything to this kid?'

Alfie turned to look at his dad. His eyes were hard. 'No, of course not.'

'Okay,' Matthew said quickly.

'Don't you believe me?' Alfie said, a thickness in his voice.

'Of course I do. Did you tell the school what this boy said?'

A pause. 'No.' His jaw was set.

'It might have made a difference to their decision. I think I should tell them.'

'No. I don't want you to.'

'Why not?'

There was another pause, and then Alfie stood up. 'Okay. I'll show you.' He left the room and returned a few seconds later, holding a brown A4-sized envelope.

'What's that?' Matthew asked.

'A kid in my class had it.'

Alfie handed the envelope to his dad. Matthew read the typed label. *Alfie Stanford - private and confidential.*

'Did this boy give this to you?'

Alfie shook his head. 'He opened it. He was saying all these things about Mum. When I told him it was rubbish, he said he had proof. He was waving this envelope about. I asked him to give it to me. He refused. That's why I got into the fight.'

Matthew opened the envelope and pulled out the folded paper. On the page, he saw a few short sentences.

It's time for the truth.

You are adopted.

Matthew's head jerked up. His son's gaze was locked on him. 'That's not true,' he said.

'None of it's true,' Alfie said.

Matthew continued reading.

Your mother was a junkie.

Your father is screwing his secretary.

You're a freak.

You were abandoned once before.

And you will be again.

'Jesus,' Matthew said softly. He swallowed the lump in his throat. 'Where did he get this?'

'He told me he was given it by a girl. He didn't know her; she just stopped him on the way into school. Claimed she'd been given a hundred pounds to hand the envelope to anyone in year seven.'

'Someone paid her?' Matthew was shaking his head.

'That's what he was told.'

'Okay,' Matthew said, deep in thought. Why would someone hand an envelope to a random schoolboy rather than giving it to Alfie directly? It had to be because whoever had done it knew that the messenger would open it before they delivered it. More importantly, they wanted to protect themselves, which meant that it was orchestrated by someone Alfie would recognise. 'We need to find out who sent you this,' Matthew said.

Alfie shrugged. 'Why? They're the ones with the problem, not me.'

Matthew agreed with that, but there was no guarantee the abuse would be the end of it. He didn't reply because he didn't want Alfie to worry more than he was already. Why would anyone want to brutally attack him, especially so soon after he'd lost his mother? It was unfathomable.

You were abandoned before. And you will be again. What did it even mean? Was that a reference to Lucy's death? Whoever had written the note knew that Alfie's mother was dead because they had referred to her in the past tense. He hesitated. Was that right? It could mean that she used to take drugs. He shivered at the use of the word *junkie.* He couldn't know whether it was just random abuse or whether it was a reference to the cocktail of lethal drugs that had been found in Lucy's bloodstream.

'I'm going to my room,' Alfie said, walking out of the lounge, leaving Matthew staring at the typed messages designed to cause such pain for his son.

27

THEN

OCTOBER 2006

St Albans, London

MATTHEW WAS SITTING ON HIS CHILDHOOD BED FOR THE LAST TIME. He'd come back home because his father was selling up. He hadn't given Matthew much notice, and it seemed he had only called his son back to empty his bedroom before the move.

When Matthew walked into the room, he realised it'd been untouched since he was last there, the best part of a year ago. But he knew it hadn't been left untouched because it was a shrine but because he'd been forgotten. However, forgotten implied that he had made some level of impression in the first place.

Packing up was strangely unemotional. He'd declined Lucy's offer to come with him and help and regretted his decision the whole day. He didn't have much that he needed to take back with him. His father had a box of stuff that belonged to his mother, and he'd asked Matthew to take it. Matthew had shrugged. He had little chance of returning the box to his mother; he wasn't even sure he would try. The bedroom furniture was part of the sale, so it was just Matthew's books and old clothes. The sum total of his childhood memories. His eyes fell on an old mathematics textbook. Pressed inside the cover was the letter he had received from Benjamin Caesar.

He slipped it out of its fading envelope and unfolded the pages. As he reread the letter in his bedroom, he recalled his amazement at being selected by someone who didn't even know him. Caesar had been nothing but supportive, and he'd also introduced him to the best thing that had ever happened, or ever would happen, to him: Lucy Summerton. Now Lucy Stanford, and soon to be the mother of their child.

There was a knock on the door, and his father walked in. He hadn't told his father that Lucy was pregnant. He'd figured he would pick a moment to tell him that weekend. And now, the opportunity had come knocking.

'I wanted to speak with you, Matthew.' Which wasn't a phrase that Matthew could ever remember his father uttering before.

'Okay. What is it?' He'd have to come back to his news.

'I've met someone.' The three words seemed to echo around the room. 'That's why I decided to sell the house. I'm moving in with her. Her name is Jan.'

'What about Mum?' Matthew knew that his parents' relationship was broken and would never be fixed, much like his own relationship with his mother, but as far as he knew, she still owned half the house.

'She'll get her share. I haven't got any choice about that.'

'Isn't she entitled to it?' Matthew asked. He tried to keep any judgment out of his voice.

'Yes, but she's...' He looked around the room, searching for an answer. 'She's not very good at looking after herself.'

Matthew nodded. His mother lived in a hostel. The last time he'd tried to visit her was to invite her to his wedding, but she'd refused to see him. He wasn't sure why, but ultimately, it was the question of whether she would ever want to see him again rather than why she wouldn't currently meet with him, which was important. She'd had some sort of breakdown all those years ago, and her choice had been to leave. It didn't look as though she was ever going to come back. Not to him. She hadn't even come to the door on the last visit, leaving her friend to tell him she didn't wish to see him.

Matthew's father lowered himself down onto the bed and looked straight ahead. His face didn't shine with the happiness of a man who had found love for the second time. He cleared his throat and started to speak.

'You see, Matthew, the thing is, you were always your mother's idea. She talked me into having children, and then she just left,' he said. 'You were too young to know what was happening, but it was clear she wasn't going to look after you.' A lump lodged itself in Matthew's throat. His father pushed on. 'It was left to me, and I did my best. Which wasn't what you deserved.' He flinched. 'I mean, you deserved more than me. I've never been good at being your dad.'

Matthew swallowed. He could taste something bitter in his mouth. He didn't dare speak. 'Now, you're grown up. I've met Jan, and you've got Lucy. I guess this is where I hand you over.' His voice dropped to a whisper. 'And wish you well.'

Matthew's voice cracked as he spoke. 'You're saying goodbye? That's it? I tried, I did my best, and I'm done?'

His father's breathing quickened, and his head jerked with a tic. 'I think so, yes.' His father finally turned to face him. Anger was etched into the creases on his forehead. 'I will never forgive your mother. And I know it's unfair, but I can't look at you without feeling angry with her. It's never gone away.'

Matthew knew that image of his father would stay with him forever. It was as if his father was looking at his mother, and his features were twisted from their usually impassive resting state into a picture of hurt—the pain of a man who felt he'd been wronged.

Matthew closed his eyes. He'd come home to say goodbye to his childhood home, not to his father, and he still needed to tell his father his news.

Or did he? The urge to withhold the information flooded over him. Why should he tell his father? He'd just excused himself from Matthew's life. But if he didn't tell him, what would that make

Matthew? And maybe it would make a difference, re-spark life into the family combustion chamber.

'Lucy's pregnant.' He was crying now, tears streaking his face. 'You're going to be a grandfather.'

His father pushed himself up from the bed. 'I'm happy for you, but I can't think of myself as a grandfather.' The engine spluttered and died.

Matthew started a retort but managed to stop himself. What was the point? His father was already walking out of the room, and a few seconds later, he was gone, leaving the door slightly ajar behind him.

Matthew dropped the letter onto the floor and curled himself into a ball on the bed. Strike one, his mother. Strike two, his family home. Third strike and out, his father. But at that moment, just as he'd been totally rejected, his tears stopped. He felt surprisingly devoid of emotion.

What had he actually lost? He'd thought his father had loved him, but that was before he met Lucy. Lucy had taught him how to love and be loved, and he knew his father had spoken the truth. Their relationship wasn't built on love but on obligation and dependence. Matthew's independence offered his father the chance for freedom.

There would be questions for another time. Such as, why didn't his parents love him? What had he done that was so wrong? But as much as he might one day want answers to those questions, he had a bigger purpose in his life right then. He was going to be a father. And, with Lucy as his guide, he vowed that their child would know love every single day of their life.

28

NOW

TUESDAY, 25 JUNE 2019

Raynes Park, London

MATTHEW GRUNTED WITH THE EFFORT OF LIFTING THE BOX AND carrying it down the loft stairs towards the kitchen. He was still working his way through his suspicions and theories. The attack on Alfie had ratcheted up the pressure, but he was sure there was a link from Caesar's original Genius Club to Lucy's death, maybe to Kathryn Farthing's murder, and even to Alfie's hate mail.

If he was going to find the truth, he needed to uncover patterns of behaviour. Then, he might be able to divine the motivations. Goldman had profiled Sammy's mother—that seemed incontestable, so Caesar, Bannister, and Goldman might have done the same with Matthew's parents.

The metal box wasn't locked, but the lid was jammed. After a few minutes of effort and with the help of a kitchen knife, Matthew eased it open and lifted the contents onto the table. His mother's papers had held no interest to him until now. He reached over and picked up an envelope with his mother's name typed on the label. Jayne Mary Stanford. He opened the flap and tipped out the contents. It looked like a contract, a few typed pages long. He caught sight of one of the parties' names in bold capital letters.

The contract was between his mother and a company called Double Helix Limited. Matthew's hands trembled as he turned the page. His peripheral vision faded as the contract demanded his total focus. He bit his lip as he absorbed the words.

This was a contract about him.

About his life.

About his *birth*.

He flicked back to the front page. The contract was dated 12 July 1983, a year before Matthew had been born. His arms jerked as he read a clause that spelt out what had happened.

His mother had paid the company to source a sperm donor.

The words *sperm donor* fizzed through his mind. His father wasn't his father, the man who had told Matthew that having him had always been his mother's idea. And here, the black-inked evidence was pressed indelibly into white paper. His mother had signed this contract, had given birth to her baby, and then, not long after, she'd left her son with a man who knew that he wasn't the baby's biological father. A man who had struggled every day to love the little boy, even as he grew into a man.

Tears trickled down Matthew's face. He'd already lost his father once. Now, it was happening all over again. What had his father said all those years ago?

You deserved more than me. This is where I hand you over and wish you well.

Quite literally, job done.

Matthew stared at the printed pages, trying to take it all in. The contract set out the payment terms, the process for his mother to select from a short list of desired characteristics for her child, and the requirement to keep the arrangement confidential.

The truth was so evident that he knew it before he turned to the last page. Perhaps his mind was giving his body a chance to prepare for the shock. Whatever the reason, when it hit him, he was numb. He balled his hands tight as he stared at the signature of the man who had signed the contract for Double Helix Limited. It wasn't a surprise, not right then, but it was a betrayal.

Benjamin Caesar.

The warmth in Matthew's chest began to spread as the numbness faded. His mother had signed up, and so, he was willing to bet, had the mothers of the other scholars.

Now, the photograph of Sammy's mother made sense. Goldman, or if not him, then one of the others, would likely have compiled a file on Matthew's mother, too.

Matthew had discovered the truth. The Genius Club *was* an experiment, and it began when Benjamin Caesar, Christopher Goldman and Henry Bannister founded their own sperm bank.

Raynes Park, London

MATTHEW OPENED his laptop and studied the photographs he had taken of Dylan's hard copy schedules. He studied the mystery numbers annotating each name, numbers that had initially made little sense and had no explicit key. He heard footsteps approaching, and Alfie walked into the kitchen.

'What are you doing?' He peered over his father's shoulder.

Matthew sighed. 'I'm trying to guess what something means.'

Alfie shrugged and opened the fridge. After a few seconds of surveillance, he closed the fridge door.

'I'm sorry. I need to go shopping,' Matthew said. 'There's an apple left if you want it.' Alfie picked it up, and Matthew heard a crunch as his son took a bite. 'Actually, Alfie, I wanted to speak to you.' His son's shoulders sank immediately, but Matthew pushed on. 'I went to see Dylan.'

Alfie turned to face his father, his expression unreadable and not helped by being partially hidden by the apple in his hand. He chewed on his mouthful and said nothing.

'It was ... fine,' Matthew said.

He saw Alfie swallow. 'I thought you didn't like Dylan.' He said it in a way that made it clear that was one hundred percent a failing of his father.

Matthew rubbed his chin. 'Well, I haven't been her greatest fan, and vice versa, but we spoke. We talked about Mum.' He paused. 'She also told me she'd been running your computing club.'

He looked at his son, who wasn't trying very hard to suppress a smile. 'Is that what she called it?'

Matthew frowned. 'No, that's what I called it. Why?'

'Oh, nothing. It makes it sound lame.'

Matthew pushed on, fighting his natural urge to want to know precisely what Alfie had been doing with Dylan. 'Anyway, you don't need to ... you can tell me where you're going in future. You don't need to worry that I'll be upset. I know she'll look after you.'

Alfie tilted his head in a manner oddly reminiscent of Dylan. 'You are still talking about Dylan, right?'

'I know, I know. What can I say? People change.'

'Well, Dylan hasn't changed, so it must be you.'

'That's what I meant.' Whether that was true or not didn't matter because, for once in recent days, the two of them had had a conversation without Matthew inadvertently driving his son out of the room.

'So, what's this thing you're puzzling over?' Alfie asked, walking over to peer at the computer screen. 'Can I help?'

Matthew smiled at him. The numbers annotating each name on Caesar's database puzzled Matthew from the outset. There was no key, no hint as to what the numbers meant, and they were oddly distributed. But right then, he would've bet all Sammy's millions that those numbers somehow related to the biological father of each student.

'Sure.' He pointed at the screen displaying the list of names. 'The two photos list eighteen names. Each name has a number assigned to it, somewhere between three and twenty-two. But there's no key explaining what it means.'

'This is something to do with the scholarship, right?' Alfie peered at the pictures.

'Yes.'

It was the first time that Matthew had looked at the spreadsheet since the discovery that Caesar had run a sperm donor facility. If Caesar were obsessed with genius and had meticulously recorded everyone's performance, surely he would track the child's genetic father? He continued explaining the puzzle to Alfie. 'Some numbers aren't there at all, and some are repeated. Seventeen appears three times. And yet there's no one, two, five, ten, thirteen, fifteen, nineteen, twenty or twenty-one.' He raised his eyebrows at Alfie. 'But twenty-two appears twice.'

Alfie was quiet as he stared at the screen. 'Looks like some sort of cipher. Can I use your laptop?'

'Sure.' Matthew stood up and let Alfie take his seat. He watched as his son opened Excel and typed up the list of names from the photographs. The familiar names of Sammy, Lucy, Alastair, Daniel, Matthew and Vanessa were at the top of the list.

Alfie added in the scores in the next column before highlighting the spreadsheet. Matthew and Daniel were the only two members with the same number, seventeen, along with a woman Matthew didn't know. Alastair and Vanessa were each separately matched with another stranger, whilst Lucy and Sammy were uniquely identified. The distribution was widespread. If he was correct, it suggested many biological fathers, with most only being selected once, which didn't fit with the smaller pool of genetic fathers indicated by the limited selection offered by the donor contract.

'What are you doing?' he asked.

'Just reordering by surname,' Alfie said as he tapped the keyboard. 'Interesting. It looks like there's a relationship between the scores and their alphabetical order. So, if we subtract their place order, we get ... this.'

He turned the screen towards his dad. Each person now had a score between one and six. Matthew's arms felt heavy as he locked onto the groups—six groups, six fathers.

'Can you order it by the new numbers?'

'Okay.' A couple of clicks later, it was as if Matthew had been immersed in cold water. 'Are you alright, Dad? You look pale.'

Matthew stared at what he felt sure had to be the paternal groups. Lucy and Alastair were half-siblings, along with Kathryn Farthing. Sammy, Matthew, and Jason Tanner were grouped together. Daniel was an only child; by contrast, Vanessa was one of six children with the same biological father.

Matthew pushed himself towards the kitchen sink and turned the tap on full just as he ducked his head down. The cold jet soaked the top of his head. He forced himself to breathe. There were so many questions, but one drowned out all the others. What the hell should he do now?

Slowly, he tuned back into the environment around him. Alfie was standing next to him, staring at him with concern etched on his face. 'What's wrong, Dad? What have I done?'

Matthew turned and reached out for Alfie. He clumsily pulled him into a hug. 'Nothing,' he said, his mouth buried in his son's hair. 'I'm just emotional. I'm sorry.'

Alfie wriggled to free himself and look at his father. 'But what does it mean? Is it some sort of ranking?'

Matthew grabbed onto that explanation. It was certainly easier than telling his son the truth. 'Yes. Yes, I think so.' Water trickled down his neck, and he raked his fingers through his hair. 'Sorry. It's just seeing Mum's name at the top. Well, it just got to me. That's all. I'm sorry, Alfie.'

'You made group two. Silver medal,' Alfie said. His voice was quiet, but Matthew could tell he was trying to bolster him, and Matthew loved him all the more for it.

He reached for the hand towel on the back of the kitchen door and used it to dry his face. 'You've been very helpful, Alfie. Thank you.'

'Sure. Anything else you need me for?'

'No, go and play on the computer. Maybe practice something that Dylan taught you at computing club.'

Alfie laughed. 'Ha. Yeah, maybe I will.' He grinned at his dad and slipped out of the kitchen.

Matthew studied the first group. Lucy, Alastair, and Kathryn Farthing. Kathryn had been murdered three years before Lucy had died. Was it too much of a coincidence? The name of the sperm donor wouldn't appear on the birth certificate, so there would likely be no public record that Kathryn and Lucy had the same biological father. He tried to imagine what he would say if he called the police - and decided that he didn't have enough evidence of a link between the deaths, not yet. All he had was tenuous evidence of a previously unknown family relationship.

Matthew picked up his phone and tried to work through the options. He glanced again at the spreadsheet and felt something twist inside him. If he was right, he should be happy. Sammy was his half-sister, but an unease was gnawing in his chest as memories of Lucy swamped his mind. She would never know that Sammy was his sister, and yet she would have been so delighted for him. He'd been deserted by his mother and then handed off by his father. For him to finally have family, especially a sister as wonderful as Sammy, would have filled Lucy's heart, and he couldn't help but think he should feel something similar. However, right then, all he could think about was that he'd just uncovered an essential link to Lucy's death.

He put his phone down and pulled out the burner phone. He needed to see Dylan.

Putney, London

IT WAS odd seeing Alfie with Dylan, but it was clear that he was relaxed in her company. They may not have been routinely laughing and joking, but Alfie looked comfortable, and Matthew supposed there was no good reason why he shouldn't be.

He felt a twinge in his gut. His relationship with Alfie was stretched. He knew he couldn't expect it to be easy. They were both still in the early days of trying to work out how to live without Lucy. Lucy had always been in the middle, with the gravitational pull to keep the two of them orbiting in the same galaxy. Routine had helped: school pick up, weekdays versus weekends, anything that imposed some structure, and that's why the suspension from school was hard; every day bled into the next.

Matthew excused himself and walked to the bathroom. It was small and functional and smelt faintly of bleach. There was a bottle of shampoo, a bar of white soap on the shelf in the shower and a hairbrush on the windowsill next to the washbasin. Matthew pulled the plastic bag from his pocket. He turned the bag inside out, being careful not to touch the inside with his fingers. He then clamped his hand, protected by the plastic glove puppet, onto the hairbrush and teased out as many strands of Dylan's hair as possible. He manoeuvred the brush away, twisting it until it released. He then replaced it and reversed the inside of the bag back into its rightful position. Once he had sealed the bag, he slipped it into his pocket. He stood silently for a few seconds before hitting the flush on the toilet.

Matthew walked back into the study to find Alfie standing. 'We're finished,' his son said.

'Okay.' Matthew hesitated, conscious that his next request would change a dynamic that Alfie had grown used to all his life. 'I need to speak with Dylan about something, Alfie. Is it okay if you wait downstairs?'

Matthew saw Alfie glance at Dylan. He was asking her for guidance rather than trusting his father, but whatever signal Dylan gave was enough for Alfie. He shrugged and left. He closed the door behind him, but Matthew felt like Alfie was shutting his father out rather than excluding himself.

Dylan looked as though she was going to say something, and Matthew gathered himself. He wasn't sure he had the patience to listen to any parenting tips from Dylan Steele. But she didn't speak. Instead, she looked at him and waited.

'I found some more information.' He unzipped his bag and pulled out the envelope. He handed it to Dylan and waited whilst she read through the contract. She didn't say anything but blinked several times, which Matthew was learning was an extreme Dylan reaction. 'It was in a box of my mother's papers.'

Dylan was nodding. 'You think it's real,' she said. It fell halfway between a question and a statement.

He nodded. He'd replayed that fateful conversation with his father over and over. It all made sense now. His father knew. Perhaps his mother had signed up alone and only told her husband afterwards. Or maybe she was already pregnant before they got together. Whatever the details, his father had confirmed that Matthew had always been his mother's idea. He'd misunderstood that at the time. He'd imagined that his mother had been keener on having children than his father and had never dreamt it could have been so extreme.

'Do you?' Matthew asked.

'I believe that Caesar was, and is, capable of something like this,' she said. 'Have you spoken to him?'

Matthew shook his head. 'He still hasn't returned anyone's calls. The consensus seems that he'll be there on Wednesday, but I'm beginning to doubt it.'

Dylan handed back the contract. 'If this is real, then it won't be the only one.'

'I know.' He scratched his chin. 'Each name on the spreadsheet you showed me has a number next to it. It's a cipher,' Matthew said.

Dylan tilted her head. 'You think it tells you who has the same donor. Do you need help solving it?'

'Alfie's already done it.' He caught her expression. 'He doesn't know why. He thought we might be grouped in some sort of genius ranking.'

'Did it tell you anything interesting?'

She seemed to be glossing over parentage as being anything worthy of interest. Matthew cleared his throat. 'Lucy, Kathryn Farthing and Alastair are in the same group.' He paused. 'You're not on it, of course, but...' He shrugged and had to stop himself from instinctively reaching for the hair sample in his pocket. He knew Dylan had been brought up by her mother. He remembered answering Dylan's door to the man she had called Adam. 'What do you know about your dad?'

Dylan looked as though she was weighing up whether to respond, but after a few seconds, she answered. 'Nothing, and whatever the truth of all of this, it won't change anything. I've lived my entire life without a father, and I intend to continue that way.'

That was one way of dealing with things and quite possibly the sanest route, Matthew thought. It was just emotionally impossible for most people.

'I thought maybe Adam...'

'No.' She looked directly at Matthew, and her eyes narrowed slightly. 'Okay. We have three people who don't know they're related.'

'They also don't know who their father is.'

'We already know Sammy's father,' Dylan said.

'Yes, Christopher Goldman,' Matthew replied. 'That's why he had a picture of Sammy's mother in his wallet. She's the mother of his daughter.' Dylan was still staring at Matthew. 'There are two others in the same sibling group as Sammy. Jason Tanner and me,' Matthew said. He swallowed hard. 'Christopher Goldman is also my biological father.'

'How do you feel about that?' Dylan asked.

Matthew wondered whether it was the first time she'd asked how he felt. 'It actually explains quite a lot.' He shrugged. 'Anyway, that means that either Caesar or Bannister is most likely the biological father of Lucy, Alastair, and Kathryn.'

Dylan nodded. 'You think Lucy is Caesar's daughter.'

Matthew's mouth was dry. 'I can't be sure, but if she is, then Alfie is Caesar's grandson, and Caesar would have known that all along.'

Dylan closed her eyes for a few seconds and then stepped towards Matthew. 'You can't tell Alfie. At least, not yet.' Her voice was a whisper.

A burst of heat burned inside Matthew. It was his decision, not hers, and if he wanted to tell his son, he would. She had no right to tell him what to do.

'I'm sorry,' she said. Matthew did a double take. He'd never heard

Dylan apologise for anything before. That was two emotional firsts in one conversation. 'I've no right to tell you what to do. Alfie's your son. I just think it would be unhelpful to tell him something like this now.'

He released his clenched fists and silently talked himself down. Alfie trusted Dylan, and Alfie needed all the support that he could get right now. 'I agree.' He fought to keep his focus on the new information. 'I think this might be the reason Lucy was killed.' Dylan stared at him. 'Kathryn and Lucy are both dead,' he continued. 'Two out of the three half-siblings have died. I'm worried about Alastair. He could be in danger.'

'Are you going to tell the others?' Dylan asked.

Matthew nodded. 'Tonight. Then, on Wednesday, I'm going to confront Caesar and force him to tell us the full extent of their experiment.'

29

THEN

MARCH 2007

Curzon Street, London

MATTHEW WATCHED ALASTAIR SITTING AT THE POKER TABLE. HE HADN'T wanted to come out that evening, but Lucy had insisted that Matthew leave her and Alfie alone at some point. He hadn't been able to settle on Lucy's motivation, but he could see that he wouldn't win the argument. So now he found himself in a private casino room drinking sparkling water as the best non-alcoholic approximation to champagne bubbles. After all, if he were to wet Alfie's head, he'd do it his way, and Alastair, of course, would do it his.

Alastair was sitting, looking relaxed, at the far end of the table. He ran his hand over his chin. Poker face. Slowly, he pushed a pile of black game chips forward. Alastair loved the casino and music, but he spent the first five minutes at the casino explaining to Matthew why casino music should be illegal. How was anyone meant to concentrate on the poker with that sonic abomination?

Matthew walked over to stand behind his friend. The other players were dressed smartly, but Alastair wore a T-shirt, jeans, and a leather jacket. Not that it mattered; the cards didn't have a dress code; they just played by the odds.

A tall, slim man was sitting next to Alastair, a business type whose loosened tie and crumpled shirt advertised that tonight wasn't his night. Envy shone from his eyes as he watched Alastair on a hot streak. The man's playing had become bolder, more erratic, as the evening had progressed, but now it bordered on desperation. No doubt Alastair had seen it happen many times. When would people learn it was a game that needed an ice-cool mind? The very best could hide behind a fraying exterior, encouraging their opponents to play them for a fool. Unfortunately for this man, he wasn't one of the very best. Even more unfortunately, Alastair was.

Alastair waved to the waitress to bring him another drink. She returned quickly, gently resting her hand on the sleeve of his leather jacket as she placed the glass of whisky next to him.

'Here you are, Mr Niven.' She smiled at him, but not just because she was paid to. Alastair was looking at the bull-like man two seats away from him. The man had been impassive throughout the game, but Matthew sensed he was simmering. Alastair had pressed his buttons and taken his money. He would need to be careful.

Alastair placed his cards on the table and waited. The other players folded one by one until only two of them were left in the game: Alastair and the impassive man. Everyone else was looking at the man to see how he would respond. He deliberately flipped over his cards, laughing as the last card fell face up. He had nothing left to bluff with.

'Take it. It's yours.' The man had an accent—maybe South African, just a hint.

He leant forward. He was well built, had a solid frame, and had his hair cut short. He looked around at the other players, tilted his head towards the door and waited whilst they slowly melted away. Without saying another word, he had emptied the room other than him, Alastair, and Matthew.

The man gave Matthew a full-bore glare. 'You need to leave.'

Matthew looked at his friend.

'Just give us a few minutes, Matt.'

'I'll just be outside.' He knew his physical presence presented no threat to the other man, but hopefully, knowing that Alastair had a friend who knew where he was offered some level of protection.

Alastair pushed his chair back, but he didn't stand up.

Matthew walked out of the room and lurked in the corridor. The door shut behind him, but he could still hear the men talking.

'You know what happens next.' The man spoke matter-of-factly, which did nothing to hide the menace.

Matthew craned his neck to listen. After a few more seconds, the man spoke again.

'If you humiliate me one more time, I will use this knife to disfigure you. Or perhaps you have a pretty girlfriend I could start on?'

'Screw you.'

Matthew took a step back. Alastair was meeting this challenge head-on, but Matthew wasn't sure that was wise.

The man started to laugh, but the sound of a slap and a grunt of pain from Alastair cut off his laughter. Matthew reached for the door but heard words, not punches, next. His hand hovered over the handle.

'If the time comes, I will remember that insult and start by cutting out your tongue.'

The door flew open, and the man brushed past Matthew like he wasn't there. Matthew glanced after him to ensure he was leaving and then turned back to face his friend.

Alastair was still sitting down, pulling the chips towards him and stacking them in piles. A bright red mark was visible on his cheek, but there wasn't a drop of sweat on his shirt. He started to count, taking his time. When he had finished, he recorded the details on a gaming slip, his pencil dancing over the paper. After a few more seconds, he picked up his jacket, pulled it on, looked up at Matthew and smiled.

'Well, on balance, I'd mark tonight down as a pretty successful evening,' he said, reaching for his drink. He raised the whisky glass in the air. 'To Alfie.'

30

THEN

DECEMBER 2010

Limehouse, London

CAESAR LOOKED OUT OVER THE THAMES. HE LIKED SAMMY AND Daniel's three-story flat, tastefully decorated as it was with modern furniture and contemporary art, yet the teacup he was holding was traditional bone china. He rested the cup down on the saucer.

They'd spent a productive hour reviewing Angel Capital's investment strategy. Caesar wasn't a formal advisor to the fund, but he knew that Sammy appreciated his input. Matthew was there, too, because Sammy wanted his feedback on using neural networks to predict stock market values. It had been a fascinating deep dive into the topic; however, the conclusion was that the models weren't yet powerful enough to add value.

'What do you think about Bitcoin?' Sammy asked.

Caesar smiled. This was what she wanted to speak to him about. The portfolio review was merely a courtesy and an excuse to corner him on crypto.

He had followed the developments around crypto assets with interest. Slashdot's story on its front page in July earlier that year had seriously increased the chatter around Bitcoin—if you were listening in the right places. A couple of months before that, someone had bought two pizzas for ten thousand coins, which was the type of transaction that might go down in folklore if Bitcoin ever hit the mainstream. However, the launch of the Mt.Gox cryptocurrency exchange, allowing investors to buy Bitcoin, was the game-changer.

'It's not for me,' he said, rubbing his hand over his beard.

Sammy looked nonplussed. 'I thought I might invest the equivalent of the price of a couple of pizzas.' She raised her eyebrows.

Caesar laughed. 'As a trade or an investment?'

'I'll hold it forever.' Sammy paused. 'I'm with Warren Buffet on that one.'

'He was talking about stock,' Caesar fired back. 'I can't imagine he'd like Bitcoin one little bit.' Buffet liked to invest in what he could understand, and, no disrespect to the Sage of Omaha, Bitcoin was as transparent as gold—digital gold.

He saw Sammy roll her eyes. Maybe he'd be proved wrong, but he wouldn't mind if he were. He didn't like the risk but knew Sammy had the stomach for it. She'd begged her mother to invest in a company called Amazon in 1997.

'Buying Bitcoin is the easy part,' he said. 'Keeping your investment safe will be the hard part. That's what puts me off.'

'I'll speak to Daniel,' Sammy said. 'He advises his clients on security for different asset classes. Anyway, is it any different from using passwords for online banking?'

Caesar smiled. 'Maybe not. Luckily for me, none of my passwords are passwords, and they're all perfect.'

Sammy laughed, but Matthew just stared at Caesar.

31

NOW

TUESDAY, 25 JUNE 2019

Fleet Street, London

MATTHEW HAD SPENT THE DAY RUNNING AND RE-RUNNING POSSIBLE conversations in his head, but finally, it was time. All his friends were sitting around the table in the busy wine bar. Matthew had wanted somewhere noisy rather than reserved and quiet. Everyone apart from him had opted for wine. He took a sip of his still water and began speaking.

'I found a contract between my mother and a company owned by Caesar. It was signed a year before I was born.' He heard Vanessa mutter under her breath. 'The contract provides for the company, Double Helix Limited, to source a sperm donor for my mother.'

'Jesus.' Alastair's eyes widened. 'And, you think it's real?'

'Yes, I do.'

There was a silence as the group shared glances. Sammy was the next to speak. 'You think my mother signed a contract, too?'

Matthew nodded. 'I think it's possible our mothers each signed a contract, and that's why we were selected. Caesar, Bannister and Goldman aren't just the scholarship's founders; they're our biological fathers.'

Vanessa was staring at Matthew, her mouth slightly open.

'Which would mean some of us are half-siblings,' Daniel said softly.

'Yes.' Matthew could see the uncertainty in Sammy's eyes as she grabbed her husband's hand. 'But Caesar was careful. That's what his rules around relationships were all about. He was trying to ensure there was no incest.'

'How could you possibly know that?' Vanessa asked.

'Because I know who's related to whom,' Matthew replied. He flinched as everyone else spoke at once. He held out his hands to quieten them down. 'I have a list of all the scholars and the people who didn't ultimately get selected.'

'Where did you get that?' Alastair asked.

'There's a key on the list,' Matthew pushed on. 'I believe it confirms which sibling group everyone is in. There are five groups.'

'Jesus, this is crazy,' Vanessa said. She took a gulp of wine.

'Who are the other two donors? You've only mentioned three names,' Sammy said.

'I don't know. Three donors account for all of us, except for Vanessa.'

Matthew handed out copies of the list, and silence descended as everyone sucked in the details.

Vanessa wiped her hands over her face and blew out a breath. 'Look, I'm the only one who had a sibling.' She paused. 'A sister I grew up with.' Matthew looked down at the table. 'I don't buy this. Not for me, anyway.'

'Maybe there's something different about groups four and five,' Matthew said. 'You're in the fourth group. Maybe just groups one, two and three are children of sperm donors.'

'There's an easy way to check,' Vanessa said. 'We can arrange DNA tests to confirm which of us, if any, are related.'

Alastair whistled as he placed the page down on the table. 'This is unreal.' He leant forward and drank a mouthful of wine.

Sammy released her husband's hand and looked at Matthew. 'We're related?'

'I think so,' Matthew replied. 'The two of us - and Jason Tanner.'

'I guess you have to take the rough with the smooth,' Sammy said, trying to force a smile. 'But surely someone would've told us? Our mothers? Or Caesar? I mean, this is unbelievable.'

'The contract includes non-disclosure clauses,' Matthew said. He could imagine his mother not thinking too hard about whether Matthew deserved to know the truth. She had lost interest in him from an early age. Perhaps he hadn't shown enough signs of genius from birth, or maybe it was just another random adventure in his mother's chaotic life.

'Even so,' Sammy said, shaking her head.

'I still don't believe it, Matt,' Vanessa said. 'Maybe your mother signed up. But these groupings—was this key explicit?'

Matthew bit his lip. 'No. It was unlabelled. Just a list of numbers, but it makes sense.'

'It could mean anything,' Vanessa said.

'What about the photograph of my mother?' Sammy asked.

'There could be another explanation for that,' Vanessa replied. 'Maybe this guy, Goldman, had a relationship with your mother. It doesn't mean he's your father.'

'Goldman had a filing cabinet full of files on different women, and he denied having an affair with any of them,' Matthew said. 'It feels more likely that Sammy's mother was selected for something or subjected to some approval process.'

'I guess only one person knows the truth,' Sammy said.

'Tomorrow's meeting's going to be a cracker.' Alastair drained this glass and looked around at the group. 'I don't know about you all, but I'm feeling kind of special right now. Anyone fancy joining me in the casino?'

MATTHEW STRUGGLED to sleep that night. It had been hard to sleep most nights since Lucy's death. At three o'clock, he gave up, dragged himself out of bed and walked into the kitchen. He poured himself a drink of water and sat down at the table. He hadn't known what to expect from the meeting with his friends. At least this time, they appeared to accept that his theory might be partially true.

Vanessa was the most sceptical, and Matthew understood why. She had grown up as part of a family, a foundation strong enough to withstand the shock impact of Matthew's theory. Her sister had died from muscular dystrophy four weeks before starting university. Alastair had told him that Vanessa wasn't going to take up the scholarship or go to university at all until her sister made her promise that she would. Alastair, Daniel and Matthew had talked about their families the first night they stayed at Caesar's house in Cambridge. Matthew thought back to the conversation that night.

'How about you guys, any siblings?' Alastair said.

Matthew shook his head.

'Me neither,' Daniel said.

'Your surname's Solarin. Have I got that right?' Alastair asked. 'Is that African?'

'Nigerian, yes. My mother came to England a couple of years before I was born. She died giving birth to me.'

'God.' Alastair was shaking his head. 'I'm sorry, man. What about your parents, Matt?'

'My mum moved out before I could walk. My dad brought me up.'

'Do you still see your mum?'

'No, not now. I did a bit when I was younger. Then, after a few years, it dwindled to only a Boxing Day visit.'

'What a bunch we are,' Alastair said. 'Still, I guess that's partly why we're here. Caesar's collection of waifs and strays.'

'Yeah,' Daniel said. 'We should be grateful for that.'

Matthew pushed his chair back and stood up with Daniel's words echoing in his head. He still couldn't process everything that had happened and the revelations he'd uncovered. Tomorrow, at least, they should all get some answers.

32

THEN

JANUARY 2013

Putney

ALFIE'S ATTENTION WAS ON THE CHESS BOARD, AND HE HAD TO DRAG the question back into focus. He was aware of Dylan standing at the doorway, watching the two of them play. He didn't know Adam's age, but he was older than Alfie's parents. He was pretty good at chess, too. Good, but not great.

'I'm six next month,' he said, scrunching his nose as he studied the formation of the pieces.

'And who taught you to play chess?' Adam asked.

'Mum and Dad taught me the rules. Dylan taught me how to win.'

It was true. His mum had told him that she'd once seen Dylan play and defeat three opponents in simultaneous games. She was a good teacher—Alfie could already beat his parents, although he wasn't sure whether they were letting him win. Dylan didn't just teach him chess, though. She had started teaching him how to code computers. Alfie didn't mind playing chess, but coding was way cooler.

Adam smiled at him. Alfie liked how the lines around his mouth almost reached those furrowing his forehead.

'And do you think that Dylan taught you well?' he asked, glancing over at Dylan, who was staring at Alfie. She had silver headphones on and hadn't spoken since Adam and Alfie had started their game.

'I think so.' There was a twinkle in Alfie's eyes as he moved the knight to its final position. 'Checkmate.' He let out a little laugh.

Adam studied the board before nodding and holding out his hand. 'Well played, Alfie.'

They shook hands, and Adam turned to face Dylan. 'You might have warned me that he was a child genius.'

'Where's the fun in that?' Dylan asked.

'Can you beat Dylan yet?' Adam asked.

The scrunched nose was back. 'Soon,' Alfie said. 'Very soon. I kick her butt at Mario Kart, though. No problem.'

Adam laughed. 'I'm sure. And don't think you'll get me to race against you. I know when I'm in for a beating.' Adam pushed himself up from the chair and took a fraction of a second to steady himself.

'Best of three?' Alfie asked, replacing the chess pieces in their starting positions on the board.

Adam shook his head. 'I need to go home and rest. Perhaps I'll swat up on some chess strategy for next time. Even old guys like me can improve.'

Alfie stared at him for a moment and then shrugged. 'Okay. Dylan, you want a game?'

'Sure.' Dylan walked over to the table. 'Let me just see Adam out. You finish setting up.'

Alfie watched her follow the older man to the front door. Adam was shaking his head. 'That's some kid you've got there.'

'You know he's not mine.'

'He's a little bit yours, I think,' Adam replied. 'He trusts you.'

Alfie could hear them speaking. He started to sing under his breath as he set up the chess pieces, ready for the next game.

'How's he doing at school?' Adam asked.

'How do you think? He's bright enough to be in secondary school. His parents don't like to push him, though. They just want him to be happy.'

'And you? What do you want for him?'

Dylan didn't miss a beat. 'I want him to be happy, too.'

Alfie smiled to himself.

'Okay, then,' Adam said. 'Same time next week?'

'Yeah, I'd like that.'

Alfie heard Dylan close the front door. He turned the chessboard around. Dylan could be white. If he were going to win, he'd do it the hard way.

33

NOW

WEDNESDAY, 26 JUNE 2019

Blackfriars, London

THE MEETING ROOM HAD A CORPORATE, CLINICAL FEEL, WITH SPLASHED colours on canvas hanging on the otherwise plain walls and a wooden table forming the centrepiece.

Matthew glanced at the place name, printed in the same typeface as the invitation. Directly before him was an envelope with his name neatly typed and a branded ballpoint pen. Five places were identically set up—five seats, five envelopes—but only four guests were present.

Matthew couldn't take his attention away from the man standing at the head of the table. Karl Irons. He looked familiar, but Matthew had never been good with faces and names. He was smaller than average, slim, and greying at the temples; his otherwise dark hair cut short. The lawyer had just confirmed Matthew's expectations. A murmur travelled around the table.

'I repeat, Benjamin Caesar cannot attend in person, but he has asked me, as his lawyer, to share certain information with you all.'

Daniel seemed to be calmly evaluating the lawyer, whilst Sammy, sitting beside her husband, pushed her glasses up her nose. Daniel and Sammy had looked relaxed enough when they had arrived. Matthew wondered whether his firm's investigation had already cleared Daniel.

Matthew waited as the host looked at each of his friends before it was Matthew's turn in the spotlight. The cold look the man directed at him instinctively made him close down his mind to guard his feelings. It felt off. This man claimed to represent Caesar—Benjamin Caesar, whom all in the room thought of as their mentor. But Matthew had never even heard of Karl Irons.

And where was Alastair? He'd said he would be here.

Vanessa flicked her red hair and half rose out of her chair. She pointed at the lawyer. 'You better start explaining this. Fast.'

Karl Irons held his hands out, perhaps in mollification or perhaps in defence. 'I'm sorry, but I want to wait until everyone's here.'

Vanessa was standing now. She wasn't tall, but she knew the secret of commanding attention. 'You might be waiting forever.' Which was true. Alastair could be erratic, and there was every chance he might blow the meeting off if he wasn't in the mood or was still in the casino. Vanessa walked round to the empty chair.

There was a flicker of a smile from Karl Irons. 'I appreciate you're used to being right, Ms Wordsworth, but perhaps you'll humour me for just a few moments?' He then very deliberately sat down and crossed his arms.

'This is a joke,' Vanessa muttered, but Matthew could tell she was slightly off balance. She sat back down, and an uncomfortable couple of minutes passed.

'How long do you plan to give him?' Sammy asked quietly.

'Just a few more minutes.'

Everyone turned as the door opened. No one said a word as Alastair walked in and slid into the seat next to Matthew. He looked rough, unshaven, and with his hair even more unkempt than usual. Matthew noticed his friend's hands trembling as he rested them on the table. Karl Irons walked over and closed the door. Matthew couldn't read from the lawyer's expression whether he was pleased, unnerved, or annoyed.

'Thank you for joining us, Mr Niven.' Karl Irons stood next to his chair. 'My client, Benjamin Caesar, as you all know, is the founder of your scholarship. What you may not be aware of is that your scholarship...' He hesitated as if he was searching for the right word, 'selection, started many years ago. Long before you attended university, in fact.'

'What do you mean? Our first contact was in our last year of school,' Alastair said, his voice raspy. It seemed he was going to push the lawyer to see what he would voluntarily reveal.

'Benjamin Caesar believes that all the scholars are exceptional. He monitored you from an early age once he had identified that you might have the correct characteristics he sought in his scholars.'

Matthew scanned the room, checking for any reactions from the others. Until the last few days, he'd had no idea that he, or any of them, had been selected for the scholarship before they started applying to university. He'd always thought that Caesar had found him through his school. He could vividly remember the excitement as he read Caesar's letter, telling him he could go to university fully funded. And now? This puppet of Caesar's was revealing the truth.

'What exactly do you mean by correct characteristics?' Daniel placed a heavy emphasis on the last two words.

'Well, it's not my place to run through the detailed requirements that Caesar insisted upon in his scholars.'

'Hold on. I want to know what you mean. Don't think you can gloss over this.' Daniel sounded calm. Vanessa, however, looked as though she were about to go nuclear.

Karl Irons pursed his lips. 'Very well. As you know, Benjamin Caesar has a keen interest in human intelligence. To be selected as a scholar, you had to show a high level of general intelligence and a particular ability in a specific area such that you might be described as gifted.' Irons paused and gazed around the room.

Matthew swallowed hard. He couldn't wait any longer. 'What about the contracts?'

'I'm sorry,' Karl Iron dropped his gaze towards the legal pad on the desk in front of him, 'Professor Stanford,' his forehead was creased with lines, 'I'm afraid I don't understand your question.'

'My mother signed a contract with Caesar's company, ' he said, reaching into his bag resting on the floor between his feet.

Karl Irons scowled. 'I'm sorry, I don't know what you're talking about. I'm not aware of any written contracts.' He turned his attention to the others and cleared his throat. 'As I was-'

Matthew slid the envelope over the table. 'Read this,' he said, feeling his friends watching him.

The lawyer sighed. 'Perhaps we could deal with any questions-'

'It's a contract to source a sperm donor for my mother.'

Irons gave a slight shake of his head. 'I'm happy to have a look at the document, Professor Stanford, but to the best of my knowledge, my client has never entered into any contract for sourcing sperm donors. It all seems rather,' he paused, 'incredible.'

Incredible. As in, impossible to believe or extraordinary, Matthew wondered. 'We need to speak with Caesar,' he said.

'I'm afraid that's not currently possible.'

'Why not?'

'My client simply isn't well enough to receive visitors,' Irons said. 'I know you came here today to hear from him, and he's very sorry that he cannot be here in person. I could try to explain what my client wanted to convey in this meeting, but luckily, we have a better option.' He pointed towards the screen behind him and picked up a remote control. 'We can hear from Benjamin Caesar himself.'

Matthew hesitated, glancing at the others. Vanessa crossed her arms while Alastair shrugged. Matthew was disoriented. He needed an explanation that would make some sense of Karl Irons' denial of the contract's existence. But the lawyer was pushing his chair to the side, and the others were now all facing the screen, which had flickered into life.

Benjamin Caesar was sitting in a chair with a wall of books behind him. If Caesar was unwell, he didn't particularly look it. Matthew tuned in to Caesar's voice.

'My passion has been to support bright children who have faced challenges in life, the sort of challenges that push people to strive to achieve. I monitored you closely as you grew up. There were other gifted children, but they hadn't ever experienced hardship, loss, or adversity.'

Matthew shivered. That was the first admission from Caesar that he had studied them all long before the scholarship interviews were granted, but Matthew was sure their patron had known about them all from their conception. Correction. From *before* their conception.

'Those children didn't interest me; more importantly, they didn't need me. Whereas with all of you, I felt I could make a difference.' He paused, and his expression looked momentarily troubled. 'I have always had conviction in my vision and methods, but recent events have caused me to reflect on what is right and what is just. So, I have something important to share with you.'

Matthew felt the breath catch in his throat. This was it. He closed his eyes to ground himself and forced himself to breathe. When he opened his eyes, he saw the lawyer staring at him. Irons looked at the contract on the table and then back at Matthew with the expression of a man who knew what was coming next.

Caesar's words echoed around the room. 'I have decided to end the scholarship with immediate effect.'

There was a gasp, and glances darted around the group. Matthew slunk back into his chair as the energy drained from his body.

Caesar was still talking. 'I've given this a great deal of thought. For so long, I believed we could continue without change, without confronting the past, but I know now that's a fallacy.'

Confronting the past. Another nod to the truth of the scholarship programme. Matthew balled his hands, and a bead of sweat trickled down his back.

'Some things just reach their natural conclusion. The scholarship has been my life's work and privilege, and I want it to be remembered that way.'

For a second, Matthew thought that was the end, but Caesar shuffled slightly in his chair and then continued to address the camera. 'I have written to each of you personally. I wish I were well enough to meet with every one of you. I owe you that much, at least, but I'm afraid I can no longer do that. You will all have questions. Some of you may even feel hurt, but I want you to know that I never intended to hurt any of you.'

Matthew's heart thumped against his chest as he stared at the envelope bearing his name.

Caesar paused to cough. It was the first time he'd looked frail. He carried on speaking.

'My lawyer will be able to answer some of your questions. He has been fully briefed and is aware of the contents of my letters to each of you.' He turned to look directly at the camera. 'I hope you can respect my decision, and I hope that you can forgive me.'

The screen faded to black.

MATTHEW WAS SHAKING. How long had that taken? Maybe five minutes. He was lost in memories of his teenage years. Some of those pieces of good fortune were beginning to click into place: it'd been Caesar, not God, looking over him.

'This is unbelievable.' Alastair was looking intently at Karl Irons.

'I understand there's much to consider here, but you have some time. As Benjamin Caesar explained, the envelope in front of you contains a document personal to you. Please read it carefully.'

'What does it say?' Sammy asked. Her voice was quiet but steady.

Irons hesitated. 'It explains what happens for each of you on the termination of the scholarship.'

Matthew could see tears in Vanessa's eyes. She didn't need any financial support, but Caesar's exclusion from her life would hit her hard, yet it would almost be the reverse for Matthew. He could live without Caesar in his life if he had to, but the truth was that he needed the money to keep Alfie at school—at least in the short term.

'There's one more thing.' All eyes turned towards Irons. 'The scholarship you have enjoyed gave you the best possible start and an enviable level of ongoing support. Indeed, some of you have enjoyed significant financial returns as a result.'

'Your point being?' Vanessa stared at Irons, eyes wide.

'You are required to pay an exit fee.' The lawyer delivered it as if reading a clause from a contract.

Matthew froze. The world slowed.

'What?' Vanessa gripped the desk in front of her and looked as if she was about to try and tip it over.

'The exit payment is proportionate to your financial position.' Irons paused and looked around the group of friends. 'I'm sure you all recognise that your life would've been considerably less successful were it not for the patronage you have enjoyed.'

'And if we don't pay?' Vanessa was still clutching the table.

'I'd think very carefully about that. My client is still an influential man.'

Matthew's head was pounding. He rested his hands on his legs to try to quieten the tremor and then gave up and picked up the envelope. He needed the ongoing patronage for Alfie. Christ, how had he let himself become so financially dependent? What would Caesar want from him? He shook his head and glanced at Alastair, who seemed lost in thought.

'Any questions at this stage?' Irons looked around again.

'If I capitalise the value of Caesar's annual investment over, say, ten years, I'd guess we're talking about, say, five million. Am I close?' Sammy spoke quietly.

Matthew's head was still spinning with the announcements—shuttering the Genius Club, stopping the funding, and demanding restitution—all after the lawyer had flatly denied Matthew's theory. He saw the lawyer's eyes harden.

'You are good with numbers, Ms Angel.'

'It's my job to be good with numbers, Mr Irons, but I don't like ultimatums, and I don't like surprises.'

'Me neither,' Vanessa said. 'This whole thing is unbelievable.'

Irons didn't seem fazed. 'All the relevant details are set out in your letter. Does anyone else have anything to contribute?'

'Just this,' Vanessa said, and in one motion, she ripped the envelope and its contents in half and dropped them on the table.

Matthew felt the urge to lash out. Alfie had just lost his mother; Matthew couldn't expose him to more change right now. A financial demand was unlikely to make much difference to Vanessa; her shareholding in her company was valued at over ten million pounds. She seemed to be objecting on a point of principle.

'Copies of the documentation will be...'

'Don't bother.' Vanessa pointed at Irons. 'I don't trust you, and I don't like you.' She gesticulated at the pile of ripped paper. 'I'm not accepting any of this until Caesar looks me in the eye and tells me himself.'

Vanessa was always direct, but something in her tone was unusual. Something beyond assertion, way beyond confidence in knowing her mind. Matthew could see the tension around her eyes and the subtle shake in her arms. It echoed her countenance at their group dinner. And as Vanessa swept a glance around the room and announced her departure, it hit Matthew with cold certainty. Vanessa was scared. Of what he was unsure, but as she hurried out of the room, he had a strong feeling that something else entirely was going on with her.

Irons coughed to refocus the room's attention back to him. 'Well, I can't say that I'm surprised. I was warned that Ms Wordsworth could be somewhat temperamental.'

He coolly regarded those who were left in the room. Matthew thought his smile was not only unnatural but also misplaced. Perhaps he thought he was building rapport? If so, he was wrong.

'I will email you a copy of the letter and the video you have seen today. Please review your letter carefully.' He reached inside his jacket and produced a small pile of business cards. He walked around the desk and calmly placed a single card in front of each of them. 'My details are on the card. I'm dealing with this matter personally, so I'd be grateful if you'd wait for me to return your call or message if I'm not immediately available.' The forced smile made another appearance. He turned to face Alastair and Matthew. 'Gentlemen, perhaps I could have a couple more minutes of your time?'

Daniel and Sammy were already on their way to the door.

'Wait for us over the road,' Alastair said. 'We'll join you as soon as we can.'

Sammy nodded and then led her husband out of the meeting room. Karl Irons walked over and pushed the door closed behind them. He turned around and rested both hands on the table.

'I wanted to let you both know that the letters you each have from my client are somewhat different to the others.'

Matthew's brow creased. Why were they being treated differently?

'My advice,' Irons smiled, seemingly more to himself than to them, 'for what it's worth, would be to keep the specifics of your letter private. I advised my client against any material differentiation between you, but he chose not to listen to me.' There was the smile again. 'A client's prerogative.' Matthew glanced at Alastair but found his expression impossible to read. 'Well, gentlemen, thank you for your time. You're welcome to use this room for the next hour or so if you'd like to.' He nodded and walked briskly out of the room.

Matthew turned his envelope over in his hands.

Alastair picked up his letter. 'Aye, good idea, Matt. Let's see what the man has to say to us.'

34

NOW

WEDNESDAY, 26 JUNE 2019

Fleet Street, London

MATTHEW WANTED NOTHING MORE THAN TO BE ALONE, BUT HE WAS drowning in the noise of a crowded wine bar. Caesar's letter and Karl Irons' advice echoed around his head. *Keep the specifics of your letter private.* Advice which made a great deal more sense after he had read it.

Other than Sammy, his friends hadn't fully bought into his sperm donor theory, and Karl Irons' flat denial hadn't helped. If they were to learn the contents of his letter, it could seriously damage their friendship; the benefit of the doubt would reverse, and he wouldn't blame them because it simply made no sense.

Alastair was waving his hand slowly in front of Matthew's face. 'You alright, Matt?'

'Sorry.' Matthew took a sip of water. His friend looked at him and waited for him to continue. 'I was just thinking about, well, us.' He could feel Sammy and Daniel watching him, too.

'To the Genius Club!' Alastair said, holding his bottle in the air.

'Keep your voice down, Al,' Sammy said. Alastair was smiling at her embarrassment. 'I never thought, when I received my invitation for this meeting, that it would be the announcement of the end,' Sammy said. 'Have you guys read your letters yet?'

Matthew flicked a glance at Alastair.

'Yeah, quite the love letter.' Alastair ran his hand through his hair before signalling the waitress to bring him another beer.

Matthew chewed his bottom lip. He had no idea whether Alastair was telling the truth. He'd been sure that the letters would reveal the truth about the sperm bank, perhaps even give each of them the name of their biological father, but his letter had contained nothing even hinting at that. He squirmed in his seat.

'The whole thing makes me so angry,' Sammy said. 'He announces the end of the scholarship out of the blue and then makes these outrageous demands. It's ridiculous.'

None of which made it sound like her letter had told Sammy anything about her biological father. *Some of you may even feel hurt.* That's what Caesar said in the video, and Matthew thought that was a reference to him finally revealing the truth. Yet it appeared that it was a request for a repayment and nothing else triggering Sammy.

Matthew saw the chance. 'He didn't say anything about being a sperm donor.' He said it as a statement but hoped it was a question, too.

'No,' agreed Sammy. 'But I think there's something in what you said, Matt. Even if he didn't acknowledge that truth, he admitted to monitoring us before we knew he existed. That's unnerving.' She shivered as if to emphasise her point.

'Vanessa was right—we need to confront him, not just meet with his lawyer,' Daniel said.

Sammy put her glass down. 'It's like we've suddenly outlived our use to him. He's effectively shuttered Cerebrum, too. We've all worked hard on that, and it's his passion project. How could he end it? It doesn't make sense, even if he is unwell.'

Alastair shuffled on the chair and rested his feet on the edge of the table. 'I'll admit, I didn't like the threat about Caesar being influential.'

Matthew scratched his temples. He had so many questions.

Caesar's not attending in person robbed him of the opportunity to confront his patron about the past, which seemed to be being rewritten with every passing day.

Daniel was nodding. 'I don't think the demands have any contractual force, but we need to take the time to work out what's going on.'

'V seemed pretty sure of her position,' Sammy said.

'When has Vanessa ever not been sure of her position?' Daniel asked.

'It's odd, though,' Sammy continued. 'She's a successful businesswoman, yet she shredded the document without stopping to ask any questions.'

'Maybe that's why she's a successful businesswoman,' Daniel said. 'Never waste time asking unnecessary questions. And never, ever, give any money away.'

'Maybe,' Sammy said, 'but I think there's more to it. Perhaps she's so focused on work that she dismissed it out of hand?'

'I was due to meet up with her a couple of nights ago, but she cancelled at the last minute because of some work crisis about a patent.' Alastair paused to swig his beer before continuing. 'She looked stressed today, even before the fireworks.'

Matthew had noticed it, too. Vanessa was always a bundle of raw energy, but that afternoon, she seemed different—slightly less in control than usual.

'We all need to take some time,' Daniel said again. 'Ben Caesar has been the backbone of our adult lives, and now that role is changing. It came from nowhere. We can't expect to rationalise that within an hour of finding out about it, no matter how much we might want to.'

A silence fell over them until Alastair sat forward and looked around the group with his eyebrows raised. 'Funny to see Karl Irons again after all this time.'

Matthew frowned at Alastair. Where did he recognise him from? Sammy and Daniel were looking blank, which Alastair seemed to find amusing.

'Nobody? Okay, our friendly lawyer, Karl Irons, was the doorman at our first-ever weekend event in the country house in Cambridge.' He grinned at his friends. 'I guess you were all too focused on other people that night to remember, but it was definitely him.'

'I thought he looked familiar,' Matthew said.

Daniel glanced at his phone. 'I was looking him up before you both came in. He checks out as a lawyer.'

'So, you think this is genuine?' Sammy pushed her glasses higher up her nose. 'We all know Caesar's story. His troubled upbringing. His passion to support us,' Sammy said. 'His drive to democratise intelligence. We all bought into Cerebrum. Why would he close it down?' She shook her head. 'Why would he give up on us? It's so unlike him. When I was building my investment track record, before I launched Angel Capital, he worked through my entire portfolio with me.'

Alastair was nodding. 'I remember V telling me that when she was having all those problems with her patents, he spent hours with her - and when they finally fixed it, she told him they needed to file the patent in joint names, but he wouldn't have it. Flatly refused. Said it would be inappropriate.'

'He's always been so generous to us,' Sammy said, still shaking her head. 'Today's decision is totally out of character.'

Matthew was thinking of Caesar and his old college friends, the inaugural Genius Club, his own contracted birth, and Lucy's death, and he knew right then that he had no earthly clue as to Benjamin Caesar's true character—not anymore.

'WELL, I don't know about you guys,' Alastair said, 'but I think we should read out our letters right now.' He leant to the side and pulled the envelope from his trouser pocket, presenting it with a flourish. 'Who fancies going first?'

For a while, no one spoke. Matthew couldn't read their expressions, couldn't tell who was comfortable and who wasn't. He didn't want to go first. He wasn't at all sure he would read it out, but refusing to would damage his relationship with his friends even more than the contents. His choices were limited. Stay silent, tell the truth, or lie.

Sammy half-raised her hand, and everyone's attention pivoted towards her. He sat back in his chair and focused hard on her words as she began to read.

'*Dear Sammy, I regret that it has come to this, but this is a formal request for a payment as restitution for the investment I have made in you over the years. You have been extraordinarily successful and have generated great personal wealth. It is a near impossible calculation to determine what element of your fortune is attributable to my patronage. In the circumstances, I have settled on a number which I think is fair.*'

Matthew watched Sammy closely as she pushed a swathe of dark hair away from her glasses and tucked it behind her ear. Matthew had no idea how much Sammy made a year, but he would guess it was well north of a million pounds. He'd put money on it if he had any. Daniel had a flat smile fixed firmly in place. His eyes were dark as they flicked towards Matthew, who immediately looked back towards Sammy.

Sammy was still reading. '*You are required to make a payment to me of fifteen million pounds. This amount is due and payable one week from the date of this letter. Yours sincerely, Benjamin Caesar.*'

'Jesus Christ,' Alastair said, leaning forward. 'Fifteen million? That's wild.'

'Who's next?' Matthew said, sounding hoarse.

'I'll go,' Alastair said, half smiling. The skin beneath Matthew's eyes was taut, and there was a slight tremor in his arms. He and Alastair had been advised not to share their letters, yet Alastair was about to read his out. 'He's taken a slightly different approach with mine.' He shot Matthew a glance before continuing.

'*Dear Alastair, you were capable of so much more. You had everything: the natural intelligence and my support, but the sad truth is that you're an addict. I know you live and fight your addiction every day, and you still function at a high level, but if you were free from addiction, you would fly so much higher.*' Alastair looked around. 'I'm not sure I can finish reading it. It's so embarrassing to read out such effusive praise.' No one laughed. He smoothed out the letter and continued reading. *'I don't want a repayment, but I can't support you anymore.'*

Alastair didn't bother with confirming the name of the letter's author, and for a moment, no one said a word. Matthew realised he'd been visualising Caesar speaking, but now his mental image was blurred. He struggled to picture Caesar writing the letter, those words, making it clear that he was cutting Alastair off.

'Well,' Alastair said, 'remind me to do this again soon.'

'I don't know where to start,' Daniel said.

'I'm so sorry, Al,' Sammy added.

Matthew's head was spinning. Had that been Alastair's actual letter? Or had he made it up, only he'd gone for something more spicy than Matthew could ever have managed? Alastair always liked to put on a good show.

Daniel was the next to go. He caught Sammy's eye, and Matthew saw her quickly look away. She looked pale—paler than usual. She squeezed her hands together. Daniel, however, seemed relaxed as he unhurriedly picked up his letter and held it in front of him.

'Dear Daniel, I regret that it has come to this, but this is a formal request for a payment as restitution for the investment I have made in you over the years. You are a successful lawyer and undoubtedly have many years of your career ahead of you.

You are required to pay me two hundred thousand pounds. This amount is due and payable one week from the date of this letter. My only other specification is that it be paid from your funds, not your wife's.

Matthew could feel himself withdraw as if to protect himself. He was the only one not to have read their letter. Sammy was looking at him, but her expression was unfocused, as if she was looking beyond him. In many ways, her decision was the easiest. Caesar couldn't enforce anything. She was wealthy. Independent. She could, and would, say no.

Daniel broke the silence. 'He can't force any of us to do any of this.'

'Easy for you to say,' Alastair said. 'What if you rely on his scholarship payments? He can stop those easily enough even if he can't enforce any repayments.' Matthew swallowed. Alastair was talking about him because Alastair himself would be comfortable enough without any funding from Caesar. His private practice made good money, certainly enough to cover his day-to-day expenses, although Alastair's night-to-night expenses might be more of a problem.

'Are you going to read yours, Matt?' Sammy asked.

Matthew dropped his gaze to the table. He unfolded his letter and stared at the words on the paper. His eyes blurred. Without exception, his friends were looking at him—waiting for what was coming next. He silently reread the words, and a lump formed in his throat.

'Would you like me to read it?' Alastair offered.

'I don't want anyone to read it,' Matthew replied. He saw his friends exchange a glance.

'No one's forcing you, Matt,' Alastair said.

He thought he caught a glint of a tear in Sammy's eyes, but the last thing he needed was pity. He shrugged because he didn't trust himself to speak. Right at that moment, he was the central focus of the group. Compassion and concern swirled around, threatening to suffocate him.

'I didn't say I wouldn't let you read it,' Matthew said. 'I said I don't want you to read it.' He stood up and handed his letter to Alastair. 'Here you go. I'm sorry, but I need to get home to Alfie.'

Usually, his friends would have shaken his hand or hugged him, but this time, they stayed seated. He hesitated and then pushed through the people standing at the bar and out the door. He pulled up his hoodie and bowed his head against the wind whipping through the London streets.

35

NOW

WEDNESDAY, 26 JUNE 2019

Fleet Street, London

Matthew turned as he heard Alastair calling after him, and he watched his friend jog over.

'I'll stroll with you,' Alastair said, pointing down the road.

Matthew started walking, a knot forming in his stomach. Why had Caesar promised to keep supporting him when he told everyone he was shuttering the scholarship? Caesar had demanded a staggering payment from Sammy, yet he offered to continue paying Matthew. Why? There'd been no mention of Lucy in Matthew's letter, but he wondered whether Caesar's actions were motivated at least in part by her death.

Matthew would have no choice but to accept Caesar's terms. His primary objective was to look after Alfie, and to do that, he needed money—Caesar's money—at least until he had an alternative.

'Look, Matt, I know you're dealing with what happened to Lucy, and you're worried about Alfie, but as your friend, I have to tell you, I'm worried about you.'

'Why?'

'Well,' Alastair glanced up at the sky, perhaps hoping for divine guidance, 'firstly, I think you've jumped to some conclusions that aren't wholly based on solid evidence.'

'And?'

'And now Caesar is treating you differently to the rest of us.' Alastair's tone was almost offhand. Almost.

'How do I know you were telling the truth about the contents of your letter?' Matthew asked.

They both stopped walking, and Alastair reached for his back pocket. He pulled out a folded piece of paper. At that moment, Matthew knew precisely what it said.

'Every word was God's honest truth.' Alastair held out the letter and nodded towards it. 'Go on. Read it.'

Matthew stared at the letter and then shook his head. 'I believe you.' But he couldn't meet Alastair's gaze.

His friend sighed. 'It's hard to know what to believe right now.'

Alastair's letter hadn't been a vote of confidence like Matthew's; it had been a disowning. So much had happened in the last two weeks, but had anything he'd learnt over the previous few days fundamentally changed anything between them?

Matthew sniffed. 'I don't know why Caesar has singled me out. I don't like it. It makes me very uncomfortable.'

Alastair reached for his pocket and unfolded Matthew's letter. 'The Benjamin Caesar Foundation for the Promotion of Disadvantaged Children is a catchy title.'

Matthew flicked a glance at his friend.

'It's not very complimentary about the rest of us,' Alastair said, handing the letter back.

The wording of the letter echoed in Matthew's head. *I have received reports on you all for many years and continue to do so. Some of the recent reports are troubling.*

'I guess it's pretty clear what reports he's been sent about me.' Alastair shook his head. 'Jesus Christ. It sounds like he's been paying people to investigate us.'

That point had been troubling Matthew, too. He'd never been aware of anyone following him, but that didn't mean it hadn't happened. He was the last person to be mindful of his surroundings, let alone the presence of a discrete investigator.

'So, are you going to accept?' Alastair asked.

Matthew took a long time to answer. 'I think I'll have to at least until I can get myself sorted financially. I depend on Caesar's funding for Alfie's school fees.'

Alastair raised his eyebrows, no doubt reflecting on how the school was currently being paid for Alfie to sit around at home.

'What about you? What are you going to do?' Matthew asked.

'Me? Drink, I should think.' Alastair pulled out a packet of cigarettes, put one in his mouth and lit it. He inhaled and blew out some smoke. 'It's the best answer I can think of.'

'So much for genius strategic thinking.'

'You just can't understand it right now; you'll recognise it one day.'

Matthew laughed. He tried to work out how he felt about his friend. He knew Alastair drank and gambled; but was he an addict?

'I thought his letter to you was harsh,' Matthew said.

Alastair shrugged. 'It was pretty accurate.'

Neither of them spoke for a while. There was a pull in Matthew's gut. He'd hoped that sharing what Caesar had written to him would release some of the anxiety he felt, but instead, it was winding tighter.

Alastair took another drag on the cigarette. 'There's something else I want to tell you,' he said, 'although I'm not sure I should encourage you.' He scratched his chin. 'Vanessa was thrown by the photo of Sammy's mother.'

'I didn't know-'

'I know, I know,' Alastair held up his hand. 'Regardless, V decided to do some digging of her own.'

Matthew dropped his gaze. 'Because of her sister?'

'Yes. She had some stored DNA samples at her lab, so she ran a test which showed that she and her sister are only half-siblings.'

Matthew's head jerked up. Vanessa had looked on edge throughout the meeting with Karl Irons. 'She had no idea?'

Alastair took a deep breath. 'No. Her father died a couple of years before her sister. She'd always thought he was her father, but now...'

He looked distant for a moment as if he was trying to peer back in time. 'Now she thinks that her parents opted for a sperm donor to avoid the risk of her being born with the same genetic condition as her sister.'

'And she thinks there's a connection to Caesar?'

'Her first challenge was coming to terms with it, but, yes. It's one hell of a coincidence. Your mother's contract. Sammy's mother's photograph.'

'I didn't think you believed me about the sperm donor.'

'I don't, not for all of us, anyway,' Alastair replied. 'Do you really think Ben Caesar is Lucy's father? And mine? And Kathryn Farthing's?'

Matthew shrugged. 'I think it's possible.' He paused. 'I don't know what's going on, but I think you need to be careful.'

'Everyone's giving me advice today.'

'I mean it,' Matthew said.

'I know.' Alastair glanced back the way they'd walked. 'I'll let you get home to Alfie.' He patted Matthew on the shoulder and turned to make his way back to the wine bar.

Matthew watched him walk away. Alastair hadn't seemed worried by Matthew's warning, and maybe he was right. The sperm donor theory had all but been proved true, but however strong Matthew's gut instinct, linking Kathryn and Lucy's deaths was another leap entirely.

36

THEN

MARCH 2015

Putney, London

ALFIE HEARD THE DOORBELL AND KNEW IT WOULD BE HIS MUM. DYLAN went to answer the door, and Alfie returned his attention to the computer screen. Dylan had marked his coding challenge and awarded him twenty-eight out of a possible maximum of thirty. He didn't like that he'd missed out on two marks.

With a sigh, he logged off and started to pack his school bag. He heard footsteps, and Adam walked in, holding a cup of tea.

'How did you do?' Adam asked.

'Okay, not great,' Alfie answered.

'Did you solve it?'

'Yes, but I dropped a couple of marks. I don't know why.'

'Dylan said she got the question from a coding competition for children aged fifteen or sixteen. Almost twice your age.'

Alfie shrugged. 'I started coding younger than most.' He swung his bag over his shoulder. 'I have to go now. Mum's here.'

'Bye, Alfie.'

Alfie nodded and walked out of the room. His mum came over and kissed the top of his head.

'How was choir?' Alfie asked.

'Lovely.' Lucy looked at Dylan. 'Thanks again. See you next week.'

ONCE ALFIE HAD SECURED his seatbelt, his mum started the car and began the drive home.

'Dylan said you did very well with the coding challenge.'

'Twenty-eight out of thirty.'

'Apparently, anything over seventy-five percent puts you in the top tier in the country,' Lucy said.

'How do you know that?'

His mum shrugged. 'Dylan told me. She took the questions from some national competition. Over seventy-five percent is usually good enough to put you into the top fifteen places. Something like that.'

'Huh.' Alfie wasn't bothered about the competition. He was still wondering where he'd dropped the two marks.

'What do you think of Adam?' Lucy asked.

'Dylan called him a hustler,' Alfie replied.

'A hustler. Why's that?'

'I've been playing him at chess,' Alfie said. 'I've improved a lot since I first played him.'

'I know.' His mum laughed.

'Well, he's improved too. I told Dylan because, logically, you wouldn't expect him to improve that much if he's been playing all his life. But he has. Dylan said he'd always been as good as he is now; he was letting me win. That's the hustle.'

'Right. Got it,' she said. 'Do you think he's still letting you win?'

Alfie didn't need to think too long about that. 'It's hard to know if he's playing his best, but he'd need to be much better to have a chance.'

His mother patted his leg but kept her eyes forward, concentrating on the traffic. 'Have you beaten Dylan yet?'

'No,' Alfie replied. 'The closest I came was a stalemate. I nearly had her, but she managed to force a draw.' His mum turned the car into their road and pulled over to the pavement to park. 'But it's only a question of time before I beat her,' Alfie said.

37

NOW

THURSDAY, 27 JUNE 2019

Raynes Park, London

MATTHEW NEEDED A COFFEE. HE FILLED THE KETTLE, LISTENING TO THE muffled thud of music coming from Alfie's bedroom. A beep from his laptop announced the arrival of a new message, but he finished making his coffee before he carried it over to the table and sat back down. He peered at the computer screen.

The email was from Caesar. He set the cup on the table and reached towards the keyboard to open the email.

Matthew,

I know that things are difficult right now. I'm sorry not to have been in touch properly and, of course, for not being able to attend Lucy's funeral. I'm afraid I am very frail at the moment. I am sure it was a lovely service.

Terminating the scholarship was a very difficult decision, and it's perhaps not surprising that some of your fellow scholars are struggling with it.

I am, however, disappointed they can't recognise my role in their success. I have asked them to make a payment, and whether they see it as fair somewhat misses the point. Their payments will help fund the foundation that I hope you will run.

Unfortunately, I expect things will get more challenging in the short term, although people are less predictable than I would like. I find myself in the strange position of not being able to trust those whom I have cherished for so long, but I can't ignore the evidence.

Please be careful.

Ben

Matthew rubbed his face with his hands. There was a dull ache in his stomach. He was drowning in claims and counterclaims. He needed to break things down and get back to first principles.

Firstly, what if Caesar was telling the truth? He wanted to create a foundation, and he wanted Matthew to run it. Caesar was who they always thought he was—a generous man who sponsored talented children facing hardship and had a vision for the future—but he knew his time was running out. He was precisely the sort of man who would pivot to use his funds to set up a foundation for disadvantaged children.

Matthew took a sip of coffee. That was one possibility, but he didn't buy it without being able to articulate precisely why. Certainly, none of it brought him any closer to the truth about Lucy's death. He reread the email.

What if his suspicions about the scholarship programme were correct? Perhaps Caesar knew that Matthew was close to uncovering the truth about his experiment, and he was trying to protect himself. Caesar might be desperate to cover his tracks and protect his legacy. He was the last founding member of the original Genius Club, and he wanted to bury their secrets forever.

Instinctively, he would turn to Caesar, Alastair, or Sammy, the people he confided in the most after Lucy, but he couldn't afford to do that now—not when he didn't know what was happening or whom he could trust.

He had to find a way to test his hypothesis and prove the sperm bank theory. He needed more specific information. He considered visiting his mother, but even if he could see her, he wasn't sure he would believe whatever she said. No, he needed proof, and that meant DNA tests. Vanessa had suggested it; she'd already tested herself and her sister. Matthew just had to hope she would be happy to run the tests for him.

Wimbledon, London

JUST AS MATTHEW approached the tube station, his phone beeped with the arrival of a new email. It was another message from Caesar. This time, the title was simply *Alastair.* He opened the message and started to read.

I know you're good friends with all the scholars, but they all have their dark side.

Alastair is in debt to a gambling cartel.

He doesn't know who he is dealing with.

To make it worse, he thinks he can gamble his way out of trouble.

Maybe you could have trusted him before, but not anymore.

Trust no one.

There was a link below the message, and Matthew held his breath with his finger poised over the phone screen. Did he want to see whatever Caesar had decided he wanted to share with him? He knew it wouldn't be the highlight reel of Alastair's proudest moments. He clicked on the link. For nearly two minutes, he watched his friend gambling, snorting powder, and partying.

Several thoughts collided in Matthew's brain. Caesar had access to a video like this, which proved his claim to be monitoring them still, or at least Alastair, after all these years. Why had Caesar, who had ignored Matthew's calls and been unable to attend Lucy's funeral and the reunion, begun emailing Matthew? And why was Caesar telling Matthew about Alastair's lifestyle and warning him to no longer trust his best friend?

Alastair had seemed hung over at the meeting with Karl Irons, but then again, he'd been to the casino the night before and flown in from Vegas a few days earlier. He'd been there, done that, and spent the next few days wearing the same T-shirt. But Alastair didn't usually show stress. His whole persona had been cultivated to be seen to be taking everything in his stride. Alastair had always lived on the edge, and based on Caesar's email, it looked as though he might be about to fall off it.

Irons had advised them not to share their letters, but Alastair had shared his regardless. Was Caesar's email designed to ensure Matthew knew the truth about his friend? If so, to what end?

Matthew had no intention of replying to the email, but he was increasingly worried about Alastair. He'd admitted to Matthew that the thrust of Caesar's letter was accurate. It was conceivable that he was also holding a losing hand with a cartel. Then there was the sibling group. Kathryn and Lucy were dead. Alastair was the sole remaining member. He needed to try again to get Alastair to take the warning seriously. He dialled his number, but the call was diverted to voicemail, so he texted asking to meet as soon as possible.

He pocketed his phone. It would take him around thirty minutes to get to Vanessa's lab, so he had plenty of time to try and decide exactly what details he wanted to share with her. Should he ask her about Alastair and any recent gambling? The two of them were close, but trying to anticipate their status was like placing your stake at the roulette wheel.

He shook his head. Everything felt like a gamble right then, but he had no choice. He headed down the steps into the underground station.

VieEdit offices, Paddington, London

MATTHEW COULD SEE Vanessa studying a piece of paper while a woman talked to her. The other woman was dressed in a pinstripe trouser suit and had bobbed hair—corporate lawyer standard issue—quite the contrast to Vanessa's bright yellow dress. But both left Matthew's jeans, open-necked shirt, and hoodie in the shade.

'In essence, they're saying that we're infringing their patents.

Except they don't say that, of course.' The woman certainly sounded like a lawyer.

Vanessa looked up and saw Matthew hovering in the doorway. 'Hi, Matt. Just give me a couple of minutes to finish with Lizzie.'

'Sure.'

Vanessa's secretary guided Matthew to the brightly coloured chairs outside the office. He rested his bag on orange and chose purple for his seat.

Vanessa's voice trailed through the air. 'Because they're scared we'll sue them for making an unjustified threat?'

'Exactly,' Lizzie replied.

The secretary looked at Matthew and pushed back her chair.

'Which I assume is what you would recommend?' Vanessa said.

'Yes. We need to defend this position hard.'

'Our patents are watertight?'

The secretary closed the door and returned to her desk, where she slipped on her headphones and recommenced typing.

Matthew could no longer hear whatever Vanessa and her lawyer were discussing. He glanced at the glossy magazines on the table in front of him. He selected a copy of Scientific American and flicked through it. He'd just decided which article to read when the door opened, and Lizzie walked out. She nodded politely at Matthew, who dropped the magazine on the table and headed to the office.

Vanessa's perfume hit him just before he was enveloped in her hug. Her frizzy hair tickled against his face. She stepped back as if to get a better look at him. 'Well, this is a surprise, Matt. Is everything okay?'

She held the door whilst indicating for him to come in. He heard the door click behind him and walked over to the floor-to-ceiling glass window. It was quite the view of corporate London. The world looked different from up there.

'I think so,' he said. 'That sounded like a heated conversation.'

Vanessa sighed. 'Yeah. You could say that.'

'Everything okay?' he asked.

'I don't know.' Vanessa walked around behind her desk and sat down. 'We've got an issue with one of our patents. Honestly, it's why I was so keen to see Caesar and why his recent decision has been so devastating.'

'You need his help with the patent?'

'No, not exactly. I've already had his help.' She opened a drawer in her desk and removed a small blister pack before she popped a pill into her hand, took a mouthful of water from a glass on her desk and swallowed. Matthew saw her catch his glance. 'They're herbal tablets. Meant to help me relax.' Matthew nodded and slid into the leather chair opposite her. 'Caesar helped me with the original patent. Now, someone else is challenging it. Specifically, one of the aspects that Caesar was heavily involved in.'

'They're suggesting you copied it?' He'd picked up that much from the snippet of overheard conversation.

Vanessa didn't answer directly. 'The only person who knows the truth about that is Caesar. And now...' her voice trailed off.

The patent concern must have explained why Vanessa had looked so fractious recently, even before she had run the DNA test. Her company, VieEdit, was a biotech company, and Matthew knew that patents were its lifeblood. There'd been a real buzz about the most recent breakthrough Vanessa and her company had made in gene editing. The future security of her company might have rested on Caesar's evidence—and yesterday, he'd turned his back on her. No wonder she was stressed.

'Anyway, enough about me,' she glanced at the computer screen on her desk. 'Why the surprise visit?'

He cleared his throat. 'I wanted to ask you a favour,' Matthew said. 'I need you to run some DNA tests.'

She raised her eyebrows. 'Okay,' she said. 'Not totally unexpected. Have you got the samples?'

Matthew reached into his bag and produced the sealed plastic bags, carefully labelled A, B, and C.

'You and Lucy,' she said. 'Who's the third?'

'I'd rather not say,' Matthew said.

Vanessa's eyes widened momentarily. 'You want to check for any half-sibling relationships?' Matthew nodded. 'Alright, I'll do it.'

'Thank you.' He hesitated, unsure whether to venture into the next topic.

'Alastair told you about my sister,' Vanessa said, holding his gaze.

'Yes.'

Vanessa grimaced. 'It was a shock. I genuinely thought it would confirm what I'd always believed.'

'Any chance it's wrong?'

'The tests aren't perfect, but it's a statistically significant result.'

'I'm sorry,' he said.

She shrugged. 'It's not your fault.' She paused. 'Although I guess I would never have run the test if you hadn't found your contract and Sammy's mother's photograph.'

Was she making an allegation? As far as his friends were concerned, he'd claimed to have found the contract in his loft and produced a photocopy of an old blog with the picture of Sammy's mother. Could any of them think he'd made it up? He wondered whether any of them had searched for the original blog online. Matthew stood up and cleared his throat. 'Hey, have you seen much of Alastair recently?' He tried to keep it casual.

Vanessa reached up to adjust one of her earrings. 'Probably no more than you have.'

'Do you think he's okay?'

'I think so.'

Matthew wondered whether she knew what Alastair's letter said. She hadn't been there when they'd all disclosed the contents of their letters, and judging by her somewhat cool response, they weren't together right now. Was that right? He wasn't sure he was reading her correctly, but there was something there, some tension.

'Okay. I just wondered, that's all.' Vanessa was looking at him, but he wouldn't say anything more about Alastair. He started towards the door. 'Well, thanks again. I hope you sort out your patent problem.'

Matthew needed to head home to Alfie. He heard his phone buzz as he entered the lift and hit the button for the ground floor. He stood at the back so the other man who had got in the lift couldn't see his screen. It was a reply from Alastair.

Yes, let's meet up. Are you free this evening from 7 pm? You won't believe the day I've had.

Raynes Park

THE DOOR CREAKED OPEN, and Alfie walked over to the sink. He grabbed a glass from the cupboard and poured himself a drink of water.

'Hey, Dad, why wasn't Dylan on that list you had? I'm guessing she might have been top.' He laughed before turning and walking back out of the room.

Matthew felt as if he'd been hit with a stun gun. How the hell had he missed that? So much for being a genius. He tried to kick his brain into action. The printout didn't have her name on it, but she would have been on the original list, which meant when Alfie had reverse-engineered the parental groupings, it had an inbuilt error for everyone who came after Dylan Steele in the alphabet.

Matthew opened up his laptop and pulled up the spreadsheet. His fingers trembled as he added Dylan's name and reworked the numbers. A few more clicks and the names were all grouped by their new parental reference number.

Sammy and Matthew were still grouped as half-siblings, and now Daniel and Vanessa were grouped together.

But Lucy now had three half-siblings, not just two.

Alastair and Kathryn were still grouped with Lucy. The new half-sibling had previously been in a different group.

Jason Tanner.

Another part of the puzzle slipped into place. Caesar had kicked Jason out because he'd tried it on with Lucy, his half-sister.

Matthew's heart thumped against his chest as a second realisation hit him. Lucy was dead. So was her half-sister, Kathryn. His pulse quickened. What about Jason Tanner? Was he also dead?

Matthew flicked back to the photograph of the spreadsheet and studied Jason's results. He had scores in the forties, fifties, sixties, and seventies and a highest score of eighty. He had been filtered out at gate three but must have been on a reserve list because he was added to the scholarship when Dylan left. He had nothing to go on other than Jason's name, approximate age, and his recollection of what he had looked like, aged eighteen. He searched on his name but no news story dominated the first page of hits on Google. He tabbed through the first few pages, hoping something would jump out. Nothing. Even a thorough trawl through the social media profiles of the many different people named Jason Tanner only allowed him to eliminate those who were clearly the wrong age. He pulled out his burner phone and called Dylan.

'I made a mistake with the groups.'

'Okay,' Dylan said.

'There's another person in Lucy's group. Jason Tanner.'

'Lucy told me about him. I guess that means Caesar kicked him out rather than risking an incestuous relationship. Who knew he had such impeccable morals?' Dylan was typing on a keyboard. 'What do you know about Jason Tanner?'

'Nothing. I can't find anything about him. I don't think any of us have had contact with him since that day.'

'You didn't ask Caesar?'

Matthew hesitated. Dylan didn't know Caesar had been a no-show. 'He didn't turn up. His lawyer was there instead. He played us a video message and then gave us each a letter from Caesar.' Matthew paused. It was time to run through the highlights—a collection of hits that still left him off balance. 'He's terminated the scholarship and demanded sizeable compensation payments from Sammy and Daniel.'

'Only Sammy and Daniel? What about the rest of you?' Dylan asked.

'I don't know about Vanessa, but I'd guess she's also been issued with a repayment demand. Alastair was slated for being an addict but wasn't asked to make any payment.'

'And you?'

'I was invited to be the paid trustee of his new foundation.' It came out as a whisper.

'What have you done to deserve such preferential treatment?'

It was a great question and one he still had no answer to. Dylan moved on to another question. 'Is Caesar dying?'

'He's unwell. We weren't given any more information than that.'

'Maybe he's dying, and someone, someone who knows about all his biological children, wants to claim the estate.'

Matthew bit his lip. Could that be the motive behind the killings? 'I don't know how inheritance laws work, but Daniel will know.' He rubbed his forehead. 'Bannister died in November 2013. His estate will have been dealt with years ago.'

'If we're right about the motive, Caesar is likely their biological father.'

Matthew ran the theory through his brain. Four children. Two dead. One alive. One unknown. 'I need to let Alastair know,' he said. 'He could be in danger.'

'Or, it could be Alastair,' Dylan said, 'and Tanner could be the one in danger.'

'It's not Alastair,' Matthew replied automatically.

There was a brief pause before Dylan replied. 'Okay. I'll see if I can find out whether Tanner is still alive,' she said.

The line went dead. Matthew stared at the phone for a moment. Could Dylan actually believe Alastair was a killer? He shook his head. Then he texted Daniel and arranged to meet him at six o'clock, one hour before he was due to meet with Alastair.

38

THEN

JULY 2018

London

Ben paused amongst the gravestones, his hand clutched to his ribs. The rain had soaked through his hair, and water was trickling down his forehead. He stepped back and lowered himself onto the bench, tilting backwards as he sat down. He exhaled deeply and shuddered as he drew in the next breath. He fumbled in his pocket and fought with the lid of a container to twist it open. His mind snapped back to the conversation with the doctor six months earlier.

'I'm afraid there's nothing we can do, Mr Caesar.' The doctor had worn an expression of professional compassion.

'How long?' Ben had been pleased that his voice hadn't wavered.

'A year, maybe two. Do you have someone who can care for you?'

It had been a good question at the time. And it still was.

A few small, white tablets spilt out, landing in a puddle by his feet.

'Damn.'

He balled his hand and flexed his fingers to drive out the cold before trying again. He placed two pills in his mouth and removed the brown leather-bound hip flask from his inside jacket pocket. The warmth of the whisky stung his mouth, and he paused for a moment before washing down the medication. Alcohol and drugs weren't the recommended treatment, but they worked magic of their own. He closed his eyes and waited for the pain to ease.

He knew that Kensal Green Cemetery was London's largest and oldest public cemetery, but Ben wasn't there to pay his respects to Isambard Kingdom Brunel or Lady Byron. There were over sixty-five thousand graves, but he knew precisely where he was going. He'd been here every year since 2011.

The pain was beginning to fade even if the rain was unrelenting. He edged forward on the seat, stood, and shuffled down the path. After a few minutes, he was standing in front of the tombstone. He knelt and reached forward. The cold, wet stone felt alive under his fingertips as he traced the name etched in a golden tribute to the dead man.

Henry Bannister. Born, 17 April 1956. Died 4 Nov 2011.

Ben was the last of them now. Christopher Goldman had died nearly a year ago. There hadn't been a service; Ben had been notified by one of Christopher's neighbours in Naples, but as with Henry, he'd been taken far too soon.

He started to shake. There was so much still to do, and he knew now that he wouldn't accomplish everything he'd set out to do with his life. The three of them had made a vow to dedicate their lives to the development of genius. Ben had chosen nurture, whilst his friends had been more radical. Henry pursued DNA sequencing and manipulation, while Christopher pushed genetic breeding.

It was hard to know whether, as time passed, he had become more cautious and conservative or whether the other two had embraced more extreme actions. Both of them leant too far toward eugenics for Ben's taste.

His plan, Cerebrum, was focused on democratising intelligence, allowing anyone to become symbiotic with computer-powered intelligence in the same way a smartphone could be regarded as an extension of an individual human. That ideal still burned bright, but it was no longer the most important thing in his life. He wanted the weight of the secrets he had been carrying to lift, and the only way he could do that was to tell the truth, finally, after all these years. The scholars deserved that.

He tipped his forehead until it rested gently on the stone. 'Oh, Henry,' he whispered.

He pushed himself upright and brushed the dirt off his trousers. Two wet patches recorded where his knees had pressed against the ground. He looked around. No one else was in the cemetery, and the light was fading. With one final glance towards his car, he straightened himself and walked away from the tombstone.

39

NOW

THURSDAY, 27 JUNE 2019

Embankment, London

MATTHEW HAD BEEN READING THE NEWSPAPER OUTSIDE THE CAFÉ FOR nearly an hour. He was early, but he'd needed the time to think. He felt his phone vibrate in his pocket. Perhaps Daniel was calling to cancel. But it wasn't Daniel. It was another email from Caesar, and this time, the title was the name of the friend he was waiting to meet: *Daniel.* The body of the email was simply a link.

Matthew swallowed hard and slipped his headphones on. He had a feeling he knew what was coming. He clicked on the link, and within seconds, he was watching a video of a man and a woman kissing by the steps of a swimming pool. The man looked like Daniel. Then he was listening to an audio clip of a man begging a woman not to stop and the woman teasing him. The man sounded like Daniel, but neither woman looked nor sounded anything like Sammy.

Matthew was vaguely aware that Daniel had something of a reputation before he and Sammy got together. Still, since then, he'd been nothing but the model of monogamy until the recent allegations at work. Everything in the clips appeared consensual, but it all cast Daniel in a seedy red glow.

It was surprising on two counts. Firstly, that Daniel would cheat on Sammy. Secondly, and some considerable distance behind the first surprise, that if he had done it, he'd been caught. His work specialisation was in reputation management for the ultra-wealthy. He had told many stories of how he'd had to unwind unfortunate consequences of the salacious activity of the loaded and the irresponsible - and he regularly bemoaned how the easiest thing to have done would be not to have transgressed in the first place.

Matthew closed the email and sat there, stunned. He didn't see Daniel until he was nearly next to him. Seconds earlier, Daniel would have been close enough to see what had been on Matthew's phone.

'Thanks for coming, Daniel. I know you're busy,' Matthew said, thinking, but busy doing what?

Daniel looked at Matthew for perhaps ten seconds without speaking. Something was off. He didn't seem pleased to be there. 'Okay. I was just going to go and grab another coffee, so how about we do that and head into the park? I haven't got long.'

'Sure,' Matthew said, following Daniel into the café.

Daniel was dressed very casually, which was quite the contrast to the smooth city lawyer look Matthew was used to. Had he already been suspended from work? They chatted politely while Daniel bought his coffee, then walked down the road and found a bench in the park.

It was early evening, and although people were walking through the park, no one else was sitting down. Matthew frowned at Daniel, trying to get the measure of him. A man he wanted to believe hadn't cheated on his wife but whom Matthew had just seen with another woman on video. He shook his head. He needed to stay focused on the legal advice he'd come for. 'I wanted to ask you what would happen to Caesar's estate on his death?'

'What do you mean?'

'What's the position for anyone who's his biological child?'

Daniel hesitated, but Matthew could tell he knew the answer to the question. 'Any living *biological* child could make a claim on his estate if they could prove they were his child with a valid DNA test,'

Daniel said. 'It's also possible for anyone who had been treated by Caesar as his child but who wasn't legally adopted to challenge the intestacy rules.'

'You're saying one of us could make a claim on the estate?'

'I think so,' Daniel replied. 'If they could demonstrate Caesar had supported them throughout adult life.' He paused. 'Harder now, after the letters. I'd say there was no chance most of us would be able to substantiate a claim like that.'

Matthew swallowed. He wouldn't describe himself as having been supported by Caesar, but he had received some assistance - and his support hadn't been switched off, unlike all the others. He wasn't about to ask Daniel to clarify that position.

'Lucy died intestate,' he said. 'I'm hoping that doesn't cause any problems.'

He felt Daniel hesitate as if trying to decide how to respond. Was that it? Or was it a reluctance to help Matthew?

'The likelihood is everything will pass to you. It can be a little more complex if Lucy's estate was worth over two hundred and seventy thousand pounds.'

Matthew shook his head. 'It won't be anywhere close to that figure.'

'Then, it should be fine, but *you* should write a will. For Alfie.'

'Won't everything just pass to him when I die?'

'Yes.' Daniel looked slightly irritated. 'Unless you remarry. But the bigger issues are appointing a guardian and whether you want Alfie to inherit at eighteen. Many people choose twenty-five, but you'll need a will to do that.'

'So, it makes sense to do it because it provides more control?'

'That's right. It also makes administering the estate easier, but setting out your wishes about Alfie is the big one.'

'Okay,' Matthew said. 'Thanks.'

'Well, if that's it, I'll be going.' Daniel started to stand. He'd hardly touched his coffee, and now he seemed desperate to leave. 'That's about as much free advice as I feel like giving you,' he said.

What did that mean? Matthew was about to ask when the answer became clear. Daniel knew about Matthew's offer from Caesar. Daniel had said *most*, rather than *all*, of them couldn't claim to be supported by Caesar. His pulse quickened, and Caesar's recent email looped in his mind. Perhaps Caesar had good reasons for making his decisions. What had he said? He couldn't ignore the evidence. Maybe Matthew shouldn't, either.

'How's Sammy?' he asked. A question so loaded it went off with a bang.

Daniel didn't answer for a few seconds. 'She's fine,' he said eventually. 'There's some stuff going on at work.' He turned and looked across the park. 'It's complicated.' His face was strained.

'I've seen a video of you and another woman,' Matthew said.

Daniel turned slowly, very slowly, towards Matthew.

'No, you haven't.' His voice was quiet.

'I know what I saw, Daniel.'

'I can't explain what you *think* you saw, but I can categorically tell you I haven't so much as kissed another woman since Sammy and I got together.'

Neither of them spoke for a few seconds. Matthew wasn't sure where to go next. He had expected Daniel to wilt in the face of a direct accusation. Was he trying to brazen it out?

Daniel made the next jab. 'Anyway, how the hell did you get a video of me?'

'I thought it wasn't you.'

They were both standing now. 'You think now is a good time to be a smart-arse?'

'No.' Matthew spoke quickly. His mind spun. He hadn't foreseen the conversation going this way.

Daniel stepped forward until his face was only inches away from Matthew's. 'Listen to me very carefully, Matthew. You're one of our closest friends, and I can't imagine what you must be going through.' He was breathing hard. 'But right now, with everything that's going on, I'm really, really, not in the mood for this.'

Then Daniel turned and walked away.

Richmond, London

MATTHEW WATCHED Alastair finish his first pint of beer while taking only his second sip of his Coke.

Alastair wiped his mouth. 'I needed that. I'm going to get another. You okay?'

Matthew nodded and pulled his hoodie tight to combat the cool evening air. He still felt shaken by his confrontation with Daniel. Moments later, Alastair placed his fresh pint on the table and sat back down.

'So, what did you want to tell me?' Matthew asked. He hadn't been given any hint as to what his friend had wanted to talk about.

'I was hoping to get two pints down me before telling you.' He took a large gulp of his drink. 'Never mind. My parents summoned me to explain my lifestyle. I went this morning. It was awful.' Alastair lit up a cigarette and took a drag. He turned away from Matthew and blew the smoke into the air. 'You know what they're like, Matt. They don't know any of my friends; I mean, they've only met you twice. As far as they were concerned, I was a paragon of virtue.' He blew the next mouthful of smoke out the side of his mouth.

'What happened?'

'Well, it took me a while to get it out of them. When I arrived, they wouldn't even speak to me. Mary made a pot of tea in total silence. Then, when the tea had been poured, and we were all sitting down, Frank leaned forward and said, *Alastair, we need to talk.*'

Matthew took another sip of coke while Alastair gulped down a couple more mouthfuls of lager. He always referred to his parents by their names, as if he couldn't entirely accept that they were his mum and dad. Matthew pushed away the irony.

'Frank said, *it has come to our attention.* Can you believe that? They're so formal. *It has come to our attention you may have been drinking alcohol, taking illegal drugs, and engaging in sexual intercourse outside of marriage.* I felt as though I was eighteen all over again.' Matthew raised his eyebrows. 'Okay, sixteen.'

'Did they tell you where they heard this from?' Matthew asked. Had they been sent the same video as Matthew?

'They received a letter but wouldn't show it to me. I think we can both guess who it was from.'

'Caesar? You think he'd do that?' Matthew thought about it. It was certainly possible based on his recent behaviour. His letter to Alastair had been blunt, and the video he'd emailed Matthew had doubled down on his view.

'Who else could it be?' He looked at Matthew over the top of his pint. 'If I were you, I'd enjoy it while you can.'

'Enjoy what?' Matthew tilted his head.

'Being the sole remaining scholar.'

The tone in Alastair's voice was light but loaded. Matthew swallowed a mouthful of his drink, and the fizz lingered in his mouth.

'Let me get this straight. You want my sympathy because your parents have found out the truth about you. And then you imply I should feel guilty because Caesar wants me to be his trustee.' Matthew put down his glass. He'd tried to keep the tone neutral but saw the flicker across Alastair's face and knew he'd gone too far.

'Steady on, Matt.' Alastair's eyes were boring into him.

'Maybe it's time for me to leave,' Matthew said, starting to stand.

'Come on. You're overreacting.'

'Am I?'

'Sit back down and finish your drink. We were talking about me, not you.'

'*You* brought *me* up.' Matthew stayed standing.

'Yeah, I did, and then you went nuts on me. Come on. Sit down.'

Slowly, Matthew lowered himself back down on the stool. Perhaps he had overreacted. 'Sorry. You just touched a nerve, that's all.'

Alastair drained the last of his beer. 'Shall we get back to talking about me then?' He walked to the bar and brought back another pint of beer and a Coke. 'Mary and Frank threatened to disown me.'

'Jesus. Really?'

'Now, we don't like blasphemy, Matt.' He grinned. 'It seemed real enough to me. They asked me about the allegations in the letter.'

'Did you deny them?'

'I was considering it when Frank showed me the photographs.' Matthew's eyes widened, and Alastair held up his hand. 'The photos weren't helpful. Pictures of me gambling, snorting coke, enjoying the company of women. The photos may as well have been me walking through a storm of hail and brimstone, following a signpost to Sodom and Gomorrah.'

Matthew almost laughed, but at the same time, he knew how much Alastair loved his parents and how he'd worried this day would come. His friend looked relaxed. Matthew had known Alastair to be that way since they'd first met, but he'd learned that the relaxed look didn't always mean he was happy.

'What are you going to do?' He wasn't sure how, if at all, he could help him.

'What does it look like?' Alastair raised his eyes to sweep around the pub garden and took another long drink. 'I don't want to lose them, but I can't change who I am.'

'Would it help if someone else spoke with them? If I spoke with them?'

'Sure. I think a quick conversation with you would change their outlook completely. Oh, don't look so offended, Matt. Be realistic. Anyway, what would you say? You all think I drink too much anyway.' The truth of that statement hung in the air between them. 'You've gone quiet all of a sudden.'

'I don't know what to say.'

'Well, I'll drink to that.'

'Why do you think Caesar's doing it? I always thought the two of you were close,' Matthew said.

'So did I. He was a father figure. I went from having one to having two. Now, it looks as though I'm heading for none.' Alastair looked puzzled. 'What? What have I said?'

'I need to tell you something. I've found another half-sibling.

Jason Tanner. He's in the same group as you, Lucy and Kathryn,' Matthew said. 'I think you might be in danger.'

Alastair wiped his hand over his face and sighed. 'In danger?' he asked. 'Of what? A more extensive Christmas card list?'

Matthew's mouth was dry. 'I think someone already knows about these relationships, and I don't think it's a coincidence that Lucy and Kathryn are dead.'

'What, precisely, *do* you think, Matt?' Alastair asked.

Matthew swallowed. He could see the hurt in his friend's eyes. 'I think Ben Caesar is your father. I think he's dying. I think Jason Tanner might have killed Kathryn and Lucy to allow him to claim Caesar's estate.' He swallowed. 'So, yes, I think you're in danger.'

'I guess I should be grateful you don't think I'm the one killing my half-siblings.' Alastair didn't sound angry, but Matthew could believe on some level he was. 'You haven't got any evidence. Have you even asked your mother about it? Or your father?' Matthew's mouth twitched. 'This is borderline conspiracy theory stuff, Matt. You'll be telling me you've been hanging out in online chatrooms next. Do you *really* think Jason Tanner is a killer?'

'I know one thing for sure. My wife is dead.'

Alastair's face softened. 'I know, and it's not fair. It's gut-wrenchingly unfair, but spinning a web of spurious theories isn't going to bring her back.' He took a mouthful of beer. 'Where did you get the list?'

Matthew did a double-take. 'Sorry?'

'The list of our names, all the names and the groupings. None of us have seen it. You've never mentioned it before, and everything you're suggesting flows from that list. I wondered where you found it?'

Matthew swallowed. 'Dylan Steele gave it to me.'

Alastair rocked backwards. 'Dylan?' He pushed out a deep breath. 'Dylan's the only other person who loved Lucy as much as you did. Do you want to put your faith in Dylan's ideas?'

'It's not her idea. She hadn't broken the cipher.'

'Are we talking about the same Dylan Steele here? She'd crack a cypher like that in her sleep.'

Matthew shook his head. 'How do you explain the contract my mother signed or the photograph of Sammy's mother?' Matthew paused. 'Or Vanessa's DNA test results?'

Alastair reached for his pint. 'I don't know,' he said. 'There's just a lot of allegations right now.'

Alastair didn't believe him. Fair enough. That was his choice, but Matthew couldn't help but think that, two days ago, Alastair might have given him more credit. Caesar's termination of the scholarship had already begun to loosen the bonds between him and the other scholars. He tried to hold his friend's gaze.

Alastair hadn't mentioned his gambling debt. He'd told Matthew what had happened to him that day, but he'd simply relayed the events. He hadn't been looking for advice. He didn't even seem to want sympathy. It was as if Matthew merely knowing the facts was enough. But wasn't that just Alastair?

Matthew glanced at his watch. 'I need to head off shortly.'

'No worries, ' Alastair said after finishing his pint. 'I think I might go for a walk along the river. It will help clear my head after this.'

Alastair stood up and slipped his leather jacket on. Then he turned and walked off into the night without looking back, leaving Matthew to wonder whether Alastair had blown him off because he felt angry or guilty.

MATTHEW STAYED SITTING at the table, his mind still looking for an answer amongst all the recent revelations. He pulled out his phone and called Dylan.

'Any progress?' he asked.

'I found something interesting. Jason Tanner was detained and then released by the police following a fight in a pub in August 2016.'

'August 2016 was when Kathryn Farthing was murdered,' Matthew said.

'Yes, and the pub was in Richmond, close to Kathryn's home.'

'Okay,' Matthew said, tapping his free hand on the table. 'Anything else?'

'Nothing else recent. He was expelled from a couple of different schools. Looks like he joined the army after Caesar kicked him out.'

Something scratched at Matthew's memory. What had Lucy said to him, something Kathryn had said? 'Someone told Lucy, ages ago, Jason was boasting about going to join the army.'

'Well, he didn't make the grade. He was honourably discharged after a year, in June 2002,' Dylan said. 'After that, apart from his fight in Richmond, he seems to have disappeared off the face of the earth.'

Matthew waited whilst the barman cleared the glasses from the table. 'None of it's conclusive, but it fits with Tanner being a suspect. I need to speak to Caesar.'

'No luck, there,' Dylan said. 'I can't find any record of him being in a private hospital—not in London, anyway—and I haven't been able to get a trace on his mobile.'

'Even if we're correct about what he did in the past, why would Caesar end the scholarship and demand payments from Sammy, Daniel and probably Vanessa?'

'Those payments would increase the size of his estate,' Dylan said.

'True, but Caesar's spent two decades supporting us all. Why change now?' Daniel had been clear the demands were legally unenforceable, and the lack of any legal bite to the payment demands had been bothering Matthew. 'What if it wasn't about the money?'

'What do you mean?' Dylan asked.

'I think the letters are meant to evidence Caesar's state of mind in his final days.'

'They *are* evidence of that,' Dylan replied.

'Only if everyone thinks he wrote them,' Matthew said. 'Daniel told me any scholar could make a claim on Caesar's estate if they can show he regarded them as his dependants. Their case would be much harder in the face of Caesar's most recent declarations.' Matthew swallowed. 'What if Jason Tanner discovered the truth and worked with Karl Irons to get everything he could?'

'Or Karl Irons discovered the truth about Caesar's children and tracked down Tanner.'

'That's more likely,' Matthew agreed. 'As Caesar's lawyer, Irons would have access to all sorts of personal information.'

'If that's what's happening, there's still one thing that doesn't make sense,' Dylan said. 'You. Why treat you differently?'

'I've been thinking about that. At first, I thought whoever was behind this cared about Alfie. Except...'

'What?'

Matthew swallowed. 'There's something I haven't told you,' he said. 'Alfie was suspended from school.'

'I know,' Dylan said.

'He got into a fight because someone was taunting him. This other boy told Alfie someone was paid to give him a letter containing all these horrific slurs he was shouting at him.' Matthew could feel Dylan's cold anger down the phone. 'I think that's linked. Now I wonder whether someone's trying to punish me emotionally rather than financially. The letters have already driven a wedge between me and the others.'

'There's a third possibility,' Dylan said. 'If two people make a claim on the estate, it doubles the number of suspects if anyone ever starts to piece things together.'

'You think I'm being framed.' Matthew shivered.

'I think it's possible. I certainly think whoever's behind this is smart enough to have built in a contingency plan, and you might be part of that.'

It was Matthew's turn to be silent. A requirement of being smart didn't help narrow down the suspect list. He needed to keep digging for information.

'I'm going to pay Eleanor Goldman another visit,' he said. 'Unless we find Caesar, she's the only person I can talk to who knows something about the origins of the Genius Club. She's the only lead we have.'

40

THEN

SATURDAY, 8 JUNE 2019

Belgravia, London

Benjamin Caesar watched as Karl Irons prodded at the fire. He'd been fussing over it, and it was a few minutes until he seemed happy the flames were taking properly.

'That should keep you warm enough,' he said.

Ben already had a blanket over his lap and was wearing a thick Aran jumper. It all helped ward off the chill, but he found it impossible to feel comfortable these days.

'We need to concentrate on the video,' Ben said.

'The video is locked.'

Ben flicked Karl a look. Karl had a vital role to play as his lawyer. He had been a good friend of Ben's since they'd worked together on one of Ben's other projects. He'd even acted as the doorman for the inaugural meeting of The Genius Club. So, there was a certain symmetry to what would happen. He needed someone to push things forward after his death, but Ben wanted to be the judge of when the recording was ready. It was an important announcement. It had to be right.

'I want to watch it through again,' he said.

'It's ready to play.' Karl lowered himself into the armchair opposite Ben.

'Good. And you'll send the invitations?' He wasn't really asking him or even talking to Karl anymore, but rather, he was testing himself. Would he have gone down this route in any event? He told himself one more time he had no choice. Fate was like a ten-tonne truck rolling down a hill. You could try to run faster, hop on the truck, or stand your ground and die, and Ben wanted to live for as long as he could.

'The invitations are ready. I'm just waiting for your final approval of the letters.'

'Hmm.' Ben rubbed his cheek. 'Email the latest drafts to me. Now, let me see the video again.'

He reached towards the table for his tablets. He hated the rattle the bottle made as he picked it up and detested the musky smell that assaulted him when the lid popped off the container. But so far, it hadn't been as bad as he had feared. He was still alive and was at peace with what he was doing.

He heard Karl sigh, but he didn't care. He forced the pills down with a mouthful of water. He had to get this done and get it done right. He owed that to his dead colleagues. Hell, he owed it to the scholars.

Ben had to admit Karl had done an excellent job with the video. He looked healthier in the shot than he'd felt for a few months.

Karl had reviewed the script, but Ben had written it. Even so, his stomach pitched as he listened to the final words. He said nothing as he watched Karl lean forward to stop the recording.

'I told you,' Karl said, 'the video's ready.'

Ben was nodding, but it didn't feel right. 'Hold on to it, for now.'

'Very well, ' Karl said, standing up and picking up his briefcase. 'I'll wait to hear from you.'

Ben watched Karl leave.

Was he doing the right thing? He planned to play the scholars his video telling them of his decision to close the scholarship. They would be shocked, but that would be nothing compared to their reaction when they read the letters telling the truth about the Genius Club. The thought that had burrowed into his brain was stretching out. He'd resisted total transparency for a long time, but the daily reminder of his mortality had caused something to shift.

Ben had never thought of himself as a coward. The only option was to tell everyone the truth, but not by video. He would tell Karl that the meeting was off and that the video and the letters could be binned. Instead, he would tell them all the truth in person. That way, he could explain it, answer any questions, and make peace.

He knew instinctively who he had to tell first. His daughter and the mother of his grandson.

He needed to speak with Lucy.

41

THEN

TUESDAY, 11 JUNE 2019

Raynes Park, London

Lucy caught sight of the white headset in the mirror and stifled a laugh. She looked ridiculous, like a character from a sci-fi movie.

She picked up the controller and, taking a deep breath, flicked on the electric current. There was the familiar immediate warmth in her temples and a mild itch as the twenty milliamperes of electric current tapped into her nerves. The first twenty minutes passed quickly, but from then on until the end of the hour, the process was uncomfortable. Eventually, the controller switched off the current, and Lucy removed the headset and replaced it in the plastic case.

She felt alert. More alert? It was hard to say these days, but she could still recall the improvement when she'd first tried it. She couldn't scientifically prove it, but pregnancy brain had felt real for her, and the brain fog hadn't lifted after Alfie was born. She hadn't wanted to try it until after Alfie was born. Bannister hadn't said she shouldn't; that was her instinctive reaction.

Her experience with the device had led her to approach Caesar about playing a pivotal role in Cerebrum. She enjoyed her poetry but was outside the Cerebrum project, which bound the others together. Caesar had rejected her suggestion out of hand at first, but she was wearing him down.

She tried not to think too hard about an electrode array being inserted into her brain, but Cerebrum was due to start human trials soon, and she was determined to be the first human patient. Her name would be written in history alongside those of her friends. She smiled to herself. The Genius Club would build a genius factory.

She'd just finished tidying all the equipment into the wardrobe when the doorbell rang. She walked down to the front door and opened it.

'Hello,' Caesar said.

Caesar had never called round to their flat before. Matthew was at work, and Alfie was at school. He must have wanted to speak to her alone.

He looked tired, and simply walking up the stairs seemed an effort. She showed him into the living room. He declined the offer of a drink and perched on the edge of the sofa with Lucy sitting in the armchair opposite him.

'What's up?'

Caesar's eyes flickered around the room, and Lucy felt a cold bead of sweat prick between her shoulder blades. She pulled herself up to avoid slouching and waited.

'I need to talk to you.' He wouldn't meet her eyes, and his hands were tapping on his lap.

'Are you okay?' It was Lucy's go-to. She worried about others. He looked ill, and she silently prepared to hear his bad news. How bad would it be?

'It's about your father,' he said. Words which were like punches to her gut. What? 'There's no easy way to say this.' He sniffed and scratched his bearded jaw before leaning back and then shuffling forward again. 'I should have told you years ago.'

Lucy's heart was hammering now. Years ago. What on earth could he mean? 'What?' Her mind was scrambling, searching for something to latch onto.

Caesar was staring at her now. His eyes were wet. Lucy held her breath.

'Lucy, I'm your father.'

The words circled her heart and pulled tight. Her chest burned. She was conscious of reaching out to feel for the arm of the chair. She couldn't speak. She wanted to scream it wasn't true, but as she absorbed the words, she knew it was possible. Why would he lie?

A spark caught inside her, and her body burned. She'd never known her father. Her eyes bore into Caesar. 'You bastard,' she said.

'I'm sorry.' He aimed the words at the floor.

Lucy was on her feet. 'Get out.' Her voice was a whisper.

Caesar pushed himself up. 'I wish I could change things, but at least I wanted you to know the truth before…' he trailed off.

'Before what?' Lucy spat out the words. 'Before you die? You want to clear your conscience?' She took a step towards him. 'Get out.' Louder this time.

'Lucy, there's something else. I need to tell you about your sister. I think you're in danger.'

Her words cracked through the air. 'I said, get out.' She watched his face crumple.

Caesar bowed his head. 'I'll talk to you after you've calmed down.' He turned and edged away.

The dull shuffle of his footsteps moved along the hallway and down the stairs, followed by a clunk as the front door closed.

Lucy forced herself to breathe and tried to clear her head. Different courses of action shouted for her attention. She didn't need to panic, not yet. At least not until she knew the truth, but she couldn't deal with this alone.

She brushed away the tears running down her face and walked to the study. She needed to speak with Matthew. Right away. She closed her eyes when the phone diverted to voicemail. She ended the call and tried Dylan's mobile, but it rang without a reply. She stood still. She wouldn't discuss what Caesar had told her with Alfie, but she had the sudden urge to hear his voice. His phone would be off because he was in school. She dialled his number, tears pooling in her eyes.

'Hey, this is Alfie. Here's the beep. Knock yourself out.'

She sucked in every word. After a few seconds, she realised it had diverted to voicemail. She ended the call.

42

NOW

FRIDAY, 28 JUNE 2019

East Dulwich, London

Matthew knocked on the door. He thought he saw the curtain in the front room twitch. A few seconds later, he heard the metallic grind of the security chain slipping into place. The door cracked open, and Matthew saw a slither of Mrs Goldman's face. She looked pale, almost haunted.

'I can't talk to you.' Her voice sounded devoid of emotion.

'I'm sorry. It's important. I need your help.' It sounded weak. She'd know he needed her help. Why else would he have travelled to see her?

'I can't help you.'

'Your ex-husband set up a sperm bank,' Matthew said. Confusion clouded her face, and her involuntary movement opened the door more widely. 'Please. I'm worried my friend is in danger,' Matthew said.

'I shouldn't let you in.'

At that moment, Matthew knew she would. She pushed the door closed to release the security chain before opening it. He stepped into the hallway and waited while Mrs Goldman shut and deadbolted the door. She didn't invite him in any further.

'I don't know anything more than I told you before.' There was conviction in her voice, but she looked brittle. 'I swear I didn't know he set up a sperm bank.' She dropped her head and rubbed her forehead. 'Are you sure that's true?' she asked.

Matthew didn't have time to cover everything. He pushed on with his questions. 'Your ex-husband is a director of a company called Cerebrum,' Matthew said. 'You told me you hadn't heard of it.'

She shook her head. 'I haven't heard of it. I have no idea what it is.'

Matthew decided to change tack. 'Do you recognise the name, Jason Tanner?'

'No.' She paused. 'No, I don't think I've ever heard that name.'

'Kathryn Farthing?'

'No.'

He sighed because he believed her. 'Karl Irons?'

'No.' Another shake of the head. 'Sorry.' She had no apparent motivation to lie to him.

Matthew had struggled with the decision of whether to tell her that her ex-husband was dead. Was it his place? The answer seemed quite clearly to be no, but how could he question her and not tell her what he'd discovered?

'Mrs Goldman. I have some news about your ex-husband.'

Something in her expression made him stop. Her hand covered her mouth, and she closed her eyes when she spoke. 'Is he dead?' She opened her eyes.

Matthew nodded. 'I'm sorry.'

She drew herself up. 'Well,' she said but left it at that.

'Perhaps I shouldn't have…' he trailed off. She'd been so anxious about him being there—far less relaxed than on his first visit—and the news of Christopher's death didn't appear to have eased her concerns. A thought struck him: 'Mrs Goldman, has someone called or visited you? About Ben Caesar? After I was here.'

She nodded, but her eyes widened.

'What happened?'

He had no right to expect her to answer. She didn't owe him anything, but somehow, she summoned the courage to talk.

'A man called here the day after you. He knew you'd visited, but he didn't seem to know why. He asked me what we'd talked about.' Matthew wasn't sure what emotion his face was showing, but Mrs Goldman rushed on. 'I didn't tell him. He mentioned Benjamin Caesar, but I didn't say anything.'

Matthew was thinking. It had to be Karl Irons or Jason Tanner, but how did they know Matthew had visited Mrs Goldman? Dylan was the only person to know before the trip, but he'd only told the others at the dinner later that same day.

'Can you describe him?' he asked.

'I can do better than that,' she said. 'I can tell you his name.'

Matthew's heart tried to burst through his chest as he waited. She looked at him and held his gaze.

'His name was Alastair Niven.'

A CHILL CREPT down Matthew's spine as he walked along the pavement. Alastair's name was ringing in his head. He thought back, looking for anything that didn't add up. Alastair had identified Karl Irons as the doorman from the original meeting. Was it possible Alastair already knew the lawyer?

Matthew shook his head. Alastair was his best friend, but if Caesar's email was to be believed, he was in debt to a gambling cartel. Was that enough to unbalance him? He had always trusted Alastair. He'd turned to him to help with Alfie.

A numbness crawled through his body as a new thought clicked into place. He believed the killer's motivation was to claim Caesar's estate, but because Lucy had died before Caesar, Lucy's potential share of Caesar's estate would have passed to Alfie.

His stomach pitched. Oh God. Alfie. How could he not have seen it until now?

He pulled his phone from his pocket, cursing Alfie for having turned off the tracking app a couple of years ago after an argument with Lucy. All Matthew could do was pray his son would answer his phone.

Raynes Park, London

Alfie hadn't answered his phone or responded to any texts in the time it took Matthew to travel home, but that wasn't out of the ordinary. The good news was Alfie had rarely left their flat since he'd been suspended from school. Matthew tried to calm himself down. Alfie would be safe and sound inside.

He turned the key and pushed open the front door. 'Alfie?' he called out. Half greeting, half question.

He jogged up the steps. It wasn't unusual for Alfie not to reply. He would be lying on his bed, listening to music with headphones on, probably staring at the ceiling and cursing at the world. Matthew knocked on the bedroom door and swung it open in one move.

His stomach dropped. Alfie wasn't there.

'Alfie,' he called again, anxiety creeping into his voice this time. He rushed into the kitchen. No Alfie. He picked up his mobile phone and called his son again—straight to voicemail.

'Alfie, it's Dad. Please call me. I need to know you're okay.'

As soon as he'd left the message, he pulled out the second phone and called Dylan. That call also diverted to the answerphone.

'It's Matthew. Alfie's missing. I thought he might be with you. Can you call me?'

He ended the call, switched back phones, and tried Alastair, even though he was unsure what to say if he got an answer. It didn't matter because the call was diverted to voicemail, leaving him no other choice.

He had to get to Alastair's as quickly as possible.

Richmond, London

MATTHEW'S TAXI was nearly at Alastair's house. Sweat was trickling down his back, and his mind ran through the various ways Alfie could be in danger.

He tried to push the thoughts aside. The odds of Alastair being the killer were remote. He had warned his son by text.

Alfie, you're in danger. Please get to a police station. Don't trust anyone. Not even Alastair.

Logically, he knew Alfie would respond if he'd seen the message and was able to, but there'd been no reply.

Matthew hit redial. Again and again.

Every time he heard his son's voice. It was him, but not him. His hand crushed around his phone, and he shuffled backwards and forwards on the seat.

None of it helped.

He'd lost his wife. And now he might be losing his son.

Richmond, London

MATTHEW HAMMERED on Alastair's front door and kept his finger pressed on the doorbell.

Nothing.

He stood on the step, unsure what to do. He struggled to believe his best friend had killed Lucy and was planning to kill Alfie. It was ridiculous, and yet nothing was making sense anymore. He smacked his fist against the door a few more times, but there was no sign anyone was in.

Perhaps he'd been rash to rush straight to Alastair's house. There could be other explanations. Maybe Eleanor Goldman's visitor had been someone else using Alastair's name. The description she'd given —average height, dark hair, and sunglasses—could have been Alastair but could equally have been Karl Irons or any number of people.

Something was scratching away in Matthew's brain. He started to jog along the road through the drizzle and saw a bus turn the corner towards him as he approached the stop. He made an instant decision and clambered on, making his way towards an empty seat. His phone vibrated in his hand as he approached the seat, and he felt himself flinch in anticipation of the message. He glanced down to read the text, but it wasn't Alfie, Alastair, or Dylan.

It was from Vanessa.

I've had the test results back. You are a match with sample A. Neither of you is a match with Lucy.

Matthew's knees gave way, and he only managed to edge himself onto the seat when he fell. Another alert signalled the arrival of a second text from Vanessa. He swallowed as he read the next message. Pressure crushed down on his shoulders as he pushed himself back up and staggered towards the front of the bus.

I cross-checked the samples against other results on our database. There was also a match with an existing record. Lucy's biological father is Ben Caesar.

Matthew balled his hands. Not only was he right that Lucy was Caesar's daughter, but Dylan was his half-sister.

The bus would take too long. Matthew pushed past the elderly couple, arguing with the driver about paying their fare with coins, and jumped off the bus. How could he have left Alfie alone? Caesar's message had been right about one thing. He couldn't trust anyone right now. His legs pumped as he sprinted down the road and spun around the corner. He saw a yellow taxi light and stepped out onto the road.

The taxi pulled over, and the cabbie yelled through the open window. 'You want to be careful, mate. I nearly ran you over.'

Matthew was already climbing into the cab. He shouted Dylan's address and leant forward to speak to the cabbie.

'Please. As fast as you can. My son's missing.' His voice cracked with the strain.

The cabbie gave a nod, and Matthew felt the taxi surge forward.

He tried Alfie's number again. *Please answer. Please be safe.* He heard a click.

Voicemail.

Putney, London

MATTHEW WAS LESS than a mile away from Dylan's house, but every minute crawled by. He was perched on the seat of the taxi. He'd already pushed forty pounds through the internal window to the cabbie and had his hand on the door handle. As soon as the cab slowed down sufficiently, he would launch himself out of there.

The ringtone from the burner phone almost made him slip off the seat.

Dylan.

He jammed the phone against his ear. 'Is Alfie with you?' He could hear the aggression in his voice, but he didn't care.

'Yes. He's at my house.'

Matthew slumped back against the seat, suppressing a sob. He could hear some background noise. 'Where are you?' he asked, his voice stretching again with emotion.

'I'm about five minutes away from my house. I've been out to collect a takeaway.'

That wasn't the sort of thing you would either do or share if you were planning a murder. Matthew's heart rate began to drop for the first time in an hour. 'I'll be at your flat in a minute.'

'Alfie wants to stay over tonight,' Dylan said in a neutral tone.

'Well, we can discuss...' he trailed off. He'd lapsed so easily into believing none of this had anything to do with Dylan. 'I'll see you shortly.'

The line went dead, and Matthew pushed himself back into the seat.

'Found him?' The cabbie's eyes were staring at him from the taxi's mirror.

'Yes.' Matthew cleared his throat. 'Thank you. I appreciate you getting me here as quickly as you did.'

'No worries,' the cabbie said as he pulled up by the side of the road.

Matthew looked out the window. There was a light on in Dylan's house. He allowed his breathing to return to normal as he imagined Alfie sitting upstairs, tapping away on a computer. He glanced down the street to see if he could see Dylan. Rain was falling hard, and an umbrella bobbed along the pavement. He couldn't see who was carrying it, but he had a feeling Dylan didn't do umbrellas.

He thanked the cabbie again, jumped out of the taxi, and jogged to Dylan's front door. He rang the doorbell. *Come on, Alfie.*

Rain trickled down his back, and he raked his fingers through his hair. He rang again. No answer. Fair enough, Dylan would have told Alfie not to answer the door to anyone. He wouldn't know it was his dad. Matthew leant with his back against the door. Dylan had said she was only five minutes away. He looked both ways along the street but couldn't see her.

He tried to order his thoughts. His main concern had been Alfie, but he knew now that his son was safe. What about Dylan? If she'd been a risk, then she wouldn't have called Matthew back, kept Alfie safe in her house, or gone out in the rain to get takeout. He could trust Dylan. Perhaps she was the only one he could trust right then.

The messages from Caesar's email account still confused him. Ignoring the details he'd been sent about his friends was hard. He shook his head. Alastair was his best friend, yet if what Eleanor Goldman had told him was true, he had been investigating Caesar, too. Why wouldn't he have said anything to Matthew? There was either nothing to tell, or he was hiding something himself, but even if there was nothing to tell, Matthew couldn't shake the feeling Alastair would've told Matthew about his suspicions. They were close. Weren't they?

Matthew chewed his lip. He'd seen Alastair's wilder side. He liked to gamble and would joke that he wanted to give other people space by living on the edge, but even when Alastair's edge was on display, so was his smile. Matthew couldn't believe it.

He heard footsteps on the pavement and saw Dylan walking along the road carrying a couple of pizza boxes. He pushed himself upright and wiped the rain from his face.

'He won't answer,' Matthew said.

Dylan nodded as she pulled a key from her coat pocket and unlocked the door. 'Why are you worried about him?' She jerked her head to indicate Matthew should go in first.

'I think Alfie inherits Lucy's share of Caesar's estate.'

He saw Dylan blink, and then she nodded. 'He's upstairs. I'll put these in the kitchen. I'll see you both in there.' She walked down the hall and nudged open the kitchen door with the pizza boxes.

Matthew ran upstairs, shouting out for his son. He wanted to give him a moment to set his mood. He knocked on the first door he came to. There was no answer. He moved on to the next room, a study, kitted out with computers, but Alfie wasn't there either.

'Alfie?' Matthew shouted.

Matthew heard a lock turn, and Alfie emerged from the bathroom, looking at his dad. 'What's the drama?'

Matthew's knees nearly buckled. He pulled his son into a hug. 'I need to talk to you,' Matthew said, releasing Alfie from his embrace. 'Dylan's back with the pizza. Let's go downstairs.'

Alfie rolled his eyes but followed his dad downstairs.

Matthew had decided there was no option other than to tell Alfie the truth or what he knew of it. He watched Alfie stuff a piece of pizza into his mouth. His son sat in silence as Matthew talked him through the history of the Genius Club and the revelations of new family connections. Alfie said nothing, but his jaw tightened as Matthew explained his theory that Lucy had been murdered.

'I know it's a lot to take in.'

Alfie was shaking his head. 'Do you know who did it?' His voice was quiet.

'No. I'm not sure yet, but I'm close to knowing.'

Alfie nodded. He lifted his head to look his father in the eye. 'If they're caught, they'll go to prison?'

'For a long time, yes,' Matthew replied.

Alfie twitched. He offered no opinion on whether the punishment would fit the crime.

In truth, Matthew wasn't sure he could help him with that. What would he do if the person who had murdered his wife was caught, and it was his decision whether they lived or died? If he was given a gun and left alone with them in the room, with only a blind, deaf, and mute monkey as his witness? *See no evil, hear no evil, speak no evil.* He shook his head. He had no idea what he would do.

Dylan made an excuse about needing to do something somewhere else in the house. Matthew was grateful to her for giving them space. They sat in silence for a few minutes. They needed an easier topic of conversation.

'Did you get my texts?' Matthew asked.

'My phone's been charging in here. I haven't looked at it in a while.' Alfie frowned. 'Do you think Benjamin Caesar's dead?'

Matthew let out a sigh. There was a long list of people who were dead. Lucy. Kathryn. Bannister. Goldman. Maybe Caesar was, too. Now Alastair was missing. Before Matthew could reply, his phone beeped with a new text message from an unknown number. He unlocked his phone and read the message.

You don't know me.

His neck tingled, and his phone buzzed with a second message.

I need to meet you and your son. I have information about Lucy's death.

'Dad? Are you okay? Who's texting you?' Alfie spoke with his mouth full of pepperoni pizza.

Matthew swallowed and felt his throat constrict. There was no way he was taking Alfie anywhere. The phone beeped for a third time.

4 pm. The Starlight Café. Baker Street. No police. Tell no one.

Matthew checked the time. It was already approaching two o'clock, and it would take him the best part of an hour to get to Baker

Street from Putney. He massaged his hands together. What was he thinking? He couldn't go.

'Dad?'

Matthew wasn't sure whether Alfie wanted to know who had sent the texts or an answer on Benjamin Caesar being dead or alive, but it didn't matter because Matthew didn't have a clear answer to either question.

43

THEN

TUESDAY, 11 JUNE 2019

Belgravia, London

BEN BURIED HIS FACE IN HIS HANDS. LUCY HADN'T EVEN GIVEN HIM THE chance to explain. Decades of controlling his emotions and prioritising intellectual development over everything else had been destroyed in a few moments. Now, he could never put the genie back in the bottle. Everything was ruined. He might live a little longer, but his legacy would be tarnished if not destroyed.

The chime of the front doorbell echoed around the kitchen. He checked the video camera feed on his phone. Whoever was calling on him was standing off to the side, out of sight of the camera. It was most likely Karl Irons. If it were Lucy, he would usher her in, but anyone else could go to hell right now.

The doorbell rang again, but Ben was making his way along the hallway towards the spiral staircase at the end. He descended to what he liked to think of as his bunker. The main room in the basement was cavernous, with each wall lined with bookshelves from floor to ceiling and a sliding wooden ladder to enable Ben to reach the higher volumes, but he didn't need any books right then. All he wanted was the comfort of his favourite chair. He folded himself against the leather, letting his feet settle on the ground, and his arms relax onto the sides of the chair.

He could still hear the doorbell ringing, but it sounded so remote it was easy to push it away. Karl would soon give up and come back another day.

Ben had the sudden urge to smoke, something he hadn't done for years, but he didn't have any cigarettes, and there was no way he was getting up to leave the house. He stood and walked over to the drinks trolley parked near his chair. He picked up the decanter and poured himself a generous measure of whisky, and then he added another slug just for good measure. It wouldn't help clear up his mess, but it sure would taste good. He savoured the weight of the glass in his hand as he relaxed back in the chair, closed his eyes and tried to push away the day's stresses.

He couldn't switch off. An ember was glowing. He'd survive this. Yes, things would be different, possibly very different, but he'd never let anything stop him in life. Why change who he was now?

A creak from upstairs interrupted his thinking. He craned his head towards the library door. After a few seconds, he shook his head and took another drink, swirling the liquid around his mouth. He'd allowed himself to become unsettled, and that wasn't like him. He needed to reimpose some discipline.

He got up and walked over to a section of the bookshelf, removing two thick volumes. He reached into the space they left behind and tapped a code into the keypad on the exposed wall. The safe door slid open. He pulled out his MacBook, carefully closed the safe, and replaced the books. He placed the laptop on the table by his chair and clicked the power button to boot it up. He took another mouthful of whisky before placing the glass down and entering his password.

The newsfeed across the top of the webpage featured a couple of entries related to Sammy winning some fund management awards, but the newest entry caught his attention—a post from Scout Two.

Scout Two was the best of the bunch and had been on Ben's payroll since the beginning. She was discrete and highly effective, so Ben had changed her brief to cover his biological children, although

Scout Two didn't know that. She was well compensated for doing her job and not asking Ben questions.

The title of the message was *Kathryn Farthing's daughter - update.*

He clicked on the link and waited for the new page to load. The multicoloured spinning wheel signalled a delay, so he tapped his fingers on the table.

He didn't know what made him look towards the door. He hadn't heard any sound. Maybe he had caught some movement in his peripheral vision, but whatever the reason, he did look up, and his thoughts melted away from the hanging webpage.

44

NOW

FRIDAY, 28 JUNE 2019

Putney, London

MATTHEW FOUND DYLAN UPSTAIRS IN HER STUDY, SITTING IN FRONT OF one of her many computers. He handed Dylan his phone and waited whilst she read the texts.

'You can't go,' she said.

'I know.' He hesitated.

'But I could,' she said. Matthew almost laughed. It was as if Dylan had read his mind. 'If it's Tanner, he won't know me. I could go and see who turns up.'

'I was thinking the same thing.'

'And if it's Alastair, then...'

'It's not Alastair.' Matthew felt the conviction more strongly than logic allowed. He simply couldn't believe his best friend was capable of such atrocities. Dylan said nothing, but he saw a slight nod, which indicated she didn't believe it either. 'Okay. Are you sure? It could be dangerous.' Which was, at best, understating it.

'I'll be fine.' Dylan pushed the keyboard away and stood up. 'It's you and Alfie who are at risk. I think it's best you both stay here. If no one knows about me, they won't know to look for you here.' She paused. 'Have you told any of the others about me?'

Matthew shook his head. Why was that? She had asked him not to, but he wasn't sure that was the reason. It was more of a gut feeling it would be best not to tell anyone else, and right then, he was glad he hadn't. His conversation with Alastair flicked into his mind. 'Actually, I told Alastair I got the printout from you.'

Dylan stared at him. 'Well, I hope you're right about him for all our sakes.'

ONCE DYLAN HAD LEFT, Matthew deadbolted the door and slipped on the security chain. She had insisted on going then, even though she could have waited another forty minutes before setting off. Before leaving, she mirrored Matthew's texts on her phone to ensure she could see any messages from the mysterious informant to Matthew in real-time.

Dylan had also started a search on Jason Tanner on the dark web and had asked Alfie to take over when she left. Matthew massaged his head as he watched his son tapping on the keyboard.

He'd debated calling the police but decided to wait and see what information they uncovered that evening. Dylan was taking a risk in attending the meeting, and he felt responsible, but if they were right and whoever turned up had no idea who she was, she would be safe enough. Anyway, he had a feeling Dylan could take care of herself.

'Is Dylan going to be okay?' Alfie was staring straight ahead at the screen.

Matthew could hear Alfie's concern. 'She'll be fine,' he said, praying he was right.

Matthew forced himself to focus. He glanced at the time—four o'clock. The informant would be at the café on Baker Street, but Dylan still hadn't replied to Matthew's messages.

He snatched up his phone the moment it rang, but it was the wrong phone for Dylan.

'Hi, Sammy,' he said.

'What's going on, Matt?' Sammy asked. 'Daniel told me about your argument last night.'

'I'm sorry. There isn't time to explain.'

Matthew felt the tension in his shoulders. He was aware of Alfie leaning forward in the seat next to him, staring at the computer screen.

'Dad?'

Matthew twisted his neck to see what Alfie was looking at. His son was scrolling through a news story. 'Sammy, I'm sorry. I've got to go,' he said.

'Hold on, Matt,' Sammy said. 'We can talk about Daniel another time, but I've discovered something interesting about Caesar.'

'Okay.' Perhaps Sammy hadn't written him off just yet. 'I've been looking into Caesar's finances.' Sammy took an intake of breath before she carried on. 'As far as I can tell, he's practically broke.'

The word spun in Matthew's head. Broke. 'What? How's that possible? What about the house?'

'He doesn't own any property. The house in London is owned by an offshore trust.' Matthew's breathing quickened. 'There's more. I checked the accounts of Cerebrum, and it turns out that although Caesar owns the company, it's been loaned several million pounds by an offshore trust.'

Matthew said nothing. If Caesar owned no assets, his estate was worthless, and Tanner had no reason to kill.

'What do you know about the trust?' he asked.

'Not much, just the name and jurisdiction. I checked against a cache of leaked legal documents, and there's a document about the London property. The trust is called the Ada Trust, and it's based in Panama.'

Another possibility occurred to Matthew. 'Maybe he has some crypto-currency stashed somewhere,' he said.

'I doubt it,' Sammy said. 'You were there when we discussed Bitcoin with Caesar years ago. He's never invested in crypto, I'm pretty sure.'

Matthew closed his eyes. Something scratched at his memory about their meeting with Caesar when they discussed Bitcoin. Caesar hadn't been against investing in cryptocurrency; he had worried about the security. And he had said something odd—odd, and yet possibly a way of finding the truth.

'Okay. Let me know if you find out anything more.' Matthew shook his head. 'Oh, and Sammy, thank you.'

He ended the call. If Karl Irons was the mastermind, he was either a bad lawyer who didn't know his client was worthless, or he knew something Matthew didn't. He rechecked the time. Dylan had to be at the meeting by now. She'd left so early that it was inconceivable she hadn't made it in time. Where the hell was she?

'Dad,' Alfie said, with increased urgency, 'you have to see this.'

His son pointed at the screen just as Matthew's burner phone rang.

'Just a second, Alfie. It's Dylan.' He answered the phone. 'What took you ... Never mind. Are you there?' he asked.

'I just walked past the café. There's hardly anyone inside. There's a guy with a beer; that could be him. And a couple. There's no one outside. I'm going in to get a drink, play with my phone and look like I'm waiting for someone. I'll leave the line open so you can hear me. Put yourself on mute.'

'Will do.' Matthew started to breathe more easily. At least Dylan was okay.

'Dad, I've found something on Jason Tanner.' Alfie was scouring the screen, still talking. 'I think this might be him, although I'm not certain. It looks like he had a troubled childhood. Arrested, expelled from school.' He pointed at the screen.

Matthew nodded. 'Dylan found that information, too.'

Alfie was still talking. 'Subsequently charged with illegal entry into Afghanistan in December 2004…' He trailed off.

'What did you just say?' Matthew asked.

'He was charged with illegal entry into Afghanistan in December 2004. He claimed he was there for humanitarian relief work post-September 11, working for aid groups run by former military personnel, but there are reports that he was active as a security consultant for journalists and…' Alfie trailed off and blew out a breath. 'Wow. His wife and six-month-old son were killed in an attack five years ago.'

Matthew stared at the screen over his son's shoulder. Jason Tanner's life had been ripped apart. Who knew what that trauma could do to someone? Matthew tried to process the Wiki synopsis of Tanner's life. There was a picture of Tanner, too. He looked young, in his early twenties, a few years after Matthew and the others had met him. Matthew gripped the desk. He could be looking at the man who'd killed Lucy. The man who was waiting at the café to meet with Matthew and Alfie.

'Send that to Dylan,' Matthew said.

Alfie's fingers were flying over the keyboard. 'Done,' Alfie said.

Both of Matthew's phones buzzed with the arrival of a new message.

One was from whoever was waiting for Matthew.

Where are you?

The other was from Dylan.

It's him. The man in the café is Jason Tanner.

IT WAS clear Jason Tanner was right at the heart of the mystery of Lucy's death, and at that moment, he was sitting only yards away from Dylan, waiting for Matthew to turn up. Matthew jumped as he heard a scuffling noise and an angry shout down the phone.

'Dylan, are you okay?' Matthew's response was instinctive, and it took him a second to recall he was on mute. His finger hovered over the button whilst he strained to hear. There was a muffled exchange and the sound of footsteps. Then the line went dead.

'Shit,' he muttered under his breath. Alfie was looking at him. 'Dylan will be careful,' Matthew said and was rewarded with an almost imperceptible nod.

A buzz announced another text arriving. It was from Dylan.

I bugged him. I'm sending you a link. He's in a car.

Would Tanner be heading to Caesar's Palace? Matthew felt heat in his chest at his use of Alastair's nickname for Caesar's house. Where was his friend? He hadn't responded to any of his messages or calls.

Matthew clenched his fists. There was nothing he could do right now, but if Jason Tanner tried to target Alastair, he knew Dylan would alert him.

Matthew clicked on Google Maps. It would take Tanner approximately ten minutes to get to Caesar's house. One option would be to wait and see what Dylan could find out, build a case, and then take it to the police, but Matthew wasn't sure. Yes, the police would need to be involved—just not yet.

He clicked on the link Dylan had sent him and waited. He could hear a man talking but didn't recognise his voice. He was sure he was listening to Jason Tanner. The man had no accent. Maybe that's what nomads sounded like, or perhaps grief had crushed it out of him.

'The Prof didn't fucking show up. Jesus, my trousers are soaked.'

Matthew couldn't hear who Tanner was talking to but suspected it was Karl Irons. Whoever it was, it was clear they were looking for him.

'Some stupid bitch spilt her drink on me as I got up to leave.'

So, that was how Dylan had planted the bug.

'Shall I come back to the house?'

There was a pause before Tanner spoke again.

'Yeah, okay. I could try his flat?'

The tingle at the base of Matthew's neck spread over his shoulders and spine. He swallowed hard. Thank God he and Alfie had stayed at Dylan's.

'No, you're right. How about one of his friend's houses, then? He could be hiding there.'

Matthew's body froze. They were hunting him and Alfie. Yes, Matthew thought, I am hiding, you murdering bastard. Somewhere you don't know about.

'Wait. You said there'd been a scout report on the feed about his movements the other day.'

Matthew started to shake. Caesar's scouts were still following him, still reporting, and it sounded as though Tanner and Karl Irons had been receiving them for the last few days. He held his breath. Surely, they hadn't tracked him to Dylan's house?

'My thoughts exactly,' Tanner's voice was animated. *'I'll see if he's hiding out in that place in Putney.'*

Matthew was already moving. He slipped the laptop and power cable into the rucksack and slung the bag over his shoulder. He grabbed Alfie by the arm and dragged him towards the stairs. 'We need to go. Now.'

Alfie stumbled after his father. 'Aren't we safe here?'

'Not anymore. They know where we are.' He ran down the stairs to the front door. Thank God Dylan had bugged Tanner; otherwise, Matthew and Alfie would have been holed up at Dylan's house while Tanner drove right up to the front door.

'Where are we going?' Alfie asked.

'Just follow me.' He closed the door behind them, and they headed out into the night, with Matthew hoping his plan would work.

Because if it didn't, he and Alfie could both end up dead.

IT WAS the busiest café Matthew could find on Putney High Street. Close enough to Dylan's house so as not to lose too much time, busy enough that they could be hidden in the crowd. He asked for a table inside, at the back. That way, he'd have a view of anyone who came in, yet be out of sight of anyone driving along the road looking for them. Hopefully.

He pulled out the laptop and plugged it in. Alfie sat down in front of it.

'I need you to hack Caesar's iCloud account.' His son stared at him. 'It's important, Alfie. I'm hoping you know how to do it?' Matthew looked away. How the hell had he ended up involving his twelve-year-old son in all this?

There was a slight nod. 'There's an easy way and a hard way. Do you know his email and his date of birth?'

'Yes.'

'Okay. Give me the details. How well do you know him? We're going to need to answer his security questions. Bizarrely, most people answer them truthfully.' Matthew saw his eyes narrow as his hands glided over the keyboard. Alfie was in his element, and he'd been taught by the best.

'Caesar's not most people,' Matthew said, but he had a hunch he might know the answers anyway.

A few seconds later, Alfie turned the screen so Matthew could see. 'We need to know the answer to these security questions. Any ideas?'

What was your childhood nickname? What was the first thing you learned to cook?

Matthew thought back to the conversation years ago between him, Caesar and Sammy. What had Caesar said? *None of my passwords are passwords.*

'It'll be a number,' Matthew said. 'Try 33550336,' he said.

The screen shimmered. 'No luck. Next try,' Alfie said.

'8589869056.'

'Not that either. These are perfect numbers, right? This one our last chance.' Alfie was already typing. 137438691328. He looked at his father.

And all my passwords are perfect.

Matthew nodded and silently prayed to a god he didn't believe in.

Alfie hit return, and then he smiled. 'Bingo. I'm in.'

MATTHEW ENDED the call with Dylan. The planning had taken five minutes.

Dylan would call Karl Iron's work voicemail. She'd already found a video of him presenting at a conference on the internet. She was confident she'd have enough voice data to convince Tanner he was speaking to the real Karl Irons.

Matthew typed an email to Caesar. He was sure Caesar was dead, and Tanner and Irons were running everything. They'd sent the emails, but as long as they thought Matthew still believed Caesar was alive, his plan might work.

Ben, what is going on? I need to see you. I'm coming over. I'll be at your house at 6 pm. Matthew.

With luck, Tanner, or Irons, would read the message and call off the chase.

If they thought Matthew was heading to Caesar's house, they'd want to be there, waiting for him. Matthew needed to ensure Alfie was safe, and Dylan suggested they move Alfie to Adam's house. They needed a location no one could know about if neither of them could be with him. None of the Genius Club knew of Adam, let alone his address, so there was no realistic chance Caesar's scouts would have any record of it. Matthew looked again at the map on his phone. The walk to Adam's house should take him and Alfie less than ten minutes from the café.

Once Alfie was secure, Matthew would head over to Caesar's, but first, he needed a favour. He knew he was asking a lot at a time when he had no right to ask for anything. He just prayed Daniel would take his call.

Daniel answered on the second ring. 'What do you want, Matt? Why are you calling me?'

'I was a total idiot to you last night. I'm sorry,' Matthew said by way of introduction. 'But I think I know who killed Lucy, and right now, he's after me and possibly Alastair.' He glanced at his son and dropped his voice. 'Maybe, even Alfie.'

'Jesus. You need to go to the police.' Daniel's response was immediate.

'I will, but not yet. I think I can find this man and stop him.'

'No.' Daniel's voice was thick with emotion. 'It's way too dangerous.'

'It'll be okay,' Matthew said. 'Everything can be done remotely. That's why I need your help.'

Daniel had access to the necessary equipment and worked closely enough with the expert security teams for his clients over the years to pick up the know-how he would need. It also helped that he had advised Caesar personally on the security for the house in Eaton Place. 'I need you to access the security for Caesar's house.'

'I'm not allowed to do that.' His tone, however, suggested some room for debate.

'You have to. I've already got access to his computer files, but I need to be able to access and control the house's security system: locks, lighting, and sound.' Matthew blew out a short breath. 'Please, Daniel. My son's life depends on it.'

MATTHEW HAD COMPLETED an initial scan through Caesar's digital files. He hadn't located the scout reports yet, but he'd found a folder of other information that looked promising.

He glanced around the café before slipping a ten-pound note under his empty mug. He'd devised a route to Adam's house that minimised time spent on any main roads. He stood up and picked up the laptop. 'Right, we'd better get going.' He pulled up his hood. 'Keep your head down.'

Matthew's heart was hammering as they walked along the road. His eyes darted around, checking for possible sightings of Jason Tanner or anyone who might be following them. His mouth was dry, but after a few minutes, they were walking down the drive of a large, detached house. Making sure to keep their backs to the road, Matthew pressed on the doorbell.

The door swung open almost immediately, and Adam was waving them in. His expression was serious, and Matthew immediately wondered precisely how much Dylan had told him.

'Come in, come in.' He closed the door behind them and smiled at Alfie before looking at Matthew. 'Nice to see you again, Matthew.' They shook hands. 'Is everything okay? Dylan sounded worried. That doesn't happen very often.'

'We just need Alfie to be somewhere safe,' Matthew said.

'I've got a taxi coming for you, as Dylan requested. It should be here any minute.' A crease formed across Adam's forehead. 'Matthew, what on earth's going on?'

Matthew's phone beeped. It was a reply from Caesar's email account.

Matthew, I will explain everything at 6 pm.

Tanner and Irons had fallen for his bluff.

'I can't explain it to you right now, Adam. I'll be back as soon as I can. Just promise me you'll look after Alfie?'

Adam nodded. 'Yes, of course.' He looked at Alfie. 'Come on, young man, let's set up the chessboard.'

Alfie turned towards his father. 'Dad, please be careful.'

'Don't worry, Alfie. I'm not going to do anything dangerous.'

He stepped forward and hugged his son. Then he walked out of the house and climbed into the taxi.

MATTHEW SETTLED back into his seat in the cab. He slipped his headphones on and clicked the link to continue listening to Tanner. He heard a door slam and another one open.

'There's no one here.'

Tanner had to be at Dylan's house. Matthew's email message hadn't made him turn back. Thank God they'd got out in time. Matthew frowned. Why hadn't Tanner turned back?

'Yeah. Leave this to me.'

Tanner must have activated his speakerphone because Matthew could hear the other person talking. The second voice was heavily distorted, and Matthew couldn't be sure whether it was Karl Irons.

'*What do you want me to do?*' Tanner asked.

'It's time for you to get back to Afghanistan. Keep your head down and wait for my call.'

'You'll take care of the Prof and the kid yourself?' Tanner asked.

Matthew swallowed at the curt, business-like discussion about him and his son.

'Yes.'

'Okay. Works for me.'

The conversation ended, but Matthew had heard enough to know Tanner wasn't the main player. That was the man on the other end of the phone call.

Everything still pointed to Karl Irons. He was in a position to know all Caesar's secrets, and he'd orchestrated the meeting to announce the closure of the scholarship and the payment demands. It had to be him who would be waiting for Matthew at Caesar's house.

Matthew closed the link and opened a previously unexplored folder on Caesar's laptop called Red Votes. There were twelve separate documents. He clicked on Red Vote 1, and the text appeared on the screen.

To be carried by a unanimous vote only: To actively encourage sexual relationships between the members without restrictions to maximise the chances of progeny.

Result: rejected.

Votes in favour: Christopher Goldman.

Votes against: Benjamin Caesar, Henry Bannister.

A chill crept down his spine as he saw the supporting document detailing research on incest.

Jesus Christ. Shaking his head, he navigated to Red Vote 2.

To be carried by a unanimous vote only: To harvest genetic material for storage to allow future gene editing.

Result: rejected.

Votes in favour: Christopher Goldman, Henry Bannister.

Votes against: Benjamin Caesar.

Matthew's stomach pitched, and his body started to tremble. He blew out a breath and forced himself to work through the rest of the votes. By the time he reached number twelve, he didn't think things could get any more shocking.

He was wrong.

To be carried by a unanimous vote only: The active encouragement of genius through parental loss.

Result: rejected.

Votes in favour: Christopher Goldman.

Votes against: Benjamin Caesar, Henry Bannister.

Matthew clicked into the research paper, and his breath caught in his throat.

Parental loss and genius. American Psychologist.

Matthew locked on to the words in the abstract.

...a scientific theory to account for the historically eminent individual or genius by relating his/her development to loss of parents...

Sweat traced down Matthew's back.

...early orphanhood was characteristic of this eminent group...

Matthew was numb. His brain refused to make the connection that what he was reading suggested. It simply couldn't be possible.

...the effects of bereavement and orphanhood are offered to explain the relationship between achievement and parental loss, as well as that between the genius and the disturbed psychotic.

Matthew checked the date of publication. 1978, when Caesar and the others were at university. The air emptied from his body as his mind returned to the first letter he had received from Benjamin Caesar.

Individuals selected for a scholarship will be noteworthy for their academic achievement, but in particular their character, their ability to respond to adversity and their drive to make a positive impact in the world.

An unusually high number of Genius Club members had suffered parental loss. Statistically too high to be random. He fought the urge to gag.

Goldman had cast the only vote in favour of vote 12.

If there was evidence orphanhood increased the chances of a child being a genius, Caesar, Bannister and Goldman could have actively sought it out, or when women signed the sperm donor contract, they could have insisted the children were told they were orphans. It was almost too much to think about, but he couldn't shut his thoughts down. He heard himself gasp.

...the active encouragement of genius...

Everything fell into place. Vote 12 wasn't a vote on whether to select children who had suffered parental loss. They'd already made that decision. Vote 12 concerned a blueprint for the next generation. It had been a vote on killing parents to stimulate genius—a genius like Alfie.

Matthew's head was light, and the colour in his vision seemed to drain away. His breathing was rumbling in his ears. It was beyond comprehension. No. It just wasn't possible. Slowly, the world started to come back into focus. He looked out the window, trying to reconnect with reality. He vaguely recognised the road they were on - somewhere close to Caesar's house.

He had known he wasn't going to meet Caesar, but now he knew for sure who he would be meeting.

Not Jason Tanner. Not Karl Irons.

But Christopher Goldman.

A man who had already killed Lucy and was now planning to kill Matthew. All in the belief it would make Alfie a genius.

45

NOW

FRIDAY, 28 JUNE 2019

Belgravia, London

MATTHEW TRIED TO GATHER HIS THOUGHTS. SURELY ELEANOR Goldman hadn't known any of this? If she'd believed Christopher was capable of anything like that, she would have told the police. She would have severed all connections, switched back to her maiden name—everything. What she already knew or suspected was terrible enough, but this...

Matthew froze. Why hadn't Eleanor switched her name back? A few clicks later, Matthew was looking at the online wedding certificate for Christopher and Eleanor Goldman. He stared at the screen. It wasn't her who had changed name; it was him. He had taken his wife's name. Before the marriage, he wasn't Christopher Goldman; he was Christopher Lovelace, which helped explain why there was so little about him on the internet. Matthew closed his eyes. Lovelace.

'The Ada Trust,' he whispered.

Christopher Goldman owned the trust that had funded Cerebrum and owned Caesar's house—the property Matthew was heading to.

The trust's name was a paean both to Christopher's birth name and Ada Lovelace, the genius daughter of Lord Byron credited with being the first computer programmer.

Matthew took a deep breath, typed Christopher Lovelace into Google, and hit search. Towards the bottom of the first page, he found a news report that drained all the energy from his body.

In 1975, a fifteen-year-old boy was awarded A grades in each of his five A-levels, which was remarkable, but what made the story even more shocking was that when the same boy was just seven years old, he had witnessed the torture and murder of his parents. His mother was a talented writer, and his father was an eminent professor of mathematics. The journalist declared the boy to be a bona fide genius.

Matthew stared numbly at the concluding sentence of the report, unable to believe what he was reading.

God moves in mysterious ways. Is it possible that the gifts of this remarkable boy were forged from the horror of his early life experience?

DYLAN ANSWERED on the first ring. 'Is Alfie safe?' she asked.

'Yes, he's with Adam.' Matthew was sitting in the taxi parked around the corner from Caesar's house. The driver was outside smoking a cigarette. 'Where are you?'

'I was following Tanner, but after he searched my house, he left and headed out of London,' Dylan said. 'I think he's going to the airport.' Matthew could hear the irritation in her voice. 'Karl Irons must be in the house.'

'Karl Irons isn't behind this,' Matthew said. 'It's Christopher Goldman.'

There was a hesitation before Dylan spoke. 'You told me he's dead.'

'I made a mistake believing what I was told.' Matthew paused. Why hadn't he checked?

'How do you know it's Goldman?' Dylan asked.

'I found a file on Caesar's computer. Goldman was the only one who voted in favour of actively killing parents for the development of genius.'

Dylan was quiet, but Matthew was sure it was incomprehension of the man rather than not immediately making the link. 'You think he killed Lucy to make Alfie smarter?' Dylan said, eventually.

'I'm sure of it.' Matthew wiped his hand over his face and then continued. 'Goldman changed his name when he married and never changed it back. His birth name is Lovelace, and if you search on his name, there's a report-'

'I'm reading it now,' Dylan said.

'He planned every stage. The sperm bank, the scholarship, all to allow him to select a modern-day version of his parents.' Matthew shivered at the idea that Christopher had always intended for him and Lucy to breed.

'God, this bastard should be shot,' Dylan said. 'Who the hell does he think he is?'

Something was scratching at Matthew's memory. 'Hold on.' He still hadn't found the scout reports, but Tanner had mentioned a feed. Matthew ran his hand over his face. He needed to focus. He opened the web browser and checked the history. One site had been visited daily as far back as he could see. He clicked on the address and waited.

A website appeared with a list of names down the left-hand side. A cold wave crept up Matthew's spine. It was all the candidates for the scholarship. The central panel had the heading *Daniel Solarin,* and a series of news headlines was posted to a bulletin board beneath it. Matthew caught a glimpse of the entries.

Update: DS has been suspended from work. According to a colleague, he is being investigated. The colleague is unsure of the details but believes a female employee has made an official ...

Update: DS presented at a conference on advising clients on issues affecting their reputation.

Update: ...launching a service working with a select network of third-party advisers, including communications experts, cyber and physical security firms, business intelligence practice...

Matthew was transfixed by what he was seeing. 'I've just found the live newsfeed on Caesar's computer.' He scrolled down the list, revealing more posts from earlier in Daniel's life, before clicking on one of the headings across the top of the page.

Urgent updates.

A new view presented itself, and Matthew opened the most recent item—a news report headed *Success from the Depths of Tragedy.*

'Oh my God.' Matthew clamped his hand over his mouth.

The report was about Kathryn Farthing's daughter, Jenny.

Three years after she'd witnessed the brutal murder of her mother, the nine-year-old girl had just sat and passed the eleven-plus. The article talked about Jenny Farthing's exceptional talent. The echo of Goldman's horror story squeezed Matthew's chest.

'What is it?' Dylan asked.

He swallowed. 'I think Goldman killed Kathryn Farthing as an experiment to test his hypothesis. He did it, and he made sure Tanner was in the area. You were correct about his contingency, but he wasn't framing me.'

'He's been framing Tanner all this time,' Dylan said.

'Yes. There's virtually no information available about Tanner. What's the chance of the only publicly recorded date of Tanner being in the country being exactly when Kathryn Farthing was murdered, and not just in the country, but at the very location where Kathryn was killed? Tanner wasn't careless; Goldman was clever.'

'He'll have made sure Tanner doesn't have an alibi for Lucy's murder,' Dylan said. 'And I bet he made Tanner order the drug cocktail. All this time, Tanner thinks Goldman is Karl Irons; he thinks he's been working with the lawyer, and they will split the inheritance.'

Matthew was barely listening. He checked the date of the report. It had been posted to the feed on the morning Lucy was killed. Was that when Caesar had realised Goldman was a psychopath—the morning when he'd seen the report?

If that was right, it was likely there had been some showdown between the two men. Matthew swallowed. He felt an unshakable conviction that Goldman had murdered Caesar, and then he'd murdered Lucy.

'You can't go in there,' Dylan said.

Matthew wiped the sweat off his brow. 'He'll be in the basement. I can lock it remotely, right?'

'Yes, but-'

'I'm going in.' He could see the driver coming back to the car. He opened the taxi door and stepped outside, saying thanks to the driver. He waited for the driver's door to close. 'I'm going to stop this monster.'

'It's too dangerous,' Dylan said. 'I can't let anything happen to you.'

The expression of concern caught him off guard. Whoever thought there would be a connection between them that outlived Lucy? But he needed to do this. He switched into the security app on his phone and logged in using the password Daniel had provided. The screen was split into sections: video, audio, light and heat. He selected the video feed.

'There's something else I need to tell you,' Matthew said, watching the taxi drive off. 'I took some hairs from your brush in your bathroom. Vanessa ran a DNA test for me.' He could hear her breathing down the line in anticipation of what he was about to say. He was staring at the screen as he spoke. There were cameras in most of the rooms in Caesar's house, but he knew Goldman would be in the basement. 'Dylan, you and I have the same father.'

There was a silence. He couldn't predict how she would react, so he just waited. He tapped on the screen to select the video feed of the basement. Daniel had assured him no one could tell he had access.

Matthew's phone beeped. He looked down to read the message Goldman had sent from Caesar's phone, and his breath caught in his throat.

I have Alfie.

If you want him to live, come into the house and walk to the drawing room.

I will speak to you there.

'No. Oh my God, no.' The world slowed. Matthew could hear his rapid breathing.

'What? Matthew, what's wrong?'

The text disappeared from his screen to reveal the video feed. The basement came into view. There were two people visible. He focused in on the body lying motionless on the floor. There was a single bullet wound visible in Ben Caesar's head, and blood had pooled on the floor. Matthew's body shook.

'Caesar's dead,' he said.

Time seemed to stretch as different emotions collided. On some level, he knew that Caesar was dead, but he hadn't been fully prepared to see his dead body.

He tapped the screen. The display took a couple of seconds to refocus. Then Matthew could see the man who had murdered Caesar, the man holding Alfie hostage, sitting in a leather chair.

Matthew had never seen a picture of Christopher Goldman, but he recognised him the moment he saw him.

Everything in his life to that point suggested that at that moment, he would fall apart, that he would fail. He would have expected that of himself, too, but something clicked inside him.

His mind was sharp, and his thinking was clear. This would be the hardest test he would ever face, but he wasn't going to fail his son.

His voice was calm.

'Listen to me carefully, Dylan. I need you to do exactly as I say.'

46

NOW

FRIDAY, 28 JUNE 2019

Belgravia, London

The front door clicked open, and Matthew stepped into the hallway. He tapped on his phone, slipped it into his pocket, and walked along the hallway. Artwork hung on the walls, but Matthew ignored everything except the door that led into the drawing-room, which had been left open. He turned into the room. It was decorated to such a standard that ordinarily, Matthew would have been nervous to breathe, let alone sit in one of the chairs, but this was anything but ordinary.

No one was waiting for him, but a single envelope was on the antique table next to a glass of water on a coaster.

Matthew looked at the envelope. He already knew what the letter inside would be. His suicide note—addressed to Alfie. He'd been brought there to die. Specifically, to die by his own hand.

It would be recorded too, he was sure, and somehow, Alfie would see it and would suffer the trauma of seeing his father taking his own life. There was no accounting for what that would do to him. Except Goldman was conceited enough, twisted enough, to think he knew. He believed trauma triggered genius.

A voice cracked through the air as an image came into focus on the wall-mounted screen opposite Matthew.

Matthew was looking at Alfie, sitting in an unfamiliar room, tapping on a computer keyboard. He stared hard at the screen, soaking in every detail. Alfie had to be somewhere in Caesar's house.

'Isn't he something?' The voice sent a chill down Matthew's spine, but he said nothing. Alfie seemed unaware of anything untoward. 'But he is young, and he will need to develop character. He needs to understand true sacrifice, and so, we come to this.'

Matthew tried to keep his face impassive. He didn't want to give this man anything, but Goldman's words echoed some of the abuse shouted at Alfie at school.

Goldman had paid someone to deliver the envelope to prevent Alfie from seeing him. Alfie would have recognised him immediately because Goldman was a family friend.

'The equation is simple,' Goldman's voice continued. 'For him to live, you must sacrifice yourself. There is a suicide note and a cyanide pill in the envelope in front of you. Sign the letter, take the pill, and Alfie will live. If you choose to save yourself, your son will die. You have three minutes.'

The voice stopped. A red countdown clock appeared beneath Alfie's video feed. Matthew didn't react. He still had three minutes to figure out precisely what to do next.

Matthew stared at his son, his face, and his eyes, trying hard not to imagine him all alone in the world. Goldman had already taken so much from Matthew—his wife, his mentor, and he'd tried to drive a wedge between Matthew and his friends. He hoped to leave Matthew with nothing so that making the ultimate sacrifice for his son wouldn't seem impossible.

Matthew glanced around the room, trying to project a sense of confidence. It was impossible to think of this man as his father. He thought of the sacrifice made by the man who had brought him up, the man who had done his duty; then he thought of Goldman and almost began to pity him. Almost.

'Take all of the three minutes, if you wish,' Goldman said, 'but I've seen your answer to the question of taking your own life to save others. I know you'll do it. Indeed, you already know you'll do it.'

Matthew swallowed. Goldman had just confirmed he'd seen the results of the morality test all those years ago.

The countdown reached the last thirty seconds.

Matthew stood up and tipped the red cyanide pill from the envelope into his hand. It looked so small, resting in his palm. All he needed to do was slip it into his mouth, sip the water, and swallow. It would be over in less than a minute.

He looked directly at the camera fixed in the corner of the ceiling and dropped the pill in the bin. Then he removed the letter from the envelope, ripped it in half and dropped the paper onto the table.

There were seventeen seconds left.

He stared into the camera lens he knew was focused on him and waited for the countdown to hit single figures. The final countdown was the slowest ten seconds of his life.

47

NOW

FRIDAY, 28 JUNE 2019

Belgravia, London

MATTHEW FLINCHED AS ALFIE DISAPPEARED FROM THE SCREEN TO BE replaced by static.

He told himself Alfie was okay, that everything had been designed to put pressure on Matthew to kill himself, that whilst Goldman was a killer, he was doing it all for Alfie. That meant Goldman didn't want Alfie to die.

Matthew cleared his throat.

'What should I call you? Christopher? Goldman? Lovelace?'

He paused and counted silently to five.

'Or do you prefer to go by Adam these days?' Matthew asked.

Hearing Matthew call him Adam was the moment Goldman would realise he was no longer in control. He'd be nervous because Matthew knew who he was, but he'd still be confident. That was the nature of the man, and that was precisely what Matthew was counting on.

Matthew pushed on. 'There's someone very keen to meet you after all this time—someone you've been careful not to meet. I'll warn you, though, he was upset to discover the man he's been talking to all these years wasn't, in fact, Karl Irons. And he was distraught to learn he won't inherit a penny from his father. He's very keen to talk to you about that.'

Matthew clicked on his phone to remotely deadlock the basement and kill all the cameras in Caesar's house. When he was confident Goldman was locked in the basement without a camera view, he ran out of the room and sprinted upstairs. The first two doors he tried swung open to empty rooms. The third one was locked.

'Alfie?' Matthew called.

'Dad?'

Thank God. Alfie was alive. Matthew blinked back his tears. 'Can you open the door, Alfie?'

Matthew heard the handle turn, and the door rattled in its frame. 'No. It's locked. Why would Adam lock me in?'

There was a touchpad on the wall displaying the numbers zero to nine. 'Hold on, Alfie.' Matthew checked the security app and scanned through the rooms, but the one Alfie was in wasn't registered. *Christ.* He needed to get Alfie out. Matthew was breathing rapidly, then typed in the first few digits of the number Pi. Nothing. 'Come on,' he said to himself. He hit two, seven, one and then eight—Euler's number. The door sprung open, and Matthew wrapped his arms around his son.

'What's going on?' Alfie's face was full of confusion.

'Come with me,' Matthew said, dragging his son to the top of the stairs. They were in the hallway, nearly at the front door, when it swung open. Matthew gestured to Alfie to stay silent.

Matthew nodded wordlessly to Dylan as she walked in. Then he bundled Alfie outside, closed the door behind them and ushered his son down the road. They had ten minutes to walk to Victoria Station, where Sammy had agreed to collect Alfie.

48

NOW

FRIDAY, 28 JUNE 2019

Belgravia, London

CHRISTOPHER SPRINTED TO THE LIBRARY ENTRANCE. THE METAL DOOR was shut, which was expected, but the touchpad that operated it was blank, which wasn't. He jabbed the panel with his fingers. Nothing happened.

He grabbed his phone. It had always worked in the library, but now it wasn't showing any signal, and that's when he knew.

He was trapped.

He was secured in the basement with no windows, and a mobile phone jammer had been activated to kill his phone signal. That was bad enough, but it was far worse than that because Matthew Stanford knew everything.

A voice startled him, and it took him a moment to realise it was coming from the ceiling speakers.

'I'm undecided right now.'

Jesus, Matthew must have let Jason Tanner into the house. Christopher slowed his breathing.

'I don't know whether to kill you or let the police take you and lock you up until you die in jail.'

Christopher's eyes darted about, unsure where to look. 'Wait. We can work this out,' he said.

'I don't think so. Not after what you've done to me.'

Christopher switched tack. 'You're an accessory to murder,' he said. He tried to sound calm and authoritative, but he could hear the fear in his voice. 'If I go down, you go down. We need to help each other.'

'I don't even know who you are.' Tanner's voice cut across him. 'You told me you were my old man's lawyer, that your name was Karl Irons.' Christopher's palms started to sweat. 'The police are only a few minutes away.'

Christopher wiped his hands over his face. If the police found him in the house with Caesar's dead body, even if they couldn't link him to any of the other murders, he'd be going to prison for a long time. 'We can still do this,' he shouted to the room, but even he didn't believe it.

'You can rot in hell.'

Christopher clawed at his head. How could this be happening to him? This excuse for a man, this total failure, was going to deny him. It shouldn't be possible.

'Come in here and face me like a man, you little bastard.' He kicked out and started hammering on the door. 'Come on,' he shouted, spinning around to face the empty room. 'Your dad was right about you, Jason. You're certainly no genius. The other deaths were necessary, but you, Jason, you I'd kill just so I don't have to look at your stupid fucking face ever again. Come down here, you pig-thick little man. Let's settle this, man to man.'

He was body-slamming the door, but it stayed firmly shut. Tanner had gone silent, and Christopher stood still after a flurry of effort. He could hear a distant police siren. He slumped against the wall and slid to the floor. He sat motionless for a few seconds before he heard a click, and the panel next to the door sprang back into life.

His heart rate jacked up. Tanner had decided to face him after all. He pushed himself up, but the door slid open before he could get to it.

Someone was standing in the shadow, and he couldn't see who it was, but they didn't look large enough to be Tanner. Then they stepped into the room. His brain processed the intruder's face, and he instantly understood why he had been outmanoeuvred.

Their name formed in his mind a split second before two bullets shattered his skull.

49

NOW

FRIDAY, 28 JUNE 2019

Victoria Station, London

MATTHEW WATCHED SAMMY DRIVE OFF WITH ALFIE IN THE PASSENGER seat. Alfie would be safe now, he thought. He felt a buzz in his pocket and pulled out the burner phone.

It's over. These are the locations you asked for.

There was a list of five places. Four of them were familiar. The odd one out was an address in Kensal Green.

He reread the message, memorised the location and then deleted the text. He pulled out the battery and slipped both elements back into his pocket. He'd find a bin nearby for the battery, then drop the casing further away.

He picked up his iPhone, switched it back on and called Daniel. 'Hi. Yeah, it's Matthew. Can you call the police? Send them to Caesar's house.' He listened carefully to Daniel's response. 'Thank you. Yes, Sammy and Alfie are on their way back to you. I'll come over as soon as I can.'

He ended the call. He'd tried to prepare himself for the task ahead of him even before Dylan had sent him Goldman's historic locations, but there was no way to protect himself from what he would find.

He would head to Kensal Green and pray his best friend was still alive.

50

NOW

FRIDAY, 28 JUNE 2019

Kensal Green, London

MATTHEW TILTED THE HEAD TORCH DOWN TO SEE WHERE HE WAS treading. The path was slippery, with wet mud smeared over tree roots, and the branches brushed his shoulders as he walked. The wind was whipping around him, his jeans clinging to his thighs, and the rain had flattened his hair against his forehead.

'Alastair.' His shout echoed around the canopied path. He stopped and listened but was rewarded only with silence.

The cold air squeezed against his lungs, and he coughed. He pushed forward. He turned left at the junction and almost immediately took the barely visible path through the trees. His heart was thumping. The beam of his head torch bounced over the ground as he turned into the clearing. At first, all he saw was clear ground. Muttering under his breath, he wiped the rain from his glasses, and that was when he saw him.

'Alastair' His throat strangled the word.

He stumbled forward and slipped. He started to fall. His knees slid over the wet leaves, and his glasses fell to the ground. Everything slowed. Logically, he couldn't be certain, but at that moment,

Matthew knew the body on the side of the pathway, rolled against a tree, was Alastair.

He clambered towards him, reaching for his friend, his fingers searching for a pulse. His hand slipped in the blood that was warm and sticky around Alastair's neck. His eyes were open, but there was no light. No soul.

His best friend was dead.

'No,' he whispered, tears sliding down his face. And then he yelled with all the force he could muster. 'No.' The word was absorbed by the trees and drowned out by the howl of the wind.

His fingertips dotted around on Alastair's neck. There was no chance he was alive. The side of his head was thick with clotted blood from what looked like a gunshot wound. His nose was broken, and his face was heavily bruised below his eyes; his expression was a frozen scream of agony. He had died in pain. He'd been severely beaten before he'd been shot.

Matthew forced his fingers between Alastair's until they were interlaced, but whereas Matthew's fingers bent round to touch the back of Alastair's hand, his friend's fingers stayed rigid.

How could the world be so very, very cruel? He held his friend's hand up to his cheek, his tears mixing with the dried blood on Alastair's hands and smearing on his cheek. He didn't care.

He screamed again, and then he rested his head on his friend's chest. Convulsions racked his body.

Sometime later, he pushed himself to his feet, gently laying Alastair's arm across his dead body. He turned and glared into the darkness, brushing away his tears.

'I hate you.' He hurled the words at the sky for anyone who would listen. Then, the strength seeped out of his body, and he sagged to his knees.

Alastair. He couldn't be gone. He just couldn't be.

There was a vibration against his leg. It took a moment for him to realise it was his phone. He struggled to slide the phone out of his pocket, his hands wet with mud, rain and blood. He saw the name on the display. *Vanessa.* Oh, Jesus. How was he going to do this? He ran his hand over his face and tried to dry his phone screen on his jeans. He jabbed at the answer call button and clutched the phone against his ear.

'Hi Matt, it's V. Any luck?' Her voice was anxious, but it wasn't broken—not yet.

Matthew took a deep breath and started to talk.

51

NOW

FRIDAY, 28 JUNE 2019

Limehouse, London

Matthew looked at his phone. How many times was that now? But Dylan still hadn't called. Should he have kept the other phone? He shook his head. Dylan could get in touch if she wanted to.

Alfie was downstairs in Sammy and Daniel's cinema room. Daniel had set him up with a stack of films and enough takeaway food to last him a week.

Vanessa was in one of the guest bedrooms. Matthew couldn't imagine she was sleeping, but at least she could try to rest. Their conversation after he'd found Alastair would stay with him forever. She had uttered a phrase, through sobs and sniffs, that had taken a moment to settle in his brain. Words had already been hard enough, but her news had made them all but impossible.

I was so keen to talk to him—well, even more than usual—because my period's a week late.

Christ, Alastair would have loved being a father. Matthew had no doubt that the sheer joy of fatherhood would have easily squashed any desire to gamble and enjoy high-end entertainment, but his friend would never have the chance to prove it. Matthew had said nothing to anyone else, understanding that Vanessa would tell others only if and when she wanted to. Tonight, she had chosen not to share it with Sammy and Daniel. Nonetheless, they hugged and cried together and swapped Alastair stories until Vanessa signalled she wanted to try to sleep.

Sammy was sitting opposite Matthew, nursing a glass of wine. 'I still can't believe it.'

Matthew said nothing. What could he say? He couldn't believe it either.

The police had discovered the bodies of both Benjamin Caesar and Christopher Goldman at the house. That much Matthew had expected, but everything beyond that was where it all went off plan.

The police hadn't found Goldman's mobile phone. Still, they had checked the audio surveillance that automatically recorded activity at Caesar's house, and they'd heard a recording of what sounded like Goldman threatening to kill Tanner and demanding that he come and face him.

They'd found Goldman himself, Cluedo-style—in the library, shot in the head with a revolver.

The police were working on the theory that Tanner had killed him before heading to City airport, which is where they apprehended him following an anonymous tip-off.

Matthew glanced at his phone again—still nothing. Dylan had disappeared off the face of the earth. He began to think that he might not ever see her again. He paused, looking within himself to try and identify what he was feeling. He recognised the emotion, but he couldn't quite believe it. It was hope—hope that Dylan was okay.

Dylan. His half-sister, Alfie's aunt. Matthew had last seen her walking into Caesar's house when Christopher Goldman—her father, *their* father—was still alive, and Jason Tanner was already on his failed escape run to the airport.

Daniel had played them all the audio clip of Christopher Goldman shouting at Jason Tanner. Only Matthew knew that the software initially primed for Karl Irons' voice had instead been programmed with the audio recording of Jason Tanner from earlier that evening. The deep fake audio had to be good enough to convince Goldman he was talking with Tanner. It must have worked perfectly. Dylan had secured Goldman's confession while he was locked in the basement. Perfect execution.

What had happened next? Had Goldman killed himself?

It was certainly possible, even probable. His plan had been shredded. He wouldn't see the outside world again. What did he have to live for?

There was, however, another possibility: an explanation Matthew didn't even want to consider.

52

NOW

FRIDAY, 28 JUNE 2019

Limehouse, London

CAESAR'S LAPTOP WAS BALANCED ON DYLAN'S KNEES. THERE HAD BEEN a cache of information: video clips, audio snippets, and report after report posted by the scouts.

Matthew had told her about Vanessa's patent problem, Daniel's investigation for sexual harassment and Alastair's problem with a gambling debt.

Dylan scrolled through the reports from the scouts about the investigation into Daniel, but there was no evidence of any misconduct. Scout Two had confirmed the allegation had been made by Alice Gardner, a secretary on a temporary contract, who had joined the firm two weeks before the allegation. Dylan's checks suggested Alice Gardner was an alias, and whoever the woman was, Dylan imagined she'd already pocketed her money from Goldman and disappeared. If not, she certainly would when the news broke. Daniel would be cleared because he was innocent.

As for Vanessa, Dylan found nothing about the patents that would be a concern, but she was sure the competitor firm wouldn't hear from their mole at VieEdit anymore. A similar modus operandi to Alice Gardner, and, no doubt, Goldman had made a similar payment.

Dylan had only extracted one piece of information, which she would ensure made its way to the authorities.

Alastair's gambling debt was real—he was in debt to some bad people. Dylan couldn't prove it yet, but she was convinced Christopher Goldman had conspired to elevate Alastair's debt into a matter of life and death. With luck, the police would follow up.

Satisfied there was nothing else she needed to keep, Dylan found the download she was looking for and hit the button to release the digital poison. After less than a second, all the data was corrupted, almost certainly irretrievably.

It made sense Caesar would have had some in-built kill switch. It was best practice for safeguarding sensitive data. The database would destroy itself if a passcode weren't used within a defined period. She'd merely accelerated the process. You're welcome, she thought.

But she hadn't done it for Caesar. She felt nothing for him. She'd done it for Lucy and Alfie. And maybe even for Matthew.

53

NOW

AUGUST 2019

Kensal Green Cemetery

MATTHEW HAD DECIDED TO GO TO CAESAR'S FUNERAL. HE COULDN'T BE sure whether Lucy would have gone herself had she been alive and known Caesar was her father, but Lucy had always had a big heart.

Matthew watched as the coffin was lowered into the ground and the priest cast the earth.

...earth to earth, ashes to ashes, dust to dust...

Matthew knew the lines that came next. As the earth fell onto Benjamin Caesar's final resting place, Matthew swallowed the bile rising in his throat. He had come in search of more answers, but the location of the funeral made it impossible. Caesar's wishes had been to be buried next to Henry, unaware when he recorded his final wishes that his chosen resting place would be so close to where Alastair, his own son, had been murdered.

Alastair's funeral was in three weeks. That would be a proper occasion for remembrance and the celebration of life.

The priest was still pleading with God.

...according to the mighty working whereby he is able to subdue all things unto himself.

Matthew had heard enough. He shouldn't have come. He turned and walked away.

VANESSA, Sammy and Daniel were sitting in the library of an old building Matthew had hired at one of the Inns of Court in London. Matthew had come straight from Caesar's funeral, and a clerk had led him up the stone stairs and escorted him into the room.

All the available walls were filled with books. Matthew ran his eye over a selection. Isambard Kingdom Brunel, Emily Dickens, Leonardo Da Vinci and Rosalind Franklin.

The Genius Club.

Matthew looked round at his friends, sitting in a circle as if ready for a book club discussion.

Sammy cleared her throat. 'I guess this is it then, the end of the Genius Club.' There was no satisfaction in her voice. She was looking at Matthew. 'What is it, Matt?'

Matthew looked around the room, his eyes dwelling on the bookshelves. 'I wanted to talk to you about an idea.' He saw the flicker of intrigue in Sammy and Vanessa's eyes. Daniel winked at him. 'Christopher Goldman left his estate to Alfie, and it's estimated to be worth two hundred and twenty million pounds.' Vanessa whistled. 'Daniel and I have applied to take over as the executors for his will,' Matthew said.

'What about Dylan? And Sammy?' Vanessa asked.

'I don't want anything from him,' Sammy said, reaching out to take Daniel's hand.

'Dylan doesn't want anything from Goldman either,' Matthew said. 'Okay, well, I've taken expert legal advice,' he shot a look at Daniel, 'and my suggestion is to create a foundation for disadvantaged children with all of us acting as the trustees.' It would take years for them to come to terms with Caesar's actions, and more specifically, his secrecy about what he had allowed others to do to them. Matthew cleared his throat and continued. 'I have a suggestion for the name,' he said. 'The Lucy Stanford and Alastair Niven Foundation.'

He saw Sammy's smile and Vanessa's full-on grin. Matthew felt as though he was swallowing sandpaper. Vanessa was walking towards him, and he could see the tears in her eyes as she hugged him.

'Thank you, Matt. I'd love to be part of it.' She pulled away from him and turned to face the others. Her face was flushed. 'I also have some news.' Her hands rested for a moment on her stomach. 'I'm pregnant.'

54

NOW

NOVEMBER 2019

Putney, London

ALFIE WAS SITTING ON A CUSHION ON DYLAN'S SHALLOW BALCONY. Dylan stood beside him, looking out over the park across the road.

'I don't suppose you'd come and live with me and Dad?'

'That's never going to work, Alfie.'

'Why not?' Alfie asked.

'Well, for a start, I don't like your dad.'

'Oh. I thought that might have changed?'

Dylan was silent for a long time. 'Yeah. What has changed is I now believe he'll be a good dad to you.'

'He's always been a good dad to me.'

Again, Dylan took her time to respond. 'You're right, Alfie. Maybe it's me that's changed.'

'You don't believe that.'

Dylan laughed as she turned back to look out over the town. 'Hey, I can see your dad. How about we water bomb him?'

'Water bombs?' Alfie said. 'You?'

'Your Mum taught me.' Dylan stepped inside and ran towards the sink. 'Come on.'

Matthew smiled as he said goodbye to Sammy and slipped his phone in his pocket. He was happy for her. And Daniel. Their miracle baby would be born a couple of months after Vanessa's. Maybe the children would grow up to be friends. It was nice to think they could be that lucky.

He turned into Dylan's road. Strangely, this route had become so familiar to him over recent weeks. He wouldn't say he liked Dylan; he wasn't sure he ever would, but he saw what she meant to Alfie, and that shadowed what she had meant to Lucy. Anyway, Alfie needed more than just him.

It had been hard to let him go, even a little, especially after everything that had happened, but Alfie had said that talking with Dylan helped more than anything else. Matthew had tried not to feel hurt at falling into the 'anything else' category, but despite the pain it caused him, he knew it didn't matter. Letting Alfie go had helped him, too. He was learning to be himself again.

Not Lucy's widower. Not Alfie's dad. Not Professor Stanford.

Just Matthew.

The same Matthew that Lucy had fallen in love with. And the same Matt that Alastair Niven had been proud to call his best friend.

Matthew enjoyed the warmth of the sunshine on his face as he walked along the street. He knew what happened next, knew where the internal conversation went. He knew he needed a distraction to divert his thoughts from Lucy's absence and from Alastair's, too. He knew he always would.

He forced himself to breathe and stopped as he momentarily closed his eyes.

He heard something hit the pavement next to him, and looking up to Dylan's balcony, he smiled as water and laughter rained down on him from above.

THE END

END NOTES

Genius Club is a work of fiction, but as suggested by the articles referenced below, perhaps only just.

https://slate.com/human-interest/2001/02/the-genius-babies-and-how-they-grew.html

https://www.nature.com/articles/497297a

https://www.technologyreview.com/2015/08/20/166465/is-it-possible-to-make-people-smarter/

https://futurism.com/is-genetically-improved-intelligence-possible

https://www.moralsensetest.com

https://www.gwern.net/docs/psychology/1978-eisenstadt.pdf

https://maxhodak.com/nonfiction/2021/09/03/science.html

ACKNOWLEDGEMENTS

I hope you enjoyed reading *Genius Club.*

I clearly remember the evening I had the idea for this novel, and walked downstairs to tell my wife. I was so excited.

The book's journey from that evening to publication almost seven years later is a story of its own. During that time, the shape of the story changed dramatically several times—I have so many deleted scenes that I would love to use one day.

Like my debut, *The Honesty Index, Genius Club* came close to securing a publishing deal, but it wasn't to be. Since then, I have worked hard on the manuscript, and I think it's better for the extra work.

I would like to thank Ellie Hawkes for her expert editorial guidance in simplifying a complex story. She delivered some home truths in a gentle tone to help me keep chipping away at the marble.

Thanks again to my agent, Jo, who worked so hard and came close to securing this book a publishing deal, and her colleague Sarah, who read earlier versions of *Genius Club* and provided valuable and encouraging feedback.

In no particular order, my thanks to:

The Faber crew: Emma, Siobhan, Tonks, Zo, Vania, Robyn, Nicole, and Alison. This story started at Faber, so you were there from the beginning and have supported me ever since.

My beta and ARC readers. I really appreciate your time and support. I want to give a special mention to Andy for his fabulous insights about Matthew and the denouement.

Kathryn Price, for her early editorial advice and enthusiasm and

Bill Massey, for knocking the wind out of my sails before helping me pick up speed in the right direction.

Richard Kelly, Rowan Coleman, and Debi Alper for their guidance and support during the various courses.

All the great editors at publishing houses who read an earlier version of the manuscript and provided feedback and hope, even if they didn't eventually make an offer.

Jason Anscomb, for my stunning cover (with a hat tip to my son, James.)

To Claire and James, once again, for everything that I still can't adequately put into words. Maybe after book three?

Finally, thank you to every one of you for reading my book. I'm forever grateful to you all.

If you loved *Genius Club*, read on for an extract from NJ Barker's debut novel.

PROLOGUE

SUBURBAN LONDON, APRIL 2009

THE SEVEN TEENAGERS WERE SITTING ON LOGS THAT FORMED A CIRCLE around the fire. A glitterball moon spun in the night sky to the ambient lo-fi techno soundtrack of the nightingale song. Around them, silhouettes of trees lurked in the shadows.

Trent Ryder shoved his hands deep into his donkey jacket pockets and flexed his fingers to warm them. The party was winding down, and the fire had dulled to an amber glow. He looked at the packet of cigarettes Paddy was holding out. With sandy brown hair, freckles, and eyes to match, Paddy was the kind of kid that parents found easy to like but hard to trust.

Trent didn't like cigarettes but accepted the offer because he had an audience. He blew out the smoke, turned and locked eyes with Lila Jain: Bollywood princess meets home counties girl-next-door. Flawless skin, radiant smile and not even a blush of make-up. Her crimson down jacket was zipped up to the neck; her breath hung in frosty clouds, her eyes reflecting the firelight.

He held her gaze for a fraction too long. He would have carried on forever, but she turned away—a bad sign. But she was smiling, a good sign.

Trent had suggested to her earlier that they do some exploring, but she'd just laughed. First, she'd laughed at him because he was being suggestive. Then she'd laughed with him because he was funny. *Good-looking, with a great sense of humour. Keen explorer. Contact Trent if you're looking for love.*

Trent sighed and watched the smoke spiral up to greet the stars as he sat flanked by Nicholas Samson and Lila, between the devil and heaven on earth, wondering how many more minutes of this bonfire to Samson's vanity he could take.

The six of them had known each other for years, but they'd agreed to give the new kid a chance. It was Samson's birthday, after all, but the evening hadn't been easy. Samson was academically precocious, already a school year ahead of his age, which maybe didn't help.

Sitting on the other side of Samson, Copper had tried to engage him in conversation, but after each question, the silence had lengthened. Trent imagined Mrs Samson insisting on the birthday party to help her son make some friends. *They just need to get to know you, Nicky darling. The real you. The completely freaky, wide-eyed nutjob that Mummy loves so dearly.* Well, maybe not those precise words. But Nicholas Samson had cornered them all in the lunch queue two fateful weeks earlier, and once Copper had said yes, the others didn't have the heart to decline. However, the idea of leaving Copper to fly solo at Samson's birthday party had been almost funny enough to swing the balance.

They still had an hour before Paddy's father was due to pick them up in his battered old Volvo Estate. Trent could think of plenty of ways he'd like to pass the time with Lila, but none of them involved smoking. He was about to stub out the cigarette when he caught her glancing at him. He took another puff—cool, nonchalant—and gave her a wink. She shook her head gently in response, her dark bobbed hair swaying in front of her smile.

Samson had led the group of friends to the clearing by torchlight and then left the light switched off by his feet. Trent was peering into the shadows, trying to count the shades of grey, when a shaft of torchlight illuminated Nicholas Samson's face, making his skin look pale and unworldly. The fire spat out a bright orange spark, which sizzled on the dry ground.

'It's time,' Nicholas said. His voice was pure gargled gravel like he thought he was auditioning for a voice-over in a horror film trailer.

Lila covered her mouth with her hand, shoulders twitching. Dub, on the other side of the fire, caught Trent's eye. Maybe Samson thought edgy was the way to go. Boy, had he read that wrong. But he could still recover it with a joke.

'Everyone has to reveal a secret,' Samson continued. 'And we all swear to keep it. Forever.' His words would have been a good effort if only Samson hadn't been deadly serious.

'Jesus, Samson,' laughed Paddy, 'this isn't the Blair Witch Project.' His voice was louder than normal. He'd rolled off his log and was lying back on the grass, propped up on his elbows. His round face was glowing, his eyes unfocused. The six-pack of lager he'd smuggled into the party was now safely hidden in his bloodstream, the empty cans kicked under a hedge at the end of the garden.

Secret. Trent folded his arms. Despite the warmth of his coat across his shoulders, a knot was gathering in his stomach. But there was no way that he'd be revealing his secret. Not here. And not to Nicholas Samson.

'I think it sounds like fun,' said Oli. You could tell she meant it. Fun was her personal stamp of endorsement. *He's so much fun. They're all really fun.* When she was sure everyone was looking at her, she flicked her blonde hair and slowly tilted her head until she caught the perfect angle for the freeze frame.

'You go first, then, Olivia.' Samson was still shining the torch up at his face because he was so, you know, fun, fun, fun.

Oli took a moment to arrange herself as if she were on the cover of a magazine and started to talk. 'Well, my favourite sixteenth birthday present last year ... was the sex.'

Trent tuned her out—not in an 'I'm so bored, I'm too cool to follow the rule' sort of way, but because his mind had flashed back to the fire. Memories clawed for his attention. He blinked and shuffled forward, pushing those thoughts away. Before he knew it, Ali had finished, and Paddy was sitting up and talking, clearly having warmed to the idea of sharing secrets.

Trent chewed on his thumb, his teeth biting into the fleshy pad until he could feel the resistance of the bone underneath. Samson's secrets game was just that. A game. And the others already knew about the fire a year ago. Even Samson would know, although Trent had never told him directly. He didn't have to. Trent could rely on others to do that. *He doesn't like to talk about it, but I should tell you so you don't, you know, say something by accident.* So they all knew about the fire, about how his parents and younger brother had died and that only he and his sister had survived. But that was all they knew.

Trent shook his head. Just because Samson said they must reveal a secret didn't mean he *had* to say anything. He could just keep quiet, even if that looked odd, as though he had something to hide.

He could hear the birdsong. More insistent than before. Everyone was laughing, Paddy the loudest. Paddy dialled everything up to eleven. A few of the group clapped as he finished his confession, although Trent had heard the story of Paddy's father interrupting his son's 'private bedroom activity' several times before.

And then Dub was talking. Dub was thin as if he only ate one square meal a day, but as tall as if he ate four. His expression matched his tone. Serious.

'... and I didn't know what to do. Whoever it was, they were face down on the grass next to the river. I was sure they were dead.'

The laughter froze and died. Anxious glances shot around the circle, and Lila blew air from her cheeks. A ripple of wind pulsed the fire, which glowed a deep red, its dying breath.

'Jesus, Dub. What did you do?' asked Oli, her eyes movie-star wide.

'I ran home and told my dad. I reckon we were back to the riverbank within ten minutes.' Dub was staring at the floor, shaking his head. The others leant in. 'But there was no one there. I checked all the local news sites for weeks. I was sure there'd be a report of a body being found somewhere, but nothing.'

Paddy slapped Dub on the back. 'Maybe it was a ghost. I

remember reading about a girl who was murdered down by the river forty years ago. She's come back to haunt you.' He raised his hands over his head and rolled his eyes back. 'I'm coming for you, Andrew Dubnyk.' His voice was a high-pitched wail. 'I'm watching you.' Paddy's laugh triggered the others. Even Dub managed a grin.

Copper was next up. Copper by name and copper by hair colour, although the hair came first. Trent couldn't imagine *she* would have any earth-shattering secrets. The only rulebooks she hadn't read were the ones she'd written. Fifteen years old but already middle-aged.

'I discovered my father's stash of porn mags at the bottom of his cupboard,' she said with the confidence of a teacher setting lines. Write it out one hundred times.

'Copper.' Paddy's mouth was wide open. 'No way. I don't believe it. Does he know?' He was clutching his stomach.

'Of course not. I'm hardly going to tell him, am I? So, that's my secret.' A flicker of a smile. 'Well, my dad's secret.' She turned to Samson, who was next in the circle.

Trent needed to decide what to say. Paddy and Copper had opted for humour. Samson was still talking, and Trent forced himself to tune in.

'... and it was all over Facebook. So my mum decided I had to move school. And that's why you are now lucky enough to have me in your lives.'

He flicked the torch off and back on again, his expression blank. There was something weirdly staged about the whole thing. Samson had suggested the game, which sounded spontaneous, but Trent wondered whether he'd planned it just to be the centre of attention.

Trent scanned his friends' faces, looking for clues about what Samson had just said. Lila wore a Mona-Lisa smile. Copper was frowning, and he caught Dub raising an eyebrow at Paddy. Trent frowned. His desire to know the secret wrestled against his reluctance to admit he hadn't been paying attention. He cleared his throat. 'Sorry. I didn't catch the beginning of that. What was all over Facebook?'

Samson flipped the torch down until it shone directly into Trent's eyes.

Trent blinked and turned away. 'Jesus. What was that for?'

'You must be punished for not listening to the secrets.' Samson's voice was hollow.

Trent shook his head. He could only take so much, and Samson's capacity for playing the oddball appeared endless. However, it was possible that he wasn't acting at all.

Lila leant towards Trent. 'His dad was accused of election fraud, and a group of vigilantes targeted him. A mob turned up at the family home.'

'Blimey.' Trent said. Everyone was staring at him. Why were they expecting him to provide a more detailed reaction? It took a few further seconds of silence before he realised they were waiting to hear his secret. A few seconds in which he locked away his emotions. He couldn't share those because if he started, he wouldn't be able to stop. He glanced at Lila, whose turn followed his.

He started to speak. 'You all know about the fire.' *The* fire. That was enough. The others looked as if they had turned to stone.

Lila rested her hand on his arm. 'You don't have to talk about that night, Trent,' she said. 'This whole thing is just a bit of fun.'

Trent cleared his throat and continued. 'Which is why,' he smiled, 'I'm not going to talk about that.' Lila punched his arm, and he saw Paddy's shoulders drop. 'My secret is,' he looked at each of them in turn, 'I have no secrets.'

'Boo.' Paddy's foghorn of derision was magnified by his hands cupped around his mouth.

'I think I'd better take my turn.' Lila was looking at Trent. He shrugged at her and felt the spotlight swing away from him and towards Lila—the natural order of things restored.

Trent sunk back into the moonlight shadows. It was only a game —not just that. It was Nicholas Samson's game. There was no reason to share anything of consequence—no reason at all.

Lila leant forward, looked around the circle of friends, and smiled. She spoke in a conspiratorial whisper. 'Okay, guys. Here's my secret.' She shot Trent one quick, intense glance, then looked back at the others. What had that meant?

Trent's brain scrambled to make sense of his feelings. Then he heard her words.

'I have a massive crush on someone.' Her hair fell across her face, so he could no longer see her expression. Did she mean *him*? Was she going to announce it here? Lila brushed her hair back again. All eyes were on her – especially his.

'I love it. A real secret,' Paddy shouted. He pointed at Oli. 'Countdown, please, Olivia.'

'Five, four...'

Lila laughed. Paddy began clapping in time with Oli's chanting. Trent held his breath.

'Three, two, one.'

'I'm not going to tell you his name,' Lila said, grinning. Trent let out a slow breath. Lila tucked a strand of hair behind her ear. 'But I will say that he's older than me.'

Trent's world tilted. He was four months younger than Lila. He scratched his nose. Were the others looking at him? He forced himself to grin and prayed that someone else would say something.

'No, no, no,' Samson said, raking his fingers through his hair. He rocked backwards and forwards. 'That's not...' He screwed his face up, struggling to find the words. Trent didn't understand why Samson was upset. But now their host was on his feet, his pointing hand sweeping around the circle of friends. '*None* of you are taking this seriously. I don't *care* about your superficial lives. Give me something *real*.'

Trent glanced at Paddy just in time to catch the eye roll.

Samson was still going. 'I told you about something important.' There was a tremor in his voice. 'Something that changed my life. And you...' He shook his head.

Copper stood up and rested her hand on Samson's shoulder. 'We were just having fun, Nicholas.'

He shrugged her off. 'I don't care about fun.'

Oli was blinking, no doubt trying to digest a worldview so

opposed to her own. Trent was caught between laughing at the whole ridiculous charade and trying to process Lila's announcement when Samson leant back and screamed into the night sky.

They all stared at him, and it must have lasted ten seconds. When he finally lowered his face, Trent could see tears in Samson's eyes. What the hell?

'You're supposed to be my friends.' Samson's voice cracked as he wiped his face. 'And friends trust each other with secrets.' He turned away from them and started walking back towards the house.

Trent risked a glance at Lila. He'd thought the two of them had something special, but it seemed he'd been wrong. His thoughts were interrupted by Samson shouting back towards them.

Trent tried but failed to express the guttural rage. He looked at Lila. 'What did he say?' he asked.

Lila was frowning. 'He said *you should have trusted me*.'

The group stood in silence and watched Nicholas Samson walk, all alone, back to his house.

NJ BARKER READERS' CLUB

If you enjoyed *Genius Club,* you can join my Readers' Club to receive a free short story, A Lesson in Character. The story is from my Kennedy Logan Thrillers series and is a one-hour read. I hope you enjoy it.

Being a member of the Readers' Club means you will have access to more free stories in the future, cover reveals, and updates on my writing. Other than around new releases, I typically only send a newsletter once or twice a month.

You can join by visiting my website: www.njbarker.com

ABOUT THE AUTHOR

Nigel lives in Kent with his wife, son, and their two cocker spaniels. When he isn't writing, he's usually trying to recover a sock from one of the dogs.

Nigel's website is www.njbarker.com

Book Cover by Jason Anscomb.

Printed in Great Britain
by Amazon

90d56705-9118-4494-af88-38bd88ea14f3R01